"*You* do *know how to love, don't you,*"

Adam said quietly as he watched Kylie nuzzle her tiny nephew's soft curls.

"Everyone loves babies," Kylie responded defensively.

"Then why don't you have one of your own instead of sharing your sister's?"

"Because I don't happen to want a husband."

"That isn't a requirement. A lot of single women are having babies these days. It's quite acceptable."

"That might be all right while the baby remains an infant, but I think a child needs two parents when it gets older." She stopped abruptly. "Why am I explaining myself to you? It's none of your business!"

"It might be." He looked her up and down. "Now that I know you want a baby but not a husband, I might be persuaded to volunteer my services."

"Forget it, pal! I don't want anything *that* much!"

He grinned. "Don't be hasty. I'm reasonably young, extremely healthy and moderately intelligent." His voice dropped to a velvet purr. "I also guarantee to make the experience painless. You might even enjoy it."

Dear Reader,

In past months I've used this page to tell you what we editors are doing to live up to the name Silhouette **Special Edition**:

> We've brought you the latest releases from authors you've made into stars; we've introduced new writers we hope you'll take to your heart. We've offered classic romantic plots; we've premiered innovative angles in storytelling. We've presented miniseries, sequels and spin-offs; we've reissued timeless favorites in Silhouette *Classics*. We've even updated our covers, striving to give you editions you can be proud to read, happy to own.

All these editorial efforts are aimed at making Silhouette **Special Edition** a consistently satisfying line of sophisticated, substantial, emotion-packed novels that will touch your heart and live on in your memory long after the last page is turned.

In coming months our authors will speak out from this page as well, sharing with you what's special to them about Silhouette **Special Edition**. I'd love to hear from *you*, too. In the past your letters have helped guide us in our editorial choices. How do you think we're doing now? Some time ago I made a promise on this page— that "each and every month, Silhouette **Special Edition** is dedicated to becoming more special than ever." Are we living up to that promise? What's special to *you* about Silhouette **Special Edition**? Share your feelings with us, and, who knows—maybe some day *your* name will appear on this page!

My very best wishes,

Leslie Kazanjian, Senior Editor
Silhouette Books
300 East 42nd Street
New York, N.Y. 10017

TRACY SINCLAIR
Proof
Positive

Silhouette Special Edition

Published by Silhouette Books New York

America's Publisher of Contemporary Romance

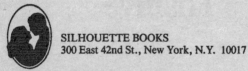

SILHOUETTE BOOKS
300 East 42nd St., New York, N.Y. 10017

ISBN: 0-373-09493-0

First Silhouette Books printing December 1988

Books by Tracy Sinclair

Silhouette Romance

Paradise Island #39
Holiday in Jamaica #123
Flight to Romance #174
Stars in Her Eyes #244
Catch a Rising Star #345
Love Is Forever #459

Silhouette Special Edition

Never Give Your Heart #12
Mixed Blessing #34
Designed for Love #52
Castles in the Air #68
Fair Exchange #105
Winter of Love #140
The Tangled Web #153

The Harvest Is Love #183
Pride's Folly #208
Intrigue in Venice #232
A Love So Tender #249
Dream Girl #287
Preview of Paradise #309
Forgive and Forget #355
Mandrego #386
No Room for Doubt #421
More Precious Than Jewels #453
Champagne for Breakfast #481
Proof Positive #493

Silhouette Christmas Stories 1986

"Under the Mistletoe"

Author of more than twenty Silhouette novels, *TRACY SINCLAIR* also contributes to various magazines and newspapers. She says her years as a photojournalist provided the most exciting adventures—and misadventures—of her life. An extensive traveler—from Alaska to South America, and most places in between—and a dedicated volunteer worker—from suicide-prevention programs to English-as-a-second-language lessons—the California resident has accumulated countless fascinating experiences, settings and acquaintances to draw on in plotting her romances.

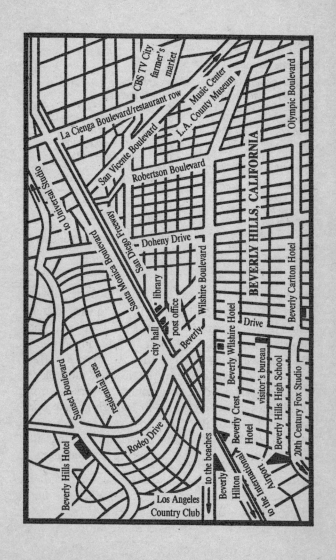

CBS TV City
farmer's market
Music Center
L.A. County Museum
La Cienga Boulevard/restaurant row
San Vicente Boulevard
Olympic Boulevard
to Universal Studio
Robertson Boulevard
BEVERLY HILLS, CALIFORNIA
Santa Monica Boulevard
San Diego Freeway
Doheny Drive
Wilshire Boulevard
Beverly Carlton Hotel
library
post office
Drive
city hall
Beverly
Sunset Boulevard
residential area
Beverly Wilshire Hotel
visitor's bureau
Beverly Hills High School
Beverly Crest Hotel
20th Century Fox Studio
Rodeo Drive
Beverly Hills Hotel
to the beaches
Beverly Hilton
to the international Airport
Los Angeles
Country Club

Chapter One

Kylie O'Connor wasn't one of those people who hated Monday mornings. She'd always looked forward to going to work. Lately, however, her enthusiasm was flagging.

Landing a job right out of law school with the prestigious firm of Bradley, Cunningham & Smythe had seemed like a bright omen. But that was before she found out what kind of cases were assigned to the low person on the totem pole.

Kylie had been fired up with the prospect of defending the poor and downtrodden. She had pictured herself as a legal Joan of Arc, bringing justice to the masses. What she spent her time on were divorce cases.

That Monday started out no differently from all the rest. She seated herself behind the desk in her comfortable office on the twentieth floor of a plush building in Beverly Hills, thinking with distaste about her caseload. The majority of Bradley, Cunningham & Smythe's clients were

Hollywood people who liked dancing but objected to paying the piper. In most of their divorces Kylie couldn't summon up much sympathy for either side.

She flipped the intercom key to speak with her secretary. "Did you finish typing that deposition from Rod Livingston, Marcia?"

"Did I ever!" Her secretary's voice was animated. "What an operator! You know, the last time he was in, he asked me to join him in his hot tub."

"After his wife gets through with him, he'll be lucky to afford a cold shower," Kylie answered crisply.

"That's so unfair! From what I hear, she was playing around, too."

"But he was the one who got caught."

Marcia sighed. "Makes you kind of wonder why they bother to get married in the first place, doesn't it?"

Those were Kylie's sentiments exactly. Of course, she'd been starry-eyed herself once, but no more. Her blue eyes darkened as she remembered Larry. They'd been so much in love—until he met a rich girl whose father could set him up in business. With both her parents dead and her prospects for wealth just that—prospects—Kylie hadn't been able to compete. Nor had she trusted her own judgment about men since. Larry had seemed so devoted. If he could fake it, any man could. She'd accepted that sorry fact and concentrated her energies on carving out a career. A woman didn't need a man to be fulfilled.

She dismissed her faithless fiancé from her mind and started to read a complicated legal brief. Halfway through it, her concentration was broken by raised voices in the anteroom. This was most unusual. Nothing ever disturbed the dignified atmosphere at Bradley, Cunningham & Smythe.

To Kylie's utter amazement, her office door flew open and a very large, extremely angry man strode in. Although he moved with the coordinated grace of an athlete, his body radiated tension. A few long strides brought him to her desk. He flattened his palms on the polished surface and leaned on them, glaring down at her with stormy gray eyes.

"I have a few choice things to say to you," he stated.

If a wolf could talk, that's what it would sound like, Kylie thought. She wouldn't be surprised if his firm lips covered wicked canine teeth.

"I told him he couldn't come in here, Miss O'Connor." Marcia peered over the man's broad shoulder, her expression a mixture of apprehension and excitement.

"It's all right, Marcia. I'll take care of this." Kylie looked at him coolly. "Who are you, and what do you want?"

"A little justice! But you wouldn't know anything about that," he growled.

"If you'll state your business, perhaps we can straighten out whatever's bothering you."

"I'll tell you what's *bothering* me, lady! What you and your client are trying to do to me is usually accompanied by a kiss."

Kylie's ivory skin warmed. "You don't have to be crude."

"I could have been more graphic," he answered sardonically. "Isn't it a little hypocritical to strip a man bare and then get offended by his language?"

"I have no idea what you're talking about," she said coldly.

"You're Donna Castle's lawyer, aren't you?" he demanded.

Comprehension dawned. So this was the legendary Adam Ridgeway, the tall, dark, handsome *and* famous photographer whose pictures appeared regularly in all the national publications. He'd covered everything from Olympic games to bloody revolutions in tiny nations.

His talent was undeniable, but his flamboyant life-style drew almost as much attention as his work. The newspapers dutifully reported every exploit, each new love affair, every unconventional act he committed.

The press had had a field day with his marriage and subsequent divorce from Donna Castle, a beautiful starlet. Their battles and reconciliations provided the tabloids with a constant source of material.

Although the media elevated Donna to star status, she possessed more shrewdness than acting ability. When her career showed no signs of going anywhere, she'd decided to parlay a thirteen-month marriage into a lifetime annuity.

Adam Ridgeway was watching Kylie with a mocking smile. "I see you know who I am."

"I do now." Her eyebrows drew together in a scowl. "Why didn't you just tell me your name instead of stomping around here like a storm trooper?"

"Would it have gotten me a warmer reception?"

"Actually, you shouldn't be here in the first place. You have a perfectly competent attorney to speak for you."

His scowl topped hers. "The words are mutually exclusive, Miss O'Connor."

"Your opinion of the legal profession doesn't interest me, Mr. Ridgeway."

"It ought to. I paid enough for it," he said grimly.

"Not to me, you didn't. I suggest you contact your own lawyer and voice your complaints."

"He's already heard them. Now I want them relayed to your client. You can tell my late, unlamented wife that I don't intend to pay her one more cent!"

"You'll be risking a contempt-of-court citation," Kylie warned.

"The court isn't the only one I have contempt for. I agreed to make monthly alimony payments for two years, and I'll fulfill that agreement. The installments are large enough to support the entire royal family of Britain, but evidently not my wife. Now she wants more."

"The cost of living goes up all the time," Kylie murmured, unable to meet his eyes.

She hadn't been Donna Castle's attorney in the divorce case, but she had inherited the job of petitioning for an increase. Kylie privately considered the legal maneuver reprehensible and Adam's anger justified. A sympathetic judge had awarded Donna excessive alimony. To ask for more was disgraceful, but Kylie had no choice. She couldn't tell Donna's ex-husband that, however.

He gave her an outraged look. "Whole families live on less *and* send their kids through college."

She tried to placate him. "Why don't you discuss this with your ex-wife? Very often these things can be ironed out without going to court."

"I couldn't talk to her when we were *married*! Why do you think we got a divorce? If she wasn't under the hair dryer, she was on the telephone."

Kylie refused to give up. She really didn't want to handle this case. "If you just sit down together calmly, I'm sure you can come to an agreement. After all, you must have shared some happy moments. Try to remember those."

He looked at her closely for the first time, his gray eyes traveling over her in a male appraisal that made her palms sweaty. Adam Ridgeway was a very disturbing man. Kylie was tempted to reach for the tinted glasses she occasionally wore as a shield when she felt insecure, but something told her he'd guess the reason.

She also resisted the nervous urge to smooth her long black hair. Since she'd just come from home, it was, no doubt, still neatly in place. She always wore her hair pulled back at the office. The severe style and her tailored suits were in keeping with the decorum at Bradley, Cunningham & Smythe.

"You're rather naive for a lawyer," Adam said finally.

He seemed slightly bemused as he stared at her. Although Kylie downplayed her appearance as much as possible, certain gifts from her Irish forebears couldn't be hidden. She could camouflage her slender, curved figure under mannish suits with midcalf-length skirts, but nothing could hide her creamy skin or the blue eyes framed by thick black lashes.

"Take my advice and come to terms with your wife," she said curtly to cover her sudden, unwelcome feeling of vulnerability. "You'll find I'm not naive in court."

Adam's momentary softening hardened. His eyes narrowed dangerously. "Don't threaten me, Miss O'Connor. I know what you're up to. Donna's alimony runs out in three months. First you're asking for an increase, then you're going to try to get it extended. Well, it won't work. Tell my ex-wife she'd better get in line at the unemployment office, because her benefits are about to run out."

With a final glare, he stormed out of the office, leaving Kylie speechless. She had no doubt that he meant exactly what he said. The result would be a nasty court battle—the first of several, probably.

Adam was right about Donna's intentions. She was a greedy, grasping woman. She would hang on like a leech, dragging him into court repeatedly. Although Kylie's office would benefit from the extravagant fees, Kylie herself had no stomach for the whole mess.

After pausing a moment to compose herself, she walked down the hall to the senior partner's office.

Maxwell Cunningham was a distinguished-looking older man with a sympathetic manner that masked a cynical nature. He'd traded his ideals for a luxurious life-style long ago.

"This is certainly a pleasant way to start the week." He smiled charmingly. "What can I do for you, Kylie?"

"I'd like to be taken off the Ridgeway case," she said without preamble. "Our client, Donna Castle Ridgeway, is petitioning for an increase in alimony. Bob Shaefer handled the divorce, and I think he should follow through."

A slight frown diluted Cunningham's goodwill. "Bob is tied up with the big asbestos case against Kesterson Manufacturing. We can't spare him for a little alimony dispute."

Kylie gritted her teeth at the reminder of where she stood in the pecking order. She chose her words carefully. "When I joined the firm, I hoped I'd be assigned cases like that."

"You will, my dear, you will," the older man said smoothly. "You're young yet. All in good time."

She didn't bother to point out that Bob Shaefer was only two years older than she. "I'm not asking for the big corporate cases, Mr. Cunningham, but I would like to handle something other than divorces."

"Unfortunately those are our bread and butter. They're an inescapable fact of modern life. You're performing an invaluable service to the firm." He smiled again, inviting her to share the irony. "You're paying the rent."

Kylie knew it was a lost cause, but she made one last attempt. "At least assign the Ridgeway case to someone else."

"What's your problem with it?"

"Donna Castle isn't entitled to increased alimony. She can support herself, or find another man to do it for her. To put it bluntly, she's a parasite. I can't, in good conscience, petition the court on her behalf."

The senior partner carefully straightened his desk blotter. "We're defenders, Kylie, not judges. Our clients are our responsibility. We owe them our loyalty."

"Even when they're defective human beings?"

"That's not for us to decide." His expression was bland. "I know you'll exert all your efforts on Miss Castle's behalf because you're a dedicated professional. That's why we asked you to join our firm."

She was expertly eased out of the office without winning her point or even gaining any assurances for the near future. She returned to her own office, filled with frustration. The situation would be the same at any other law office, she knew. She'd simply have to practice patience until she achieved junior partnership status, which carried some clout.

When the week passed without any further explosions from Adam Ridgeway, Kylie decided he'd taken her advice and come to an agreement with his wife. She couldn't imagine him swallowing his pride, but even the mighty had to make concessions. The knowledge didn't bring her much satisfaction.

By Friday afternoon Kylie had all but forgotten Adam. Until Marcia brought in her appointment list for the next week. It showed a court date on the following Wednesday. *Ridgeway* v. *Ridgeway*.

"This must be a mistake." Kylie frowned at the sheet of paper. "I didn't request this date."

"That's what you have a law clerk for," Marcia answered.

"I wish the clerk hadn't been so efficient. I wanted to give the couple time to come to an agreement."

"That's like expecting a lion and a lamb to agree on a dinner entrée."

"They'd give each other indigestion." Kylie groaned. "Adam probably didn't even talk to her. I was hoping it wouldn't come to this."

"I know what you mean. You're not going to be his favorite person next Wednesday."

"It wasn't my idea to ask for more support," Kylie answered defensively.

"You're representing his ex-wife, though. That makes you the enemy, too."

Kylie sighed. "I suppose so."

"She must be crazy to have let him get away. He's the sexiest man I've ever seen."

"He also has a foul temper. Besides, you don't know what he was like to live with."

Marcia grinned. "I'd be happy to find out. Unfortunately he didn't notice me."

"It's an experience I could have passed up," Kylie said grimly, stuffing papers into her briefcase. "Well, I'm not going to let him spoil my weekend."

"Got a hot date?"

A smile curved Kylie's generous mouth. "With a charming young man."

"It's about time! You don't go out nearly enough." Marcia's pert rather than pretty face lit with eager curiosity. "Where are you going? Someplace exciting?"

"That depends on what you consider exciting. We'll probably go to bed early."

The young secretary's eyebrows rose. "Talk about still waters running deep! This guy must be really special."

Kylie's eyes glinted mischievously. "He is."

"Where did you meet him? What's he like?"

"I've known him for eight months. He's twenty-nine inches tall, he has black hair and blue eyes and I adore him."

"Thomas!" A disgusted look replaced Marcia's animation.

"Yes, I'm baby-sitting for the weekend."

"So what else is new?" Marcia asked cynically. "You're the world's biggest pushover, you know that?"

"Susan doesn't impose on me. I enjoy taking care of Tommy."

Actually, Kylie considered it a privilege. Since she'd almost certainly never have a child of her own, her kid sister's baby fulfilled a deep maternal instinct. The majority of her weekends were devoted to baby-sitting.

The arrangement worked out well. Like many young couples, Susan and her husband, Neal, were constantly struggling to make ends meet. Paying a baby-sitter would be an added burden, yet they needed time alone together.

Kylie had too *much* time alone, so Thomas was a welcome diversion. The only trouble was that she hated to part with him when the weekend was over. For those two days he belonged to her completely. When Susan came to pick him up, it was almost like giving away her own child. Kylie dimly realized it wasn't the healthiest of situations, but she shrugged off the unsettling thought. As Tommy got older he'd become involved in his own activities. The problem would take care of itself.

Kylie had chosen her town house because of the small garden in back; she liked the idea of being able to sun herself in privacy. Tommy's arrival made the enclosed yard even more useful. He got plenty of fresh air outside in his carriage.

That Saturday morning Kylie was up early. She had put on her usual weekend attire of jeans and a favorite shrunken sweater. It was a joy to dress casually and go without makeup—not that she usually wore much. Her eyebrows were naturally arched, and her thick lashes were as black as her hair. That was another bonus of the weekend—not having to slick her hair back in its accustomed prim style. As she knelt over a bed of marigolds, a long strand obscured her vision, but she didn't care. The sense of freedom was worth a little inconvenience.

She swept the intrusive hair away with her forearm as the doorbell sounded inside the house. "I'm in the garden," she called. "Come around the back." She didn't look up when the gate creaked open. "Just let me get this last dandelion, and I'm all yours."

A deep male voice answered quizzically, "I've played second fiddle in my time, but never to a dandelion."

Kylie's head whipped around, and her mouth dropped open. Adam Ridgeway was standing over her. He looked just as intimidating in jeans and a plaid shirt as he had in an expensive suit, despite the smile on his face. Or maybe because of it.

Kylie was abruptly aware of her position—rear in the air and hair tumbling wildly around her flushed face. She scrambled to her feet and pulled at the hem of the tight sweater that had hiked up to expose her midriff.

"What are you doing here?" she demanded.

"Admiring the view." He folded his arms over his impressive chest, looking her up and down. "Your little sister's clothes look good on you."

"What I wear in private is no concern of yours," she said coldly.

"I never would have suspected you *had* a private life," he drawled. "I pictured you poring over obscure law books seven days a week, looking for legal ways to pick a man's pocket."

She lifted her chin challengingly. "I get Saturdays and Sundays off for good behavior."

The mockery in his eyes turned to gray ice. "You certainly earn them."

"I don't conduct business in my home, Mr. Ridgeway. If you have something to say to me, see me in my office—with your attorney."

"I get as much satisfaction out of him as I do out of you." He scowled.

"They tell me things are bad in Patagonia, too," she answered flippantly.

He closed the distance between them, looming over her menacingly. "If you were a man, I'd break you into so many pieces they could use you for a jigsaw puzzle."

Kylie stood her ground. "That's the way cavemen settled things. We're supposed to be more civilized. Today we have courts."

"Invented by high-priced lawyers, no doubt."

"I gave you some free advice. I told you to settle with your wife and avoid a court battle."

"Forget it! I'm looking forward to my day in court. We'll see who wins when all the facts are presented."

"If you're so eager to face the judge, what are you doing here?"

"I can't appear on Wednesday. I have an assignment in Vancouver."

Kylie looked at him with annoyance. "You can get a continuance. All you have to do is contact your lawyer."

"I tried, but he's out of town for the weekend." He glared back at her with equal annoyance. "Don't you people ever work?"

"As you just pointed out, it's a weekend."

"I knew you'd have some excuse," he muttered.

Gritting her teeth was getting to be a habit around this man. "The legal profession doesn't go out of its way to inconvenience you, Mr. Ridgeway. I received my notice of the hearing yesterday, so you must have, too."

"There was a stack of mail in the box, but I didn't get around to opening it till this morning."

Kylie got the picture. Either he'd spent last night somewhere else, or he'd been entertaining at his place. He certainly wasn't suffering from lack of consolation!

"Evidently being burned once hasn't diminished your enthusiasm for the opposite sex," she commented waspishly.

"Would it make you happy if it had?" he asked derisively. "Sorry to disappoint you, Miss O'Connor. A man might give up collecting expensive art, but that doesn't mean he ceases to go to museums."

Before she could answer, Susan came through the gate carrying Thomas in her arms.

"It's such a glorious morning, I thought you'd be back here. Are we—" She stopped abruptly when she caught sight of Adam. "Hello, I'm Susan, Kylie's sister. I'd offer to shake hands, but they're a little full at the moment."

Adam's smile was completely natural, allowing Kylie a glimpse of the way he could act when he didn't have a chip on his shoulder. "Can I help you out?" he asked. "That young man looks big enough to carry *you*."

Susan laughed. "He isn't heavy. I always stagger like this when I walk."

Kylie saw her sister stare at Adam with frank curiosity, plus a female awareness he no doubt generated in most women.

"Are you some kind of repairman?" Susan asked.

"I'm not noted for it. Why would you think that?"

"Kylie doesn't usually—I mean, you look so... competent."

"Not if you put me in front of a defective washing machine." He chuckled. "I'm much better with animate objects."

"I don't doubt it for a moment," Susan murmured.

"Mr. Ridgeway is a photographer," Kylie said curtly. "And he was just leaving."

She was annoyed at both of them. At her sister for being impressed by this blatantly macho male, and at Adam for being there in the first place.

"Not yet." His expression hardened. "We have some unfinished business."

As the tension between them mounted, Susan said, "Ridgeway. Are you *Adam* Ridgeway? The famous photographer?"

He slanted a sardonic glance at Kylie. "Some people consider me infamous."

Susan was too excited to notice the veiled hostility between them. "I love your work! The exhibit of your photos at the County Museum last year was positively smashing."

"I'm glad you enjoyed it."

"You're a genius. That picture of the skier at the winter Olympics seemed to jump right out of the frame. You must lead a fascinating life, covering all those exciting events."

"It has its moments," he answered modestly.

"You didn't tell me Mr. Ridgeway was a client," Susan said reprovingly to her big sister.

"He isn't." Kylie took the baby out of her arms. "Hadn't you better be on your way? Arrowhead is a long drive."

"That's true," Susan agreed reluctantly.

"You're a skier, too?" Adam asked. Arrowhead was a popular ski resort in the winter months. "Now I know why you enjoyed that particular photo."

"As an amateur photographer I appreciate how difficult it must have been to get a good focus against all that blinding snow. My husband and I do ski, but we have to settle for the water variety this time of year."

"Be sure to wear a life jacket," Kylie cautioned.

Susan gave Adam a laughing glance. "If she isn't taking care of Thomas, she's taking care of me. I keep telling Kylie she ought to have six kids of her own. She's definitely the maternal type."

He gazed at Kylie speculatively. "That's something I never would have suspected."

"Why else would she insist on taking Tommy off our hands almost every weekend?" Susan asked. "I'm starting to feel guilty."

"Neal's going to be calling any minute to find out what's keeping you," Kylie said impatiently.

Adam waited quietly as Susan issued a spate of late-minute instructions. His impassive gaze was fixed on Kylie and the baby in her arms.

"Goodbye, Mr. Ridgeway." Susan turned her attention back to him. "I'm sorry I don't have more time to talk to you, but maybe we'll meet again."

"It's entirely possible," he agreed pleasantly.

Silence fell after Susan left. Kylie shifted the baby's weight. "As you can see, I'm quite busy. If you'll call your attorney on Monday morning, he'll arrange for a continuance."

Adam answered as though he hadn't heard her. "Is this really the way you spend your weekends?"

"What's wrong with it?"

"The fact that you can even ask!" he answered incredulously.

"I happen to enjoy taking care of Thomas." She raised her chin pugnaciously. "Different strokes for different folks, Mr. Ridgeway."

"How old are you?" he demanded unexpectedly.

"Twenty-eight." Kylie had been startled into answering, but she recovered immediately. "What's that got to do with anything?"

"You ought to be living your own life instead of your kid sister's."

"I am! I have a very *full* life. An interesting job and . . . and . . . a very full life," she concluded lamely.

"Don't you do anything but work?"

"Of course I do."

"Like what?"

"Well, I—" She hugged the baby protectively. "I don't have to justify my life-style to you."

"How about men?" he persisted.

"How about them?" she asked derisively.

"Don't you date?"

"Occasionally, but men aren't my first priority."

"You're a beautiful, intelligent woman," he said slowly, looking at her with a comprehensiveness that made Kylie's heart beat faster. "I can't believe you're content to sit home alone night after night."

"What you're really saying is *sleep* alone," she replied tartly.

"That, too, although I'm not talking about casual sex. Clearly you aren't the type to be promiscuous, but everyone needs love."

"Love is just another four-letter word," she said bitterly. "You, off all people, ought to know that."

"I've been knocked down but not out," he answered with a touch of humor. "You, on the other hand, are afraid to risk stepping into the ring. Isn't that rather cowardly?"

"That shows how much *you* know! I once believed in love and fidelity—all the so-called nobler emotions. I was engaged to a man who was everything I dreamed of. We were going to conquer the world together, starting at the bottom and working our way up. Until he met a girl whose father could eliminate most of the rungs."

"Those kind of men exist. Women, too. You cut your losses and get on with your life."

"I have," Kylie answered tersely.

"No, you've built a protective wall around yourself."

"Only a masochist sets herself up for another fall."

"Only a pessimist expects one," he countered.

"In my business you see them all too often."

His lip curled. "You ought to get into another business."

"How would you like it if I said that to you?" she flared.

"I don't go around gouging people."

"You think I like that part of it?" she demanded. "I went into the legal profession because I wanted to help people." A note of self-mockery colored her voice. "I expected to defend the oppressed and bring justice to the masses."

"So what happened?"

"Landlords and grocers aren't equally altruistic," she answered dryly. "They get testy when their bills aren't paid."

"Okay, maybe you'll get a shot at doing good after you're older and more established. But that doesn't mean you have to put your personal life on hold."

She looked at him squarely. "You don't like me, Mr. Ridgeway, but—"

"Don't you think it's time we progressed to Adam and Kylie?" he interrupted.

"All right...Adam. You'd like to see me get my comeuppance when we face each other in court, so why this lecture about getting more out of life?"

He stared at her intently. "Maybe I did picture you as the devil's disciple, but I realize now that was unfair. You have a job to do—even though I think you could be more gainfully employed selling aluminum siding. No, let me finish," he said when she threatened to erupt. "Seeing you away from the sterile environment of your multiple-named law firm makes me realize you're a person, with all the hang-ups the rest of us have."

"You might have hang-ups; I don't," she said stubbornly. "I know exactly where I'm going."

"Where is that, Kylie?"

"I'm going to become a partner so I can handle the kind of cases I believe in."

"Who are you going to share your triumphs with?"

"I don't need anybody."

"I can't believe that. Do you really want to spend the rest of your life alone?"

How on earth had their conversation become so personal? Kylie wondered in amazement. Just then the baby made a contented sound and reached up to grab a strand of her hair. When she touched his cheek with infinite tenderness, he gurgled with pleasure. Kylie nuzzled the soft curls on top of his head, oblivious to Adam for the moment.

"You do know how to love, don't you," he observed quietly.

Adam was an unwelcome intrusion into her private world. She wished he'd leave. Lifting her chin defiantly, Kylie said, "Everyone loves babies."

"Then why don't you have one of your own instead of sharing your sister's?"

"Because I don't happen to have a husband."

"That isn't a requirement. A lot of single women are having babies these days. It's quite acceptable."

"That might be all right while the baby remains an infant, but I think a child needs two parents when it gets older." She stopped and looked at him with outrage. "Why am I explaining myself to you? It's none of your business!"

"It might be." He looked her up and down. "Now that I know you want a baby but not a husband, I might be persuaded to volunteer my services."

"Forget it, pal! I don't want *anything* that much!"

He grinned, enjoying himself hugely. "Don't be hasty. I'm reasonably young, extremely healthy and moderately intelligent." His voice dropped to a velvet purr. "I also guarantee to make the experience painless. You might even enjoy it."

Her mouth suddenly felt dry. Even though she didn't like the man, Kylie had no doubt of his ability to deliver what he promised. Those sparkling gray eyes and that sexy male body had undoubtedly induced many women to become willing participants in "the experience." She banished the thought hurriedly.

"I'm sure your talents have been honed to perfection," she remarked coolly, "but your genes aren't right."

"What's wrong with them?"

"Who'd want a baby who was apt to mug the family cat?"

Adam's white teeth gleamed. "Don't you want your son to be able to defend himself?"

"The possibility of fathering a daughter never occurred to you?" she asked sweetly.

He pretended to look thoughtful. "That *would* be a problem. Little girls are supposed to be made of sugar and spice, but ours would have a disposition like a sailor denied shore leave."

"Precisely. The entire notion is like your temper—totally irrational."

He let that pass with merely an arched eyebrow. "Okay, if we can't have a baby together, how about dinner?"

"No," she answered.

Thomas, perhaps sensing her tension, started to fuss. When rocking him in her arms didn't help, she placed him in the carriage.

"Why not?" Adam persisted.

"Because I'm not hungry."

"You will be. Where would you like to eat once you are?"

She made a sound of exasperation. "I have neither the time nor the inclination to stand around arguing with you. *I* have things to do, even if you don't."

He shifted his weight to one hip. Hooking his thumbs in the low-riding waistband of his narrow jeans, he gazed at her derisively. "Don't panic. My invitation didn't have any strings attached. You don't have to sleep with me afterward."

"You're damn right, I don't!" Her blue eyes sparkled with anger.

"Is that what keeps you sitting home by the fire, Kylie? You're afraid someone's going to make a pass at you?"

"Don't be ridiculous."

"You can't blame guys for trying. You're a very beautiful woman," he repeated.

As his appraising glance traveled over her, lingering on the sweater stretched snugly across her breasts, Kylie felt a creeping warmth. The man was undeniably sexy. She kept her eyes trained on his chiseled face, afraid they might otherwise stray to his lean hips and muscular thighs.

"You can always say no," he concluded mildly.

"I just did." She picked up the tote bag of baby paraphernalia Susan had brought and held it against her chest.

He chuckled. "I haven't exactly made a pass—yet."

"And you won't get a chance to," she stated. "You obviously think it's your mission in life to go around liberating repressed females, but I don't happen to desire your services."

"You admit you're repressed, then?"

"No! That's not what I meant at all."

"You're absolutely sure I couldn't talk you into bed if we went out together?"

"You can bet the farm on it," she said firmly.

"We'll find out tonight, won't we?" he asked softly.

"Oh, no, you don't. I'm not falling for anything that obvious. You're trying to trick me into going out with you."

"Of course." He smiled infuriatingly. "You're too chicken to accept any other way."

Kylie was almost incoherent with rage. She longed to wipe the superior-male smile off his face. "You've got yourself a date, buster,'' she snapped. "And don't blame me if it doesn't turn our the way you expected."

"I like surprises," he said smugly. "See you at eight."

He was opening the gate when she remembered her nephew. "Wait! I can't go out with you tonight."

He paused to look at her with mild contempt. "I might have known."

"It isn't what you're thinking. It's Thomas. I can't leave him."

Adam smiled sardonically. "It's time you experienced the down side of motherhood. Get a sitter."

The gate clicked shut as she gazed after him indignantly. She would have run after him, but the baby's fretting turned into a full-blown bellow. His diaper was wet, and he demanded immediate attention.

For a short time Kylie was too busy to worry about the callow way she'd let herself be manipulated. After changing Thomas and putting him into his crib for a nap, she tiptoed around the changing table and the chest of drawers decorated with nursery cutouts.

The one-bedroom apartment had seemed spacious when she moved in, but that was before she'd shared it with a baby. Since he spent so much time with her, Kylie had duplicated all of his equipment, which was extensive. She was surprised at the sheer quantity of things one tiny boy required.

While Tommy slept, Kylie usually read or gardened, but that day she couldn't settle down to either. Adam Ridgeway's visit had been too upsetting. How could she have let herself be pressured into a date with that obnoxious man?

He'd maneuvered her expertly, knowing if she got angry enough, temper would cloud her better judgment. She couldn't even break the date. That would merely confirm his suspicion that she was a frightened, frigid female, which was insupportable.

But what on earth would they talk about all evening? They had absolutely nothing in common. He wasn't remotely interested in her as a person. Adam Ridgeway wanted only one thing from a woman, and she wasn't the kind who would give it to him.

Was that why he'd tricked her into going out with him? He thought it would be amusing to add a repressed spinster to his list of conquests? Kylie's mouth set grimly. He'd find she was more than a match for him—in or out of the courtroom!

A sudden thought hit her like a thunderbolt. She couldn't go out with Adam! Since she was his wife's attorney, it would be a clear conflict of interest. They shouldn't have any contact whatsoever outside the courtroom. She had not only an excuse, but an obligation to break the date.

That should have made her happy, but the realization left Kylie with very mixed emotions.

Chapter Two

Kylie tried to reach Adam at intervals during the afternoon, but all she got was his answering machine.

The recording on it was indicative of the man. Instead of a polite excuse about being unable to come to the phone at that time, followed by detailed instructions on how and when to leave a message, his response was clipped and to the point: "This is Adam Ridgeway. Leave me a message."

Kylie did, but he didn't return her call. At first she thought he was merely out for the day, but when evening approached, she started to get annoyed. He had to have gone home to change clothes. Surely he didn't expect to take her to dinner in blue jeans. Although with a man like him, nothing was certain. Maybe he hadn't bothered to listen to his messages. That would be typical, too. He struck her as very cavalier.

She'd simply left a request for him to call her, not wanting to break their date without making sure he understood the reason. But at seven o'clock she was forced to leave her complete message on his machine and hope he'd get it in time.

Adam was stepping out of the shower when the phone rang. He strolled into the bedroom, toweling his hair dry as he listened to Kylie's amplified voice. He'd gotten home a short while ago and played back his messages, but he had no intention of returning her earlier call. His even white teeth gleamed in a sardonic smile at her stilted excuse.

"I'm afraid I can't keep our date tonight." It was seven o'clock now, and Kylie's tension was evident. "Not for the reason you're thinking. It's simply that it would be unprofessional. I—I'm sorry, but it wasn't a very good idea in the first place."

"You're not running out on me, lawyer lady," Adam said softly as the machine clicked off. "You and your kind have pushed me to the limit. Now it's my turn to give *you* a hard time."

He stalked around the bedroom, yanking open drawers and banging them shut again, his naked body taut with anger. Women like Kylie were the worst! They wanted revenge against the whole male gender because they were frigid themselves. Making love to her would be like cuddling up with a block of ice.

And yet... Adam's tight jaw relaxed as he remembered the way she'd looked with the baby in her arms. Was there a real woman under that prickly exterior? In that moment, when her guard was down, he'd seemed to glimpse a warm, caring human being, a woman capable of great feeling. She'd looked appealingly vulnerable, arousing an unexpected urge to treat her gently.

Adam's expression hardened as he buttoned his shirt. Kylie O'Connor was about as defenseless as a great white shark. *He* was the poor fish. But no more! Tonight he was going to speak his piece, and she was going to listen.

By seven-thirty Kylie had given up expecting to hear from Adam. She'd have to break the date in person. He would have made a useless trip to her place, but it was his own fault. He'd purposely avoided calling her, so he could take the consequences. She didn't waste much sympathy on his ruined evening. A man of his talents could get any number of willing replacements to fill the hours.

Kylie's tension mounted as the minutes ticked by. Until the inevitably unpleasant encounter with Adam was over, she couldn't work on the briefs she'd brought home from the office or even watch television. When the doorbell rang promptly at eight, it was almost a relief.

Adam's eyebrows rose as he stood in the entryway looking at her. Kylie had considered changing clothes; she'd even pulled several outfits out of her closet before deciding against them. But why should she bother with her appearance just to argue with Adam? Hopefully he'd be in and out in five minutes.

"You look lovely, but you shouldn't have gone to so much trouble," he said derisively.

She thrust her hands into her back pockets and glared up at him. "Don't panic. Your reputation for escorting glamorous women isn't in jeopardy. I'm not going out with you."

"I might have known you wouldn't honor a verbal commitment," he said contemptuously. "I should have gotten it in writing. Then I could have sued you."

"You don't have to be abusive."

"How am I supposed to act, pleased at being stood up at the last minute?"

"I tried to call you. Why do you have an answering machine if you don't ever listen to it?"

"We had a date, and you're breaking it," he said stubbornly.

"I never should have accepted it in the first place."

"But you did." His jaw set in a hard line. "Aren't lawyers supposed to fulfill their agreements? Or does that only apply to their victims?"

Kylie sighed. "Let's not get into another discussion of the legal profession."

"Because you can't justify it?"

"That's just one of the many things we disagree on. Without laws we wouldn't have an ordered society; we'd have a jungle where the strong would prey on the weak," she said heatedly.

His mouth curved cynically. "Under your system, the so-called weak are presently mopping up on the strong. I'd rather take my chances in the jungle."

Kylie didn't doubt it. He looked lean and mean enough to beat any odds. "Do you have to bring everything down to a personal level?" she demanded.

"It's *my* ox that's being gored, lady."

"And it's your own fault! You aren't interested in the kind of woman who wants a home and children. All you care about is sex and glitter. Well, if you marry someone who shares your own shallow values, you have to expect the experience to be costly." Kylie's cheeks were flushed.

"Why should I be the only one to pay for a mutual mistake?"

Her passion died abruptly. That was an inequity she'd questioned herself. "I guess because you're the one with the money," she mumbled.

"Am I supposed to pay for the rest of my life?"

"The hearing is solely to increase your remaining support payments."

"Which have only three months to go. Can you promise I'll be a free man after that?"

She couldn't look at him. "I don't... That decision will have to rest with your ex-wife and the judge."

His rugged face might have been carved out of stone. "We both know she's prepared to hang on like a leech. And you're going to encourage her until it isn't profitable anymore."

"We don't encourage litigation," Kylie protested.

"Really? Would you keep Donna on as a client without the prospect of receiving fat attorney's fees?"

Kylie's gaze shifted uncomfortably. "Bradley, Cunningham & Smythe isn't a charitable organization. We expect to get paid for our services, the same as you do."

He gripped her chin and jerked her head up, forcing her to look into his stormy gray eyes. "I'm not talking about Wynken, Blynken and Nod. I'm talking about *you*, Kylie. Do you go to bed every night with a clear conscience?"

Her lashes fell. "Nobody ever said life was fair."

"Nobody said you couldn't try to change it, either."

She pulled away from him. "When I was young and innocent I thought I could. Or at least make a small dent. But that was before I found out the prizes go to the people with the fewest scruples."

"So you want to be one of them? Your convictions couldn't have been very firm if you were willing to sell out that easily."

"What good would it do me to swim against the current if it means I'm not in a position to help anyone eventually?"

"That's a convenient rationale," he said sardonically. "Is that what you'll tell yourself when you're awarded a juicy slice of the pie? A piece I'll be paying for unjustly, I might add."

"You can't know how the judge will rule," she protested. "He could easily decide you have a valid objection. There are a lot of things in your favor."

Adam's gaze was suddenly piercing. "Your heart isn't really in this case, is it?"

"Donna Castle is my client," she answered unemotionally.

"That's not what I asked you."

Kylie chose her words carefully. "Every client is entitled to the best representation I can give him or her if I'm the attorney on the case."

"Even if you don't believe in the validity of the claim?"

"Yes. It isn't up to me to decide. That's what the judge is for. I can only hope he'll be fair."

"So you intend to go into court and give it everything you've got?"

"I have to. I might not be able to do anything about other people's principles, but I can't compromise my own."

Adam stared at her for a long moment while Kylie returned his gaze unflinchingly. "You're quite a woman," he said finally.

"Thank you—I think."

His firm mouth curved in a smile. "You're right, it was a compliment. Which surprises me as much as it does you."

"Does that mean you understand my position?"

"Not in a million years. I'm going to clobber you in court, but we can have a very stimulating time arguing about it in private."

"That's just the point. We can't, Adam."

"Afraid you'll lose?" he taunted. "Don't worry, it will be off the record."

"You don't understand. I can't talk about the case with you. You shouldn't even be here."

"Okay, we won't talk business." His eyes warmed as he looked at her. "I can think of more rewarding things to discuss."

"We shouldn't have any contact at all," she said earnestly. "It's completely unprofessional."

He grinned. "I'm willing to get personal if you are."

"I'm serious, Adam!"

"I am, too," he said slowly, his laughter fading. "An hour ago I thought your natural habitat was the North Pole, but I'm beginning to see a different aspect of you."

"Your compliments don't exactly err on the extravagant side," she said wryly.

"That's because I'm busy shifting gears." He smiled appealingly. "I'm usually a very gallant fellow."

"Perhaps that's your trouble."

"The fact that I like women?"

"Indiscriminately," she said curtly.

"How can you say that? You don't even know me."

"I know *about* you."

"Isn't that called hearsay evidence?"

Her mouth compressed into a straight line. "Your amorous adventures have been well documented."

"Not during my marriage. That's one thing you can't hang on me."

Kylie was reminded of the impropriety of his being there. Her disapproval changed to anxiety. "You really have to leave, Adam."

"Is that how you settle an argument when the other side is winning, run for cover?"

"It has nothing to do with winning or losing. I explained to you that meeting like this is improper."

His amused glance swept lazily over her slim body. "If this is your idea of a compromising situation, you don't get around enough."

Kylie stiffened. "Not as much as you do, obviously."

"We'll have to remedy that. Your life doesn't have enough fun in it. That's why you're so hard to get along with."

"If my personality is that obnoxious, I can't imagine why you'd want to stick around," she said coldly.

"Maybe because I'm a pushover for silky black hair and powder-blue eyes," he murmured.

Kylie steeled herself against the husky note in his voice that seemed to vibrate deep inside her. "You married a blonde," she pointed out.

"That was one of my mistakes."

"Another is thinking I'd fall for such blatant flattery," she replied angrily.

"Do you always react this way to compliments?"

"Only when they're insincere. You don't even *like* me."

He chuckled. "That isn't one of the requirements for admiring a beautiful woman."

"You're utterly detestable!" she stormed. "You'd even be capable of making love to me!"

"Entirely capable," he assured her, his eyes dancing with mirth. "But would you mind if we had dinner first?"

Kylie didn't trust herself to answer. Adam had her at a disadvantage when he brought things down to a sexual level. She was clearly no match for him in experience. He was so overpoweringly masculine that he made her feel like an untried teenager. That was something he must never find out.

She stalked to the door and threw it open. "You've had your fun. Now, kindly get out of my house!"

He sauntered over and stood very close to her, looking down with a mixture of amusement and speculation. "I wonder if our pending lawsuit is your real reason for wanting to get rid of me." His fingers trailed down her cheek before tracing the outline of her lips. "Or could it be because I remind you that you're a woman with normal needs and desires?"

He left her standing there, staring speechlessly after him as he closed the door softly.

Kylie didn't move until she heard Adam's car drive away. Then anger penetrated her trancelike state. Of all the arrogant, conceited, condescending males! He was absolutely certain that he was the one who could awaken Sleeping Beauty with a kiss. She was surprised he hadn't tried it!

Tiny ripples of excitement ran through her veins as, completely against her will, she pictured what such an awakening would be like. Adam had honed lovemaking to a fine art. He had effortlessly made a small caress almost unbearably sensuous. Her cheek still tingled from the touch of those long fingers. For one inexplicable moment she'd wanted him to take her in his arms and kiss her with tenderness and passion.

The realization was appalling! Her experience with men might be limited, but it was enough to know that Adam was bad news. She couldn't hold his interest for more than one night. Not that she wanted to. But it was a good thing he wouldn't have any reason to come near her after the hearing.

At first Kylie was afraid Adam might keep pestering her. She sensed he wasn't the type to give up easily. But if she'd had any doubts about his real motives—to seduce her away from the opposition in his upcoming hearing—they were soon dispelled. He didn't call her after that night, either at home or at the office.

She tried to blot him out of her thoughts, but he kept popping up annoyingly. A tall, athletic man seen from a distance would remind her of Adam. Or a deep, impatient voice heard in a crowded elevator.

Kylie decided her preoccupation with the man reflected her reluctance toward the coming hearing. Adam would be explosive if he lost, insufferable if he won. She wished the whole messy thing was over with.

Unlike Kylie, her client was looking forward to the confrontation. She phoned the day before the hearing.

"What are you going to wear to court?" Donna asked.

Kylie was nonplussed. Of all the questions she might have expected, that wasn't one of them. "Well, I...I hadn't thought about it. Why do you ask?"

"We shouldn't show up in the same color. It would look like we'd been to a clearance sale. I have this marvelous little red dress if you don't plan on wearing red."

"I never wear red," Kylie stated.

"Really? I've always found it very effective. Men notice you right away."

"Since this isn't a trial and there is no jury, I don't think it matters what you wear tomorrow, Miss Castle," Kylie said unemotionally.

"That's where you're wrong. A woman's appearance is always important. You never know who you'll meet."

Did she expect to find Adam's replacement at an alimony hearing? Kylie stifled a sigh. "I wouldn't get too dressed up. You're asking for an increase in your support payments, remember."

"Don't worry. I'll only wear costume jewelry."

"That should convince the judge you're a needy case," Kylie answered dryly. "Well, I'll see you at the court-house tomorrow morning at ten o'clock."

"That's such a ghastly hour, but I suppose it can't be helped this time."

Kylie picked up the inference immediately. "If we lose tomorrow, I'm afraid that's the end of the line. Since your alimony runs out in less than three months, we wouldn't have time to petition again."

Donna gave a tiny laugh. "Maybe the judge will extend my payments. After all, Adam makes a fortune, and I'm unemployed. He's really obligated to take care of me."

"For the rest of your life?" Kylie asked sharply, un-consciously echoing Adam's sentiments.

"Until I get on my feet, anyway," Donna answered smugly.

She might, if she ever got off her rump. Kylie tried to keep the disgust she felt from showing in her voice. "All we're concerned with tomorrow is increasing the amount you presently receive. Please be in court on time." She hung up before the other woman could reply, not caring that she'd been brusque.

Kylie's eyes were still sparkling angrily when her secre-tary brought in some papers for her to sign.

"You look as though you just got an obscene phone call," Marcia observed.

"How did you guess?"

"I was only joking! Did you really?"

"You could call it that. Donna Castle hinted that she intends to keep me on a retainer."

"What's wrong with that?"

"She's a conscienceless little gold digger," Kylie replied hotly.

Marcia grinned. "Here at Bradley, Cunningham & Smythe, we don't screen their morals, only their bank accounts."

"That's disgusting! Some of our clients would make Dillinger look like a purse snatcher."

"Well, look at it this way: everyone deserves a fair trial. It's called the American way."

"But that's exactly the trouble. We don't represent all segments of the population, only those who can afford to pay. Do you realize we don't take any pro bono cases?"

"A lot of other law firms don't, either."

"That doesn't make it right. I'm finding it harder and harder to justify my salary. How long can I ignore the really needy cases simply because those people can't afford my services?"

"Don't do anything foolish," Marcia warned. "If you quit, they'd only replace you with someone more amenable to their ways. What would that prove? It wouldn't change office policy."

"I suppose you're right," Kylie answered morosely. "But from now on I'm through being the tame lapdog around here. Sooner or later Mr. Cunningham will have to let me do some pro bono work. He owes it to me for dumping all these sleazy divorce cases in my lap."

Kylie felt a mixture of anticipation and dread as she dressed for work the next morning. The hearing that day was apt to be stormy. Nothing, she was beginning to believe, was ever peaceful when Adam was involved.

Her pulse beat faster as she speculated about his conduct toward her. Would there be any remnant of the desire she'd glimpsed? Kylie stared at her reflection, recalling the look in his eyes as he'd caressed her cheek.

She forced the image from her mind. Adam's intention had been to intimidate her, until he'd decided seduction would be more effective. When he found out neither worked, he'd written her off as a crusty old maid. Today in court he'd be his usual domineering self.

Kylie brushed her hair until it crackled, then clipped it neatly back with a tortoiseshell barrette. She shrugged on the gray pin-striped jacket that matched her calf-length skirt and picked up her briefcase. Adam Ridgeway might be able to bully other people, but he didn't affect her in the slightest.

As an afterthought, she tucked her tinted glasses into her purse.

The hearing was held in the chambers of a domestic court judge. The proceedings were less formal than an actual trial. Both lawyers and their clients sat on one side of a huge desk, facing the judge.

Kylie was disconcerted at the seating arrangement. She understood the wisdom of separating Adam and Donna, but without quite knowing how it had happened, she found herself sitting next to Adam. His attorney and Donna sat on either end.

Adam's behavior from the moment he entered the room gave warning that he was going to be difficult. He surveyed Kylie from head to toe with a mocking gleam in his eyes.

"You must give me the name of your tailor," was his first salvo. "Mine never achieves that macho image."

Kylie swallowed her anger. "Perhaps he doesn't have as much to work with," she answered sweetly.

He laughed out loud. "Score one for the ladies' team."

"I'm glad to see you're such a good loser."

"That's because I don't have any image problems." He looked again at her severe suit and high-necked blouse. "I don't feel the need to hide behind a disguise, for one thing."

"I'm not hiding anything," she said indignantly.

"Yes, you are, and very effectively." His voice dropped to a confidential tone. "Fortunately, I remember the sexy body under those yards of gray flannel."

Her color rose, but before she could frame a withering reply, Donna claimed his attention.

"Aren't you even going to say hello?" she pouted.

His face hardened. "How much will it cost me?"

She sighed dramatically. "I'd hoped after all this time you'd be more civil."

"You mean docile," he snorted.

"Don't be bitter, darling. *I'm* not." Donna's lovely face was wistful. "I still remember all the wonderful times we had together."

"Including the time you locked me out in the rain, and the time you tore up a complete fashion layout?"

"I prefer to remember the black chiffon nightgown you bought me to make up after the argument, and how we turned off the phone for two days," she said softly.

Kylie pushed her chair back, stood up abruptly and walked away. She didn't want to hear any more.

"How's it going, counselor?" Steve Randolph, Adam's lawyer, strolled over to join her by the window.

"Pretty good," Kylie said absentmindedly, glancing over at the other couple. "Listen, Steve, I have a feeling we could settle this case before the judge gets here."

"Is your client ready to drop her demands?"

"No, I had a reconciliation in mind."

"Forget it! My guy wants out."

"Don't be too sure. His wife wants him back, and I have a feeling what Donna wants, Donna gets."

The blond woman had moved to the seat beside Adam and was caressing his lapels as she talked earnestly in a low voice. His face was inscrutable, but he wasn't moving away.

This was Adam's kind of woman, Kylie thought, feeling an unexpected pang. She was glamour personified. Donna had decided against the red dress and had worn a black one instead. The somber color set off her pastel beauty, making her seem fragile and defenseless.

Steve was appreciative but unimpressed. "Not this time. She had her chance, and she blew it. Adam wouldn't take her back if she were Cleopatra reincarnated."

"I still think you should sound him out," Kylie said stubbornly. "What's the point in slugging it out in court if they have a chance of settling their own differences?"

"I never knew you were such a romantic," he teased.

"I believe in the sanctity of marriage," she admitted.

"Too bad your client doesn't. I could tell you stories that would make your proper little toes curl."

"Why does everyone think I'm so proper!" Kylie exploded. She was good and tired of being stuffy Miss Prim while the Donna Castles of the world walked off with all the rewards.

Her raised voice attracted Adam's attention. His grim expression faded as he smiled at her. "You can't have it both ways," he said.

Donna's eyes narrowed at the look on his face. She stared at Kylie in disbelief, but with wariness, as well. Before she could resume their conversation, Adam stood up.

"When is this thing going to get started?" he asked. "It's already twenty minutes past ten."

"Relax, Adam," Steve advised. "We have to wait for the judge."

"He's late. It's no wonder the courts are so backed up," Adam said disgustedly as he walked over to join the other two. "I keep my appointments on time, and I expect the same courtesy from other people."

Steve's mouth curved cynically. "Judges are only prompt at election time."

"Remind me not to vote for this one."

"That's your privilege, but I'd rather you didn't mention it till the hearing is over." Steve laughed.

Adam jingled some coins in his pocket as he gazed at Kylie. "I don't know what I'm doing here anyway. I could have just sent my checkbook. Isn't that right, Miss O'Connor?"

"Are you offering to settle, Mr. Ridgeway?"

"Not on your life! You're the one who runs away from a fight, not I."

"I did not run—" Kylie stopped abruptly.

Once again he had her at a disadvantage. No one must know they'd met privately, even though it didn't really have anything to do with the case. Adam had spent most of the time getting personal.

"As I recall, we were arguing about my love life." His good humor was suddenly restored. "You made unsubstantiated allegations, then refused to listen to my defense. Wouldn't you call that a cop-out?"

Steve looked narrowly at Kylie's tight-lipped expression. "When was all this? Have you been harassing my client?"

Donna had been growing more and more annoyed. She wasn't used to being ignored. She joined their group, her mouth drooping petulantly. "You'd think they'd at least provide coffee if they were going to keep us cooped up here for hours."

Steve glanced at his watch. "It shouldn't be much longer now."

A few moments later the judge entered. He was a middle-aged man with permanent frown lines and a businesslike manner. After greeting them he glanced through the brief on his desk as they took their seats.

Kylie had intended to sit on the end this time, but Adam was too quick for her. He seated Donna in that chair and again took the one next to Kylie.

The judge looked at her. "This petition states that Miss Donna Castle is asking for an increase in the amount of support paid to her by her ex-husband, Mr. Adam Ridgeway."

"That's correct, Your Honor."

"Isn't this rather unusual? There are only two more payments due. Assuming this month's obligation has been met."

"It has, Your Honor," Steve said quickly.

"Miss Castle is appealing to have the award made retroactive to include this month, since our court date was originally set for three weeks ago," Kylie said. "Mr. Ridgeway requested the postponement."

"Yes, I see that. But even so, the agreement is almost terminated."

"That's true, but we all know about inflation. People living on fixed incomes suffer hardship whether the period is two months or two years."

The judge nodded and flipped through the papers in front of him. "Miss Castle presently receives—" He raised his head and looked at her in amazement. "You can't live on this sum?"

"It isn't nearly as much as it sounds," Donna said defensively.

"Young woman, do you know what the national average income is for an entire family?"

Adam snickered under his breath.

"I'm not very good with figures." Her lower lip quivered appealingly. "My husband always took care of the finances. I guess I probably waste a lot of money, but I can never turn anyone down. You know...charities, and friends who need a helping hand. Things like that."

The judge looked considerably less stern. "Perhaps you should have a business manager."

"I'm sure you're right, but it's rather late for that. If someone had suggested it to me sooner, I might have been able to save some money." She bit her lip delicately, gazing at him with troubled eyes. "I don't know what I'm going to do when my alimony runs out."

"Your Honor, Miss Castle alleges that most of her income goes to charity," Steve said. "Even if that were true, it's her choice. We contend, however, that she spends huge amounts on clothes, furs and beauty treatments."

"I have to look good," Donna flared. "I'm an actress."

"Oh, really?" Steve's voice was heavy with sarcasm. "When's the last time you had a part?"

"Mr. Randolph!" The judge looked at him with disapproval. "We're more informal here in chambers, but you're still expected to address the court, not engage in a dissertation with the plaintiff."

"I'm sorry, Your Honor. But I think Miss Castle has made my point for me. She has a profession she could pursue if she were really desperate for money."

"That's completely beside the point," Kylie interjected swiftly. "Mr. Ridgeway agreed to support his wife, and she's entitled to the same style of living he enjoys."

"I once asked her to go fishing with me, and she had a panic attack," Adam said unexpectedly. "The only thing that cured it was a shopping trip to Saks."

"That's a lie!" Donna flashed. "Why are you trying to give everyone the impression that all I did during our marriage was shop?"

"Because I'm too much of a gentleman to tell them the other things you did."

"You weren't any saint!"

"Let me handle this," Kylie said urgently.

"I don't notice you doing anything," Donna raged. "What kind of a lawyer are you, anyway?"

"A better one than you deserve," Adam remarked.

"I want this to stop immediately," the judge thundered. "Let's have some respect for the court."

"I regret my client's momentary lapse," Kylie apologized. "She was simply overcome by the injustice of her situation."

"My client is the one who's the victim of injustice," Steve said. "He's been more than generous. We contend that Miss Castle can continue to maintain her former standard of living on what she was originally awarded. Especially since many of her expenses are paid by other men."

"That's not true!" Donna exclaimed.

"I really must protest, Your Honor," Kylie said.

Steve shuffled through some papers in his hand. "We can prove that on at least one occasion, her rent was paid by a Mr. Warren Whitley."

Donna's face reddened unbecomingly. "That doesn't... I mean, it was just a favor. I'd run out of checks, and Mr.

Whitley very kindly offered to write one for me. It was merely a friendly gesture."

"Very friendly, I'd say," Steve remarked dryly. "Miss Castle also received some shares of stock from a Mr. George Andreas."

"Irrelevant, Your Honor," Kylie said. "What does this have to do with my client's expenses? She's entitled to receive gifts."

"Gifts are flowers and candy. We're talking about money," Steve said. "She could cash in the stocks to pay her bills if she needed to."

"That should be up to Miss Castle's discretion," Kylie said. "It isn't opposing counsel's function to tell her how to spend her money."

"It is when she's trying to get more out of my client. He's already being squeezed like a fat lady in a size six girdle."

"That will do, Mr. Randolph," the judge admonished.

Kylie reached for her tinted glasses. An appalling picture was emerging. Donna was playing the field with more men than the L.A. Rams! No wonder Adam was so bitter about her. Kylie felt distaste shudder up her spine.

Adam leaned closer to her. "You win some, you lose some."

"Miss Castle has clearly violated the spirit, if not the letter, of the agreement," Steve was saying.

"I disagree, Your Honor," Kylie said without looking at Adam. "We bitterly resent these innuendos. Miss Castle is entitled to have friends of the opposite sex."

"You're not seriously asking the court to believe that's all they were!" Steve exclaimed. "She accompanied Mr. Whitley to Las Vegas for a weekend and spent several days on Mr. Andreas's yacht."

"You've been spying on me!" Donna screeched. "Who gave you the right to pry into my private affairs, you no-good creep?"

"That will be all, Miss Castle," the judge said sternly. "I think I've heard enough. Do you have anything to say in conclusion, Miss O'Connor?"

"Yes, Your Honor. I'd like to point out that my client's morals are not on trial—although we're certainly not conceding any wrongdoing. Mr. Ridgeway's attorney has attempted to create a smoke screen. He's criticized Miss Castle's spending, while conveniently ignoring her charitable contributions. She's a very giving woman." Kylie ignored Adam's snicker. "The plain facts are that Miss Castle can't live on her present income. You and I might consider it more than adequate, but she's accustomed to a different life-style—a way of life her husband introduced her to. He hasn't changed his habits, and I submit that it isn't fair that she should have to change hers. We're asking you to grant increased spousal support."

The judge looked at her impassively. "I'm afraid I'll have to deny that request. It's remotely possible that Miss Castle has difficulty living within her income, even though it seems very generous to me. She has, however, found ways of supplementing it. My suggestion would be that she get a job—" he paused "—or widen her circle of acquaintances."

Donna looked balefully after the judge as he left the room. "Lousy male chauvinist!"

"I'm sorry," Kylie said tonelessly.

"You should be. That's what I get for having a female lawyer."

"You were never a particularly good judge of character," Adam said. "Miss O'Connor is a woman of very high principles." His gaze swung to Kylie. "I thought she did a very good job, considering that the deck was stacked against her.''

Donna's eyes narrowed with rage. "I'm beginning to get the picture. Was she the one who tipped you off about Warren and George? Isn't that called collusion?''

"Take it easy," Steve said. "That kind of talk could put you on the other end of a lawsuit.''

Kylie picked up her briefcase. "If you'll excuse me, I have another appointment." She felt a sudden need for fresh air.

Adam followed her to the door. "Now you know how the captain of the *Titanic* felt.''

"Don't gloat, Mr. Ridgeway, it doesn't become you.'' She started down the hall to the elevator.

Adam accompanied her. "I wasn't gloating, I was offering condolences.''

"Phony ones! You're almost as pleased at putting me down as you are at defeating your wife.''

"That's where you're wrong. I know how important it was to you to win.''

"No more than it was for you.''

"But for a different reason. I'm sure today represented a battle of the sexes for you, a chance to prove your equality." He shook his head. "What a waste. I never regarded you as anything *but* an equal.''

With an arched eyebrow she asked, "Is that why you told me I needed a man?''

"I don't think I put it that way. I merely indicated that everyone needs someone.''

"In this case, meaning you?''

"I'm definitely available.''

"You just got one wife off your back, Mr. Ridgeway. Don't you think you should take a breather?" The elevator doors swung open, and she stepped inside.

"My offer didn't include marriage," Adam called before the doors closed.

Kylie's color rose along with her temper as everyone in the elevator stared at her.

Chapter Three

Kylie thought a lot about Adam in the days following the hearing. She rather expected him to phone to gloat over his victory, but the days lengthened into weeks with no attempt on his part to contact her.

A man like Adam could never be completely forgotten, yet after a couple of months he became an ambivalent memory. Kylie's secretary, however, made sure the memory didn't fade completely.

Marcia had been quite smitten by Adam. She read every bit of news about him and duly reported it to Kylie. "Adam Ridgeway just got another award at a big dinner in New York," she announced one morning.

"Hunk of the year?" Kylie asked caustically.

Marcia sighed ecstatically. "He is in *my* book. I'm sorry we won't get a chance to sue him again."

"You're right. I'm afraid Miss Castle is going to take her business elsewhere." Kylie wasn't depressed at the prospect.

"She won't need a lawyer for a while—except maybe to look over a prenuptial agreement. According to the gossip columns, she's about to take another trip on the sea of matrimony, courtesy of her Greek shipping magnate."

"That should make Adam happy," Kylie commented. "He'll be off the hook permanently."

"Until the next bimbo sinks her claws into him," Marcia observed sadly.

"She'll have her work cut out for her. I think Mr. Ridgeway is pretty soured on the institution of marriage."

"It's just as well." Marcia grinned. "Think how many women he's making happy."

"As long as their relationship is conducted horizontally," Kylie replied waspishly.

"You wouldn't hear *me* complaining."

"Don't you have a brief to type?" Kylie asked, ending the discussion.

The days flowed by in a predictable stream. Kylie went to work every morning, pleaded cases in court and often brought work home with her. Occasionally she went to a movie with a woman friend or had dinner with a male colleague. It was the life she'd chosen, but every now and then something seemed unaccountably missing.

Only the weekends with Tommy lived up to expectation. Watching him grow was a continuing delight. He was taking his first shaky steps now, so Kylie added a playpen to her other baby equipment.

She set it up on the patio where he could watch while she gardened. Tommy decided it was great fun to throw his toys onto the grass and see Kylie retrieve them.

"Exercise classes would go out of business if every household had a baby," she declared after stooping to pick up a stuffed rabbit and a rubber ball for the tenth time. "Give your tired auntie a break." She sank down on a chaise next to the playpen.

Thomas chortled happily and switched his attention to a set of plastic blocks.

Kylie closed her eyes, enjoying the warmth of the sun on her bare legs. With the arrival of June, her weekend uniform had changed to shorts and a halter. Her creamy skin was already tinged with a golden tan that would deepen as summer wore on.

How long would Thomas be content to amuse himself in his playpen? she wondered. Was it worthwhile to start looking over the financial statement submitted by her latest client's estranged husband?

Kylie decided it wasn't. Tommy would get restless, and she'd have to interrupt her work as soon as she laid it out. Besides, the day was too pleasant to spoil. The sordid realities of life could wait until Susan took Thomas home.

She lowered her chaise a notch and relaxed with a sigh of contentment. Tommy emulated her by rolling over onto his back and playing with his toes. A short time later both Kylie and the baby drifted off to sleep.

A shadow blocking the sun woke her. Kylie opened her eyes and blinked at the tall man standing over her. Adam's appearance was so unexpected that she could only stare speechlessly at him.

His eyes traveled from the curve of her breasts, enticingly highlighted by the skimpy halter, down the length of her slim legs. "I like this outfit even better."

Kylie sprang to her feet. "What are you doing here?"

"Don't you ever say a simple hello?"

"Not to uninvited guests."

"You're not still harboring a grudge over losing the case, are you?"

"Certainly not. I'd forgotten all about it," she said dismissively.

"Then why the less than cordial greeting?"

"I wasn't expecting . . . I mean, you surprised me." She felt especially vulnerable in her present brief outfit.

"I forgot." His amused eyes rested on her perturbed face. "You're the lady who likes to plan her whole life—so much time for work, so much time for recreation. I presume this *is* what you call recreation?" He glanced over at the sleeping child. "Is he still the only male in your life?"

"That's none of your business," she snapped.

"You're right," he agreed surprisingly. Then he added, "At least not yet."

"Not ever."

"Are you so sure, Kylie?" His voice was a honeyed purr.

"Damn sure."

He folded his arms over his broad chest. "Okay, you're a lawyer. Convince me."

She glared at him in outrage. "I don't have to convince you of anything! I want you out of here immediately. This is my yard, and you're trespassing."

"Why do you feel so threatened by me?" he asked softly. "Are you afraid I might convince you to leave your nunnery and enjoy the pleasures you've forbidden yourself?"

"Your conceit is truly staggering!" she exclaimed angrily. "If I ever did want to indulge in forbidden pleasures, as you so euphemistically put it, you'd be the *last* person I'd choose as a partner."

"Don't knock it till you've tried it." He looked appraisingly at her slender yet provocative figure. "I think we'd be terrific together."

"That's something you'll never find out." Kylie's nails made small crescent marks in her damp palms. "Did you honestly think all you had to do was show up here and I'd lead you into the bedroom?"

He laughed. "I knew it wouldn't be that easy. I'm prepared to give you the full treatment first—romantic dinners, flowers, the works."

"At least you're honest," she said disgustedly. "That's the only point in your favor."

"I plan on showing you a few more."

"Why?" she asked bluntly. "Did you run through all the available talent in town? Your passion for me can't be that burning. You didn't even bother to phone in two months."

"Ah, so you *did* notice." He smiled smugly at her blush. "Actually, I was waiting until you couldn't use Donna as an excuse for not going out with me. I just made my final alimony payment."

Kylie was thrown off balance. Was that really the reason he hadn't contacted her? "It wasn't an excuse," she said haltingly. "Your attorney could have used it as grounds for an appeal if the decision had gone against you."

"Well, that's all in the past anyway." His slightly friendlier smile softened the sharp planes of his rugged face. "The future is what counts."

Tommy took that moment to make his presence known. Their voices had wakened him, and he was bouncing against the side of the playpen, demanding attention with incoherent sounds. When he held his arms up, Adam walked over to him.

"You're shorter than my usual rivals, but I don't think height is going to give me any advantage this time." He lifted the little boy out of the playpen. "I've got experience on my side, though. What do you have to say about that?"

The baby patted his cheek and said, "Da Da."

"He called you Daddy!" Kylie exclaimed. "Do you realize those are his first words?"

Adam laughed. "Boy, is he ever confused."

"Wait till I tell Susan," she said excitedly. Kylie held out her arms, but Tommy ignored her. He was entranced by Adam. "You have a way with children," she remarked, slightly miffed at being rebuffed.

Adam held the youngster high in the air, raising and lowering him while the baby squealed delightedly. "I'm the quintessential uncle. I play with them, bring presents—and leave when they get fussy."

That probably summed up his attitude toward women, too, Kylie thought soberly. It was an important point to remember.

The gate clicked open to admit Susan and Neal.

"What are you doing here so early?" Kylie asked in surprise.

"The cocktail party was a bore," Susan answered.

"What she really means is that everyone was going on to L'Auberge, and we couldn't afford it," Neal said, a trifle sullenly.

"Who needs one of those French dinners that drag on for hours," Susan remarked brightly.

"Not on a Sunday night when you have to get up early the next morning," Kylie agreed with a veiled look at both of them.

"Mr. Ridgeway," Susan called, turning her attention to Adam. "How nice to see you again. I'd like you to meet my husband, Neal."

"Call me Adam, please." He held the baby against his shoulder and extended his hand.

"A pleasure," Neal said. "My wife told me about meeting you."

"Adam must think we live here." Susan laughed. "I'll take Thomas, and we'll get out of your hair."

"He hasn't had his bath yet," Kylie objected. "Why don't you two go have dinner and come back for him later?"

"I have a better idea," Neal said. "Let's get some take-out food and eat here."

Susan gave him an annoyed look. "I'm sure Kylie has other plans," she said pointedly, sending her husband a significant look.

He got the message belatedly. "Oh, uh, sure. It was just an idea."

"An excellent one," Adam said smoothly. "How does fried chicken sound to everyone?"

"You mustn't feel obligated to stay," Kylie said swiftly to him. "Adam just stopped by," she explained to the others.

"You mean I'm not invited?" he asked.

"I'm sure you have something more glamorous to do," she replied evenly.

"Your concept of my life-style has always been faulty."

Susan seemed to sense her sister's tension but didn't know how to undo the damage. "Well, I guess it's settled then. Is everyone agreed on fried chicken?"

While the men went out to get dinner, the women set the round table on the patio.

"I'm sorry Neal put his foot in it," Susan said tentatively. "I guess we both assumed you were spending the evening with Adam."

"It can't be helped." Kylie concentrated on arranging the silverware.

"He seems awfully nice."

"Yes, he can be quite charming when he wants to be."

Susan digested that in silence for a moment. "Do you see much of him?"

"This is the first time in two months."

"Really?" Susan's raised eyebrows were expressive.

"It's true. Don't start imagining things," Kylie said. "There's nothing going on between us."

"Then why is he staying for dinner? He seemed rather keen on it."

"Maybe he's dying for fried chicken. Or maybe he's doing it to annoy me. How should I know?"

"Why does it annoy you? Most women would be delirious to spend time with him."

"You've got that right, anyhow. Adam Ridgeway has a whole harem of women waiting for his favors. They're all beautiful and glamorous. Why would he want to eat fast food off of paper plates with me if he didn't consider it a big joke?"

"You can hold your own with anybody," Susan said loyally. She looked appraisingly at her older sister. "Especially in that outfit."

Kylie had forgotten her scanty attire. "Finish setting the table for me, would you? I have to change."

Susan followed her to the bedroom instead. "I wish you'd lighten up a little. Adam's dreamy, and he's obviously attracted to you."

"We're complete opposites," Kylie answered stiffly.

"That's good. You need someone adventurous. Your life has been stuck in neutral for too long."

"Good Lord, not you, too! I *like* my life the way it is." Kylie stepped out of her shorts and into a pair of jeans.

"Adam could make it a lot more exciting."

"Maybe for a while."

"What's wrong with that?"

"I'm not a teenager who goes from boyfriend to boyfriend every other week."

"Promiscuity is out of date—haven't you heard? Monogamy is in."

"The word hasn't filtered down to Adam yet," Kylie said grimly, buttoning her denim shirt.

"I'll bet he's not half as bad as you're painting him." Susan gazed at her speculatively. "What have you got to lose by being friendly? Unless you're afraid you can't handle him."

"Don't be ridiculous!"

"Okay, then prove it."

"You're as bad as Adam," Kylie declared in exasperation. "You must both think I'm a child."

Susan sighed, getting up off the bed. "Well, if you're determined to spend your life practicing law and nothing else, I guess I can't stop you."

"I don't know why everybody assumes my life is so sterile," Kylie protested. "I have dates like anyone else. I went out to dinner with Bob Shaefer just last Wednesday."

"That's encouraging. Where did you meet him?"

"He's an attorney in my office."

"That must have been stimulating."

"It was to me," Kylie said coolly.

"What did you do, exchange briefs?" Before Kylie's outrage could erupt, Susan said hastily, "All right, I won't say any more." She left the room, only to pop her head in the door once more. "Except for one thing. If you're trying to discourage Adam, that outfit ought to do it."

As they were driving to the shopping center in Adam's Jaguar, Neal said, "I didn't mean to put you on the spot back there. You and Kylie looked like an item."

"Don't worry about it," Adam replied easily, sidestepping the implied question.

"I'll admit I was kind of surprised. Kylie's a great gal, but she's not big on men."

"Perhaps she just needs to meet the right one."

"If you're speaking personally, I wouldn't count on it—unless you're a needy case. Kylie's a pushover for people who need her."

"Like you and your wife?" Adam asked casually.

"What do you mean?"

"She takes care of your child most weekends, I understand. That doesn't leave her much time for a social life of her own."

"Are you saying we take advantage of her?" Neal demanded. "Kylie is crazy about Thomas. She says we're doing *her* a favor."

"I'm sure she feels that way."

Although Adam's tone hadn't been challenging, Neal clearly felt the need to vindicate himself. "She could say she was busy if she had something to do."

"Or you could get a sitter and ask her to join you." This time Adam's voice held a hint of steel.

"But that's the whole point. Kylie baby-sits because we can't afford to hire anyone." Neal looked resentfully around the luxurious car. "Guys like you don't realize how much it costs to support a wife and baby."

Adam swallowed a smile. "You're quite right. I don't know anything about babies."

"I didn't, either. I didn't even want any until I got established. Not that I don't love Tommy," the young man added hastily. "He's a terrific kid."

"What kind of work do you do?"

"I manage a small men's store." Neal's laugh was harshly self-deprecating. "That's the title they gave me instead of a raise. Actually I'm an all-around flunky."

"If you don't like the work, why don't you do something else?" Adam asked mildly.

"Because I need a regular paycheck coming in every month."

"What would you rather be doing if you had the choice?"

"I took a course in public relations in college. It was really my kind of thing." Neal's face lit with enthusiasm. "Boy, would I like to mingle with all those movers and shakers!"

"You'd be good at it."

Adam turned his head to look at the younger man. Neal could have starred in one of those teen surfing movies. His blond good looks had undoubtedly made him a campus heartthrob, the kind elected class president and voted most likely to succeed. It must have been a shock to find out the real world was more than a popularity contest.

"It's a hard field to get into, though." Neal was answering Adam's comment. "Maybe if Sue and I hadn't gotten married right out of college. I made the rounds of all the PR offices, but when we found out Thomas was on the way, she had to quit her job and I had to take what I could get." His mouth twisted bitterly. "So here I am at twenty-three, stuck in a dead-end job."

"Only if you want to be. Have you ever considered writing publicity releases for an office on spec? Or you might try to latch on to a rising young comedian or singer and build a reputation on your own."

"You make it sound easy."

Adam shrugged. "Easy is staying where you are."

"That isn't much of a choice," Neal sighed. "Well, it's not your problem. I don't even know why I'm telling you all this. Maybe because I probably won't ever see you again."

"What gave you that idea?"

"I didn't think you and Kylie—I mean, she didn't seem too friendly."

"Take my word for it, you'll be seeing a lot of me." Adam's voice was confident.

Kylie had remained in the bedroom after Susan left. It wasn't the first lecture her younger sister had given her. She was always urging Kylie to stop being so conservative. Usually the advice made no impression, but this time her criticism felt uncomfortably pointed, since it was identical to Adam's.

Was she turning into a dried-up old maid who kept her emotions in mothballs? Was that why she shunned most social situations?

Kylie rejected the notion violently. Hadn't she had dinner with Bob Shaefer only a few nights ago? Her resentment died as she remembered how dull the evening had been. As Susan had surmised, they'd discussed their case loads and office politics.

Suddenly all the vague dissatisfactions of the past two months crystallized into open rebellion. She wasn't living; she was existing! But from now on, things were going to be different. Maybe Adam wasn't the solution, but he was sure one heck of a good start. If he hadn't given up on her.

Kylie was so deep in thought that she didn't hear the men return. She was startled when Adam himself appeared in the bedroom doorway.

"Susan wants to know where—" He stopped when he saw her sitting on the edge of the bed, her head lowered. "Is something wrong?"

She stood up. "No, I, uh... I just came in to change clothes. It gets chilly when the sun goes down. What does Susan need?"

"She's looking for a large platter."

"I'll get it."

"Wait." Adam put his hands on her shoulders as she started past him. He looked searchingly into her face. "If it really bothers you to have me here, I'll leave."

"No, don't do that," she said swiftly.

He hesitated. "I can make up a convincing excuse."

"Please don't go, Adam. I don't know why you'd want to stay after the way I've been acting, but I'd really like you to." Her blue eyes were wide.

He was slightly wary. "Any reason for this change of heart?"

"I simply realized that I haven't been very hospitable."

"It never bothered you before."

She slanted him an appealing glance. "Would you prefer me the other way?"

A slow smile curved his firm mouth as he gazed at her lovely face. "No, this is a definite improvement. How long can I count on it to last?"

Kylie laughed, feeling young and lighthearted. "Until something sets one or the other of us off. We both have rather short fuses."

"Arguing won't be so bad." He put his arm around her shoulder and led her toward the door. "Just think how much fun we'll have making up."

Kylie was suddenly reminded of the method he'd used to make up with Donna. Did Adam expect to bring her a black chiffon nightgown and reduce her to mindless compliance? His lean body brushing against hers gave ample evidence of his capability.

She drew away as they went through the door. Adam was entirely too experienced, and she was too vulnerable. She would have to be extremely cautious. The idea was to turn her life *around*, not upside down.

Dinner was a festive affair, due to Adam's presence. He told them stories about glamorous places around the world—Biarritz, Gstaad, Vienna. Although he didn't try to monopolize the conversation, they all asked endless questions. Neal was especially fascinated.

"How do you get to the top of the heap?" he wondered aloud.

"By climbing up one step at a time," Adam said.

"Everything looks simple after you have it made," Neal observed.

"It wasn't for me," Adam answered firmly. "I got forty dollars for the first photograph I sold, and the film cost me fifteen."

"It must have been a long time ago," Neal said. "That wouldn't put gas in your Jaguar now."

"I didn't have fancy wheels then. You have to pay your dues first."

"For how long?" Neal's handsome face was set in lines of discontent. "I don't want to wait until I'm too old to enjoy things."

Adam smiled wryly. "You'd be surprised what a comfort material things are to the elderly."

Neal reddened. "I didn't mean—"

"Of course he didn't," Susan rushed in. "You're in the prime of life. You're a very sexy man," she said frankly.

Adam looked at Kylie with a raised eyebrow. "All the counties aren't in."

"I'm sure my vote isn't important," she said.

He grinned. "I'd like to be elected by a big majority."

Kylie didn't want to be reminded of how vast his constituency was. She stood up and began to clear the table. "Is everyone ready for dessert? I have some ice cream in the freezer."

"Adam bought a lemon meringue pie," Neal said. "We're also indebted to him for dinner."

"That doesn't seem right," Susan protested. "This was Neal's idea. If it weren't for him, you and Kylie would be dining out in style."

"Not necessarily. We'd probably have had an argument, and she'd have sent me packing."

"Or you'd have found some excuse to leave," Kylie replied, not entirely convinced they were joking.

"You mean Neal and I are actually the attraction?" Susan teased, her comprehensive glance going from Adam to her sister.

"How's the guy going to answer a question like that?" Neal answered for him.

"Thanks. I owe you one." Adam chuckled.

Susan offered to help clean up after dinner, but Kylie declined her assistance. "There isn't that much to do," she said.

The young couple left in a flurry of activity. Tommy's clothes had to be gathered up, his favorite toy located and his diaper bag packed. Then while Neal bundled up the sleeping child, Kylie walked Susan to the car. When they finally drove off and Kylie returned to the house, Adam was still sitting at the table.

"I'm sorry," she apologized. "It's always hectic getting them organized."

"Sit down and have another cup of coffee," he said as she started to pick up the dessert plates. "You've been hopping up and down all night."

"I enjoy having them," she said quickly, sensing an implied criticism.

"You have a nice family," he remarked, quieting her fears. "Are there any more of you?"

"No. Susan was born after our parents had given up hope of having any more children. That's why there's such a big age difference between us."

"Not that vast, surely."

"Six years. Susan was only starting first grade when I was ready for junior high."

"Time has a way of catching up when you reach adulthood."

"It's hard for me to think of her that way. I guess she'll always be my baby sister."

"And is Neal your baby brother?"

Something in Adam's voice alerted Kylie, although his expression was pleasantly questioning. "I worry about him a little," she said slowly. "Sometimes I wish they hadn't gotten married so young."

"It must have been right out of college."

Kylie nodded. "She was twenty, and he was twenty-one." She stirred her coffee absently. "Between them they dominated the important campus activities. Married life was a change in itself. Then, when Thomas came along, they had instant responsibilities. I think Neal would have preferred to wait awhile."

"He played an integral part," Adam said dryly.

"Oh, I'm sure he's delighted. It does tie them down, though."

Adam shrugged. "That comes with the territory. Susan seems able to handle it."

"But you're not so sure about Neal?"

"I think he has some growing up to do."

"They're crazy about each other," Kylie insisted. "They went together for years."

"Nothing like marriage to break up a beautiful friendship," Adam replied ironically.

"That's a rotten thing to say," she flared. "Surely you're not equating Susan's marriage with your own?"

"It was just a bad joke," he soothed. "I hope they break the *Guinness Book of World Records* for wedded bliss. Come on, I'll help you clear the table."

Kylie was glad to drop the subject. Adam couldn't be expected to be rational about marriage, but his evaluation of Neal hit home. She'd been vaguely uneasy about Neal's restlessness for some time.

Kylie's tension eased as she and Adam worked in the kitchen together. She'd told him to go into the living room, but he'd declined.

"It will only take a couple of minutes if we both pitch in."

"You were the mighty hunter who went out and bagged the bird," she protested. "This is my job."

He raised one dark eyebrow. "Don't tell me a liberated lady like you thinks a woman's place is in the kitchen?"

"Definitely not. But I do believe in an equal division of labor."

"You had me worried for a moment. I thought you were turning all soft and feminine on me."

His laughing comment hurt, although she had only herself to blame. Jeans and a denim shirt weren't exactly soft and feminine. Even as she was wishing she'd listened to Susan, Kylie had a feeling of hopelessness. She couldn't compete with the kind of women Adam was accustomed to. Clothes were only part of it. She didn't know the first thing about being provocative.

"No rebuttal?" he asked when she didn't answer immediately.

"You learn not to challenge overwhelming evidence." Kylie was glad that loading the dishwasher gave her an excuse not to look at him.

Adam held back the shining curtain of hair veiling her face. "What's wrong, Kylie?" His voice wasn't bantering anymore.

"Not a thing. We're almost finished."

He took a plate from her resisting fingers and set it on the counter. "Look at me," he said quietly, gripping her shoulders when she would have moved away.

"You're not going to turn into one of those kitchen Romeos, are you?" she asked lightly. "The ones who think a small pinch of something refers to the cook?"

He didn't smile. "Something's bothering you, and I want to know what it is."

"You're imagining things."

"No, I'm getting to know your moods. Was it something I said? Something I did?"

She realized he wasn't going to give up. "It's nothing really. I don't even want to be soft and feminine. I hate clinging vines. Still, it's a little deflating to be told I'm not attractive."

"You have to be kidding! It was a joke."

"I know that. I'm joking too." She accepted the fiction, turning away.

He pulled her back and studied her face wonderingly. "Is it possible you don't know how lovely you are?"

She returned his gaze steadily. "You needn't give me the full treatment. My feelings aren't *that* hurt."

His hands tightened, and he shook her slightly. "If you didn't freeze every man who tried to say a civil word, you'd have them camped on your doorstep. I just happen to be more persistent than the rest."

"Or you're bored with scintillating blondes and lush redheads," she said ironically.

"Do you really think that's why I'm here tonight?"

Kylie looked at him uncertainly. He *had* seemed to enjoy himself, although the evening couldn't possibly compare to his customary forms of entertainment. Did Adam really think she was sexy?

He smiled at her doubtful expression. "Your trouble is, you don't listen when I speak. I've openly stated my intention of making love to you."

"They say barking dogs don't bite," she answered, pretending he wasn't serious.

The pretense took great effort because she was quiveringly aware of him. The warmth from his big hands burned into her shoulders and set up a chain reaction throughout her entire body.

"If that's a challenge, I accept," he said.

His arms circled her waist, drawing her against the hard length of him. Kylie's hands went up automatically, but they were crushed against his chest as he tightened the embrace and lowered his head.

She was rigid in his arms, instantly defensive. But Adam's kiss was a masterpiece of persuasion. His mouth was warm and seductive, his tongue coaxing. When she kept her mouth tightly closed, he nipped gently at her bottom lip.

Kylie's waning resistance diminished further when his stroking hands moved sensuously down her back. Helplessly her lips parted for the implicit male entry of his tongue.

Adam's seduction was masterful. For a stirring moment she surrendered to her senses. Every fiber of her being vibrated to the wonderful sensation of his mouth, his hands, his taut body. She whispered his name, twining her arms around his neck and straining closer.

"My sweet, passionate darling," he murmured, burying his face in the soft cloud of her hair. "I knew there was fire under all that ice."

His husky words brought her to her senses. She was shaken and appalled at her unbridled reaction. How could she have let her guard down so easily?

She drew away, unable to look at him. "Does it surprise you to discover I'm a normal woman?"

"It delights me. Now we'll have to work on your fear of involvement."

"You don't want to get involved. You just want to go to bed," she flared.

He chuckled. "If that isn't involvement, I don't know what is."

"A one-night stand isn't my definition of the word," she answered curtly.

"Nor mine."

He reached out and hooked one hand around the back of her neck. Kylie stiffened, expecting another amorous onslaught, but Adam merely stared at her consideringly.

"I have a feeling that when we make love, it's going to be something special," he mused.

A shiver ran up her spine, but she kept her voice even. "You can tell that from one kiss?"

A slow smile lit his face. "It's all *I* need for proof, but I'd be happy to supply further examples for your consideration."

"That won't be necessary," she said hastily.

"What would you rather do instead?" He lounged against the kitchen counter watching her, as relaxed as a giant cat.

How could he switch his emotions on and off like a light switch? She struggled to appear as casual as he. "There's always television."

"Okay, if you want to settle for spectator sports." He opened a cabinet and started rummaging around.

"What are you looking for?"

"Popcorn. You can't watch TV without popcorn."

Kylie was wary at first, concerned that Adam had some trick up his sleeve. But he was so completely natural that her tension soon vanished.

They sat together on the couch and watched an old movie. It hadn't been very good originally, but it proved to be more amusing the second time around. They made fun of the acting, the fifties hairstyles, the dialogue. Adam put his arm around her casually, more with affection than passion.

As it got later and he made no further moves, she let herself relax against him, filled with contentment. When he slowly stroked her hair, Kylie closed her eyes and rested her head in the crook of his neck, enjoying the subtle male scent of him. A short time later she dozed off.

She awoke instantly when Adam lifted her in his arms and started to carry her into the bedroom.

"What are you doing?" she asked sharply.

"Taking you to bed."

"No, you're not! Put me down this instant!" She started to struggle, but he held her easily.

"All in due time." He banged his knee on the crib and swore under his breath as he placed her on the bed. "This damn room is an obstacle course. No wonder you sleep alone."

"And I intend to go on doing so!"

"Right. We'll have to go to my place."

"If you think for one minute—"

He pinned her shoulders down. "Has anyone ever told you that you talk too much? Even for a lawyer." He leaned down and kissed her briefly. "Get some rest. You fell asleep out there."

Kylie felt exceedingly foolish when she realized Adam had merely carried her to bed with no ulterior motive. "I'm sorry," she mumbled.

"My ego might not survive, but that's okay. Anything else I can do, like undress you? ... I didn't think so. All right, I'll try again tomorrow night. See you at eight." He bumped into the changing table this time, with an appropriate comment.

Speechless, Kylie watched him go. Her anger had faded into a variety of other emotions. Her body tingled from the touch of his hands, and her lips could still taste his brief kiss. Adam affected her like no man ever had—not even Larry, her former fiancé.

She actually regretted letting Adam go. But as the hot tide of her overwhelmed senses receded, common sense took its place. Adam could teach her to loosen up and enjoy herself, but that's as far as it must go. His physical attraction was too great. He only wanted her body, but what if her heart happened to go with it? Falling in love with him would be disastrous.

Kylie glanced around the dimly lit, cluttered room, smiling wistfully at Adam's annoyance. It might have been wonderful to be lovers, she thought almost wistfully, but it was going to be great fun being friends.

Chapter Four

For perhaps the first time in her life, Kylie found it difficult to concentrate on work the next day. Her thoughts kept leaping ahead to her date with Adam. When Marcia came in with some typed contracts, she found Kylie gazing out the window.

"Is anything wrong?" the secretary asked uncertainly.

"Not unless you know something I don't." Kylie smiled, swinging her chair back to face the desk.

"Did you have a nice weekend?" Marcia probed tentatively.

"I had a wonderful weekend!"

"Don't tell me. Thomas cut a tooth."

"Not quite, but he did say his first word."

"Did you phone the newspapers?"

"No, they only get excited about bad news. This was a joyous event." Kylie laughed at Marcia's disgusted expression. "Bring me the Farraday file when you have a chance."

Her secretary's disapproval had changed to excitement when she buzzed Kylie a little later. "Adam Ridgeway is on line one."

Kylie picked up the phone, trying to keep her own eagerness out of her voice.

"Yes, Adam?"

"You sound busy."

"No more so than usual. What can I do for you?"

"You already know, but you won't cooperate." His chuckle had a deep, masculine sound. "I said I'd pick you up at eight, but there's been a change in plans."

"Oh." Kylie wouldn't have believed she could be this disappointed. "Well, that's all right," she said, rallying her pride.

"See? After only one evening with me you're learning to be more flexible. Be ready at six instead."

"But I thought—"

"Is there a problem?"

"No, I—I thought you were breaking our date."

"No way. And you aren't, either," he said forcefully. "I'll see you later."

"Adam, wait! I don't know if I can be ready that early."

"I'll pick you up at the office. That will save time."

"No. I...I want to go home and change." Kylie had no intention of going out to dinner in her plain wool suit. For once, Adam was going to see her in something feminine.

"Then leave early. The courts won't go out of business—unfortunately." He hung up before she could react.

When Kylie walked out of her office promptly at five o'clock, Marcia's jaw dropped.

"Do you feel all right?" she asked.

"I feel fine," Kylie answered crisply. "Take my calls, and I'll return them in the morning." She was aware that Marcia would find some way to satisfy her curiosity, but not now. She'd have to rush to get home and be ready on time.

Kylie knew a long bubble bath would have relaxed her, but she settled for a quick shower before hurrying to get dressed.

The contents of her closet depressed her. If only she had something smashing to wear. A shopping trip was definitely in order, and at the earliest opportunity. Turning over a new leaf meant an entire new wardrobe.

Adam didn't seem disappointed when he arrived. His eyes glowed with approval as they traveled over her slim figure. She'd chosen a clinging navy knit that softly outlined her firm breasts and rounded hips. Navy and white pumps called attention to her long legs.

"You look fantastic," he said admiringly. "I've never seen you in a dress before."

"I didn't know where we were going. Is this all right?"

"It's perfect. Do you have a warm coat?"

"I don't think I'll need one," she said. "Knits are quite warm."

"Take a coat," he ordered.

Once in his Jaguar, Kylie didn't pay any attention to the direction Adam took. She was content merely to be with him. But when she happened to glance out the window and realized they'd driven as far as the airport, she asked their destination.

"Do you like seafood?" he asked.

"Love it. Did you hear of a new restaurant out here?"

"No, it's been in the same place for years. They have the best cracked crab and French bread anywhere."

Kylie was mystified when he drove into the airport and stopped at the valet parking area. Airports weren't generally known for good food. When he led her into the terminal building and down a long corridor to the departure gates, she was bewildered.

"Where are we going?" she asked again.

"To San Francisco," he answered calmly. "You can't get fish any fresher than at Fisherman's Wharf."

"You must be out of your mind!"

"Relax." He grinned as she stopped dead in her tracks. "I only booked dinner reservations, not a hotel room. After a slightly sensational meal, we'll fly home."

Kylie allowed herself to be led onto the plane, although she had a distinct feeling of unreality. "You're really crazy, do you know that?"

"Why?" He buckled her seat belt.

"Because sane people don't fly three hundred miles for dinner."

"It's only an hour's flight. Anyplace in L.A. would take as long on the freeway. This way I get to look at you instead of the road."

"How about the expense?"

"Not to worry. I've got a pocketful of money now that I'm no longer supporting the answer to a retailer's prayer."

"Have you seen Donna?" Kylie asked tentatively.

He shook his head. "She's replaced me with a man who has more toys."

Adam sounded unconcerned, but Kylie wondered if deep down it bothered him. Obviously he cared enough to keep up with news of his ex-wife. She studied him covertly through long lashes.

"How did you two meet?" she asked. "I've always wondered."

He smiled sardonically. "Like the curiosity you feel when you look at a mule? It's the result of an unlikely pairing, too."

"I'm sorry," Kylie murmured, gazing down at her lap.

"No, honey, *I'm* sorry." He covered her clenched hands. "God knows my marriage was an open book."

"I didn't mean to touch on old wounds."

"There weren't any real wounds—on either side. That's the sad part."

Kylie couldn't believe that two people could live together, make love together, share their lives and then feel nothing when it was over. She tried haltingly to explain her convictions.

"That's very sweet," he said. "I wish it were so."

"It *is* so," she insisted. "My parents were married for over twenty-five years. Most of their friends were, too. And look at Susan and Neal."

"You should have quit while you were ahead," he said dryly.

"You don't honestly think their marriage is in trouble, do you?"

"No, of course not," he soothed. "Don't pay any attention to me. I'm just a cynic."

"You've had a bad experience. You'll get over it."

He hesitated. "I could agree that my condition is temporary, but I want to be completely honest with you. I think marriage is an absurd convention that's totally unnecessary in the modern world. That piece of paper keeps people together long after they have any reason for staying."

"How about children?"

"They're victims, too. How many couples remain in a loveless relationship because of the children? Or else the kids are bounced back and forth between manipulative parents after a bitter divorce.''

"So you think the human race should die out?''

"Not at all. When two people agree that they really want a baby, they should have one.''

"With no commitment?''

"That's a pretty *big* commitment—more binding than a meaningless document.''

"Society can't function that way," Kylie said helplessly. "You have to have laws.''

"When you find a way to make love and fidelity mandatory, let me know.''

She was appalled. Adam thought his views were advanced, but he was more closely related to the tigers of the jungle. They went their solitary ways, too, only teaming up with a female when they had the urge to mate.

Adam squeezed her hand. "Don't look so upset. No one's going to abolish marriage. Couples will still walk down the aisle with hope in their hearts.''

"Doesn't that tell you you're wrong?''

"Maybe," he conceded. "Or maybe it's only wrong for me.''

Kylie's heart twisted as she looked at his handsome face. "At least you know not to make the same mistake twice.''

His mouth curved. "What's that old saying? Those who forget the past are forced to relive it.''

Their conversation was interrupted by a stewardess who stopped at their seats with a cart containing drinks. After they'd made their selection, Adam changed the subject.

Kylie was vaguely depressed, although she knew it was foolish. She'd certainly been aware of his views before now.

He sensed her mood and set about dispelling it. By the time they arrived in San Francisco she was laughing at his wealth of funny anecdotes.

A taxi took them to a small restaurant on Fisherman's Wharf, off the main street where tourists ate. Adam was greeted like a long lost friend by the proprietor, a portly Italian man.

"Where've you been?" he demanded. "My place isn't good enough for you any more? You prefer those fancy Beverly Hills restaurants?"

"Don't blow it for me, Sal. I told Miss O'Connor *this* place was fancy."

"And she believed you?" Sal turned to Kylie. "I got a couple of feet of the Golden Gate Bridge I'd be willing to part with."

"Thanks, but I never buy real estate that doesn't have ground under it," she answered.

"This one's smart," Sal said to Adam. "How'd you get her to go out with you?"

"She had a free night, and she was hungry."

"You came to the right place. I have some fillet of sole that's so choice I changed the spelling on the menu to s-o-u-l. Sit down, and I'll go cook it for you myself."

Adam led Kylie to a table by a window overlooking the water. Small fishing boats bobbed at anchor along the pier, rolling toward each other and then away, like a group of old gossips.

Without being asked, a waiter brought steaming cups of clam chowder and a basket of warm French bread.

"You're going to get what Sal thinks you should have," Adam explained.

Kylie tasted the soup, then rolled her eyes. "If the rest of the meal is like this, he can choose for me any day."

The owner joined them for a glass of red wine and reminiscences. The two men evidently went back a long way.

"My waitresses used to fight over who got to wait on this one," Sal told Kylie. "They all wanted him to take them into his darkroom."

Adam shook his head. "Don't listen to him. Sal is a frustrated fiction writer."

"Oh, yeah? Remember Helen Tosca? She's married with three kids, and she still stops in every now and then to ask about you." Sal turned to Kylie. "I can't see it myself, but he's evidently quite a guy."

Kylie gazed at Adam as the two men bantered. Clearly, Adam was indeed a rare person. Anyone whose life he touched would never forget him.

After dinner Kylie expected to return to the airport, but Adam said there was no hurry. "The planes run every hour."

"But I have to go to work in the morning," she protested.

"So do I."

"It's ten o'clock already. If we leave right now, we still won't get home until midnight."

"That was only important to Cinderella." He took her hand. "Let's walk over to the chocolate factory and have a soda."

Kylie was about to renew her objections when she realized how foolish they were. She was having a wonderful time. What were a few hours of lost sleep?

They walked past the cannery, an old brick building that had been converted to restaurants and small shops. Beyond it was a park where the cable car made its turnaround. Even at this hour tourists were lined up, waiting to get on, shivering in the brisk wind that blew off the bay.

"Are you warm enough?" Adam put his arm around her and held her coat together at the throat.

"Yes. I'm glad you told me to bring a coat. It's amazing how chilly it is here in June."

"Mark Twain once said the coldest winter he ever spent was a summer in San Francisco."

"I thought you were merely being arbitrary about the coat. Why didn't you just tell me where we were going?"

He smiled down at her. "You'd have argued about it."

"That's true," she admitted.

"Are you sorry I didn't give you the chance?"

"It's been a wonderful evening," she said softly.

"And it isn't over yet." He bent his head and kissed her.

Adam's lips were cool, but they heated her blood. It was a brief kiss that left her wanting more. Kylie had sense enough to be grateful they were walking down a populated street.

Ghiradelli Square had actually been a chocolate factory many years ago, but it, too, had been converted to a tourist attraction. The courtyard was highlighted by a lovely fountain of bronze mermaids frolicking in a circle. It was the work of Ruth Asawa, a noted Japanese sculptress, and Kylie and Adam paused to admire it.

Part of the original factory had been preserved at the back of a large ice-cream parlor. Kylie was fascinated by the conveyor belts that carried a satin stream of chocolate to huge rollers that sent it cascading into a copper vat.

She forgot all about the time as they sat at a round marble table and had tall sodas topped with whipped cream. It was Adam who finally made the decision to leave.

The Los Angeles streets were uncharacteristically empty when they drove from the airport to Kylie's apartment. It was almost three in the morning.

"If we'd stayed a little longer, you could have dropped me off at the office," she joked as he walked her to her door.

"Are you sorry?"

She laughed. "I might be tomorrow, but I'm not now."

Adam didn't join in her laughter. Instead he lifted her chin and looked deeply into her eyes. "I don't ever want you to be sorry in the morning, honey. The choice is up to you. No pressure, no regrets. I want you very much, but only if it's right for you, too."

The moonlight glittered in his eyes, creating a hypnotic effect. How could anything be wrong when she wanted him so badly? she decided. In just a short time Adam had brought new meaning to her life. How could she refuse the part that would make it complete?

As she swayed toward him, he took her in his arms. His mouth was sensual, evoking images of darkened rooms and intertwined bodies. The corded muscles in his thighs reinforced the fantasy. Desire coursed through her veins like wine, blotting out all other considerations.

His arms tightened at her response, and his mouth grew more urgent. She clung to him as his kisses feathered over her closed eyelids. She moved against him instinctively. Her surrender was complete, but Adam didn't take advantage of it. Incomprehensibly, he put her gently away from him.

"You're tired, and your defenses are down. I don't want you to make a decision this way." His deep voice vibrated with regret. "Think about what I said, sweetheart."

She watched in bewilderment as he got into his car and drove away.

When reaction set in, Kylie went through all the stages of anger, hurt and embarrassment. Adam had known how receptive she was. He'd rejected her deliberately! Maybe that had been his intention all along—to show he could win the battle of the sexes.

But when she finally calmed down enough to be rational about what had happened, she realized Adam had been thinking of her, not himself.

Their desire was mutual, yet he'd sensed her deep reservations. Not many men would have practiced restraint when victory was virtually assured. Adam was even more special than she'd imagined.

Kylie was late to work the next morning, again eliciting her secretary's shock. Although the two women were on friendly terms, Marcia evidently hesitated to question her. Kylie was only open about her personal life up to a point.

Adam's call later in the morning must have given Marcia a clue, however. "Adam Ridgeway on line one," she chirped, as she had the previous day.

This time Kylie didn't attempt to sound indifferent. "Hi," she said softly.

"I see you made it to work."

"With one eye closed. The man in the car next to me thought I was winking at him."

"That must have made his day."

"I'm glad you called. I want to thank you for a wonderful evening."

"It was different, anyway."

"You might have set a dangerous precedent. If you invite me to an Italian dinner, I'll expect to have it in Rome."

"Funny you should mention that. I've been thinking of going to Europe. How would you like to come along?"

"I'd love it."

"Really?" He sounded surprised.

"Who wouldn't? Unfortunately, I have to work."

"Don't you ever take a vacation?"

"I've already had one."

"What did you do?"

Tommy had developed a bad case of croup, and she'd taken a week off to help her sister. The baby was so fussy that she'd stayed at their house so Susan and Neal could get some sleep. Kylie suspected Adam would disapprove, so she didn't answer his question.

"I have to go," she said hastily. "There's a call waiting."

"Wait. How about a hamburger after work?"

"I have a meeting," she said regretfully.

"What about coming over to my place afterward? Nothing fancy. I'll have the popcorn ready, and we'll go to bed and watch television."

Kylie didn't let herself imagine what that would be like. She knew it would be pure bliss. But nothing significant had changed between them. Adam had made it clear that only sensual enjoyment would be involved. She couldn't yet accept those circumstances.

"I'm still thinking about your parting instructions," she said lightly.

"Okay, then I'll see you tomorrow night. We'll go dancing, and I'll seduce you shamelessly on the dance floor."

Kylie hung up slowly. Adam didn't seem at all bothered at having his overtures rejected. He talked a lot about making love to her, yet he treated it as a joke. Was he setting some elaborate trap that she was too naive to recognize? She rejected the notion impatiently. Adam was right. Lawyers analyzed things too much.

* * *

That week was magical. Kylie went out with Adam twice—including the promised seductive dancing—and agreed to spend Saturday and Sunday with him. She felt slightly guilty when she called to tell her sister that she wouldn't be taking Tommy either day, but Susan was delighted.

"Fantastic! Are you and Adam going away for the weekend?" she asked.

"Of course not!" Kylie answered sharply.

Susan chuckled. "You don't have to sound so outraged. People do it all the time."

"People who barely know each other?"

"You've spent almost every night this week together."

"Three nights. And not the way you mean."

"I might have known." Susan laughed. "Okay, I don't suppose I can expect you to change *that* fast. I'm just delighted that you're finally doing something more rewarding with your evenings than working. Where's Adam taking you?"

"I'm never sure. Skydiving, for all I know."

"Sounds exciting. I'll watch for you from my backyard."

"What are you and Neal doing this weekend? I hope you weren't counting on me."

"Don't give it a second thought. It's time Neal spent some time with his son, instead of running to every sporting event in town. We're not college kids anymore."

Kylie thought she detected a slightly grim note in her sister's voice. It disturbed her. *Were* they having problems? As close as she and Susan were, Kylie couldn't bring herself to ask.

Adam filled Kylie's life with color and gaiety. He took her to places she'd never been and wouldn't have expected to enjoy. Whether it was a glittery, ear-splitting nightclub or a magically silent, woodsy backpack trail, everything was fun with Adam by her side. She thought about him constantly, even in the midst of business conferences, which was upsetting.

She tried to tell herself it was simply the novelty of getting a big rush from a man who was practically a celebrity. Any woman would be flattered. But Kylie couldn't lie to herself. She was afraid she was falling in love with Adam—and it disturbed her.

What would happen when he lost interest and moved on? It was a constant fear in the back of her mind. How could she resume her old, drab life after knowing Adam? It would be even more hopeless than before, since no man could ever take his place.

Kylie tried to hide her insecurity, knowing the fastest way to scare him off would be to reveal how much he meant to her. She wasn't always successful at concealing her fears, however.

"What's bothering you, honey?" he asked one Saturday afternoon in his Jaguar. She had been staring at his strong profile with an unconsciously wistful expression on her face.

"Nothing," she answered quickly.

"I know you better than that." He took one hand off the wheel and twined his fingers in hers.

They were driving to one of his mysterious destinations. All Kylie knew was that he'd told her to dress casually.

"You weren't listening to my brilliant repartee," he teased. "Am I sharing your affections with another man?"

"The only other man in my life is Thomas," she said lightly. "And I've seen precious little of him since you started monopolizing my time."

"Let him get his own girl. You're mine." When she didn't answer, he turned his head to look at her. "Aren't you?"

"If you say so."

"I just did. Now I'd like to hear you say it."

"I'm all yours."

Kylie had meant to sound joking, but her voice had a slight throb to it. Just the touch of Adam's hand in hers was enough to make her heart beat faster.

His fingers tightened. "When you look at me like that I'm tempted to turn around and head back to my apartment. Disneyland will still be there tomorrow."

"Disneyland! Is that where we're going?"

"Don't you want to?"

She began to laugh helplessly. "It's perhaps the last place I would have thought of. How can you be so sophisticated one minute and such a big kid the next?"

He grinned. "My tastes are eclectic."

"I know. You've opened up a whole new world for me," Kylie said candidly. "I'm a different person since I met you."

"You're the same sweet person, Kylie." Adam drove into a huge parking lot. He wheeled the Jaguar into an empty space, cut the motor and turned to gaze at her affectionately. "You've just learned that life is full of choices."

"What happens if you make the wrong one?" she asked in a muted voice.

"You chalk it up to experience." He kissed the tip of her nose. "Come on, let's go ride the Matterhorn."

Kylie's thoughts were troubled as she walked beside Adam to the gates of the vast amusement part. Didn't anything ever touch him deeply? If only she could be like that.

The festive atmosphere soon dispelled her sober mood. They walked hand in hand through the crowded streets, pausing to greet a giant Mickey Mouse or to wave at the driver of a horse-drawn carriage.

Fantasyland and Adventureland were only a few steps apart, but their progress through them was slow because Adam refused to miss a ride. They swooped along the steep curves of the Matterhorn, traveled up a river in a pirate ship and rode through darkened tunnels where surprises appeared around every turn, making Kylie repeatedly clutch Adam's arm. He didn't seem to mind her involuntary clinging-vine act in the least.

As they strolled away from Mr. Toad's Wild Ride, Kylie remarked, "I'm thirsty. A hot dog would be nice, too."

"You'll spoil your dinner," Adam warned.

"Aren't we just going to eat at one of the snack bars?"

"Not a chance. Tonight we dine in splendor."

"I'd just as soon stay here if you don't mind. It's easier than going all the way home to change clothes."

"You won't have to."

"I can't go out someplace elegant dressed like this," she protested. Her white linen skirt and striped blouse were scarcely suitable for a fine restaurant.

"Trust me," he said.

That was the problem, Kylie reflected fleetingly. She was beginning to trust him too much, which could prove dangerous. But then Adam dragged her off to another attraction, and she abandoned her nagging doubts.

It was getting dark by the time Adam was satisfied they'd seen everything. Instead of retracing their steps to the exit, however, he took Kylie on an elevated monorail with silver cars that carried them over the park to a large hotel on the other end.

He guided her through a busy lobby, not to the dining room as she expected, but to a private elevator located around the corner from the public elevators.

"Where are we going?" she asked warily.

"You keep asking that question." He smiled.

"Because you never tell me anything."

"It's more fun that way. It also prevents you from objecting to something I know you'll enjoy."

Since they were obviously going to a hotel room, Kylie planned to object a lot. It would be different if he'd asked. She might very well have agreed. But taking her acquiescence for granted was too high-handed.

She was prepared to tell him so when the elevator opened onto a softly lit foyer. Beyond an open door was an interior so luxurious that she was dumbstruck.

A huge, white-carpeted living room was furnished with deep couches strewn with pillows. Polished tables held rosy-shaded lamps, and soft music was coming from somewhere. Beyond the floor-to-ceiling windows, lights were starting to come on. Disneyland, with it turrets and banners, glittered like a make-believe country. The whole setting was unreal.

Kylie turned to Adam in bewilderment. "This looks like someone's home."

"They do a nice job, don't they? Come see the rest of it."

A large dining area opened off the living room. It was lit by a crystal chandelier and boasted a mahogany table long enough to seat twelve.

"Where do you think the bar is?" Adam glanced around. "They assured me it would be well stocked." He opened the doors of a large breakfront. "Ah, here it is. What would you like to drink?"

Kylie remained where she was. "Aren't you going to show me the bedroom?" she asked cynically.

"It must be down the hall. I'll make drinks while you're getting cleaned up."

Her mouth thinned as she voiced her private grievance. "You might have asked me first."

"I just did." Adam was emptying ice cubes into a crystal bucket. "Would you like a tall drink or a short one?"

"You know perfectly well what I'm talking about! Is this some sort of ultimatum? Tonight's the night, or the band plays 'so long, it's been good to know you'?"

As his puzzled look changed to one of comprehension, Adam's face hardened. "You think I brought you here to seduce you?"

"I'll admit you've been remarkably patient," she snapped.

His eyes flicked over her tense body appraisingly. "It hasn't been that much of a hardship. The work it would take to thaw you out might not be worth the effort."

Kylie gasped with indignation. "If you feel that way, why have you been wasting your time with me these past few weeks?"

"Has it ever occurred to you that I might enjoy your company? Although God knows why! You're argumentative, suspicious and close-minded." He walked over to glare down at her. "You're also the most repressed female I've ever encountered."

"That's what really bothers you, isn't it?" she flared. "The fact that I don't find you irresistible."

"It might, if you found *any* man attractive. Poor Kylie." His anger seemed to die abruptly, replaced by uncharacteristic resignation. "You don't know what you're missing."

"I'm sure you're marvelous in bed," she said stiffly.

He shook his head sadly. "I was speaking of love in general, not sex or my own prowess. I couldn't make love to you, Kylie. It has to be mutual to be fulfilling, and you don't know how to give."

The phone rang unexpectedly. Adam picked it up. His voice was expressionless as he listened and then said, "We've changed our minds. Please cancel it." He hung up and turned to Kylie. "I'll take you home."

"Who was that?" she asked uncertainly.

"Room service. I ordered dinner served up here." He gazed at her steadily. "Whether you believe it or not, that's *all* I had planned."

Kylie was overcome with embarrassment and regret. She realized he was telling the truth. "I'm sorry," she mumbled miserably.

He shrugged. "It's not important. Are you ready?"

"Please, Adam. Can't we ... couldn't we still have dinner?"

"It wouldn't be very pleasant."

"I suppose not." She bit her lip. "You're right about me. I've spoiled everything. I've been suspicious of you from the start, but only because I couldn't see what else besides ... besides sex you'd want from me."

His face softened as he looked at her lowered head. "If I'd merely wanted to take you to bed, I'd have given up long ago."

"What else could it be? You said yourself that I'm argumentative and have a closed mind."

"Don't forget repressed." His eyes twinkled.

Her fair skin flooded with color. "That, too."

Adam's face sobered. "You're a very complex and interesting person, Kylie. One moment you're an articulate, confident woman, the next you're a wide-eyed child, thrilled over pleasures you never experienced before. I've enjoyed broadening your horizons. Your delight was reward enough."

"You left one thing out of my education," she said in a low voice. "I'm not a very good judge of character."

"I was working up to that."

"Will you give me another chance?" She held her breath waiting for his reply.

He appeared to consider the matter, a smile tugging at the corners of his mouth. "Okay, but only because it's a long drive home on an empty stomach."

Adam called room service back, and a delicious dinner soon arrived.

They sat across from each other at one end of the long table, where flickering candles provided an intimate pool of light. The wavering flames reflected in Adam's eyes and cast intriguing shadows over his strong face. He had never looked more virile or attractive. Kylie quivered at the thought that she'd almost lost him.

In a fervent desire to make amends, she hung on his words and agreed with everything he said. Adam looked at her strangely but didn't comment.

Finally he said, "I heard a joke you might find amusing. Did you know they're considering using lawyers instead of white rats in laboratory experiments? There are more lawyers in the world, and you don't get as attached to them."

Kylie stiffened. "That wasn't funny the first time I heard it," she said coldly.

He started to laugh. "I know, but I figured it would bring you back to normal. You were being so saintly I expected you to sprout wings and fly out the window any minute."

"There's no pleasing you," she complained. "I was only trying to be less argumentative."

He reached across the table and squeezed her hand. "Just be yourself, Kylie. That's the woman I was attracted to."

The small compliment made her glow.

When they'd finished dinner, Adam suggested taking their coffee into the living room. "Let's relax for a few minutes before starting back."

They sat on the couch and looked out at the lights of Disneyland in satisfied silence.

After a few moments he said reflectively, "That would make a great picture on a cloudy night."

"Wouldn't a full moon be better?"

"Only for a picture postcard. With cloud cover you'd get the surreal feeling of a mythical kingdom suspended in space." His eyes narrowed. "I'd use a filter, and fast film to streak the lights."

"You don't usually talk much about your work," she remarked.

"There isn't much to say. Wide-angle lenses and F-stops don't make for stimulating conversation, except perhaps to another photographer."

"Susan says you're a genius."

He turned his head to smile at her. "You don't agree?"

"I'm ashamed to say I didn't see your show at the museum. Could I come to your studio someday?"

"Any time." His gaze sharpened as he examined her features. "I'd like to photograph you."

She wrinkled her nose. "I take terrible pictures."

"I don't believe it. You have exquisite bone structure." He held her chin in his palm and traced her brow and the curve of her cheek. "Your skin is flawless, too. I wouldn't have to do any retouching."

Kylie's heart began to beat rapidly. He was so close that she felt a little overwhelmed. She moistened her lips nervously. "I must need lipstick."

"Your mouth doesn't need anything. I'd photograph you just like that, with your hair slightly mussed, and the moonlight shining in your eyes." His gaze traveled over her breasts, but clinically. "Not in those clothes, though. If you weren't such a prude, I'd drape you in a length of chiffon to veil your body without concealing it. I can see you as a modern Aphrodite, rising half-naked from the waves."

Her whole body pulsed at the thought. "It sounds like a centerfold in one of those men's magazines." She managed a small laugh.

Her comment took a moment to register. Then his detached manner changed to awareness. The fingers exploring the contours of her face became caressing, and his voice dropped to a husky pitch. "This photograph would be just for me."

The words she was about to use to fend him off died on her lips. Why was she denying herself something that was both right and beautiful? Adam thought she didn't know how to give, but he was wrong. It was difficult to come right out and tell him, though.

He looked fondly at the thick fan of lashes feathering her flushed cheeks. "Don't worry, angel. I'll take such a proper portrait you can show it to your grandmother."

"I'd rather be Aphrodite just for you," she murmured.

His surprise turned to incredulous joy. When he reached for her, Kylie clasped her arms around his neck and lifted her face, trembling with anticipation.

Adam's kiss fulfilled all her expectations. His tongue plunged deeply, taking fierce possession as his hands roamed over her pliant body. It was the first time he had allowed his leashed desire full rein. She pressed closer, wanting to feel all of him.

Within moments she was lost in a world of pure sensation. Every kiss drove her yearning higher. Every caress made her throb with longing. When Adam groaned and dragged his mouth away from hers, she stared at him questioningly.

"We'd better go," he said, drawing a ragged breath.

"Go?"

"This wasn't what I planned, sweetheart," he said regretfully.

"I know, but it's all right."

He stood up. "No, it isn't. You'd never be sure."

Kylie stood up, too, and put her arms around his waist. "I'm through analyzing your motives. Just make love to me, Adam."

He disengaged her arms a little roughly. "Don't make it harder, Kylie."

She couldn't believe what was happening. This was the second time he'd done this to her. How long could she continue making excuses for his rejection? Desolation settled over her like a smothering blanket. She turned her back to hide her shame and embarrassment, but not before Adam had seen them.

He pulled her back into his arms. "Don't look like that, angel!"

She held herself stiffly when he wouldn't let her go. "You'll have to excuse me. I don't seem to learn by experience."

"Why do you persist in misunderstanding?"

"Stop being kind, Adam! You did warn me," she said bitterly. "When you said you couldn't make love to me, I was just too dense to realize you truly don't want to."

He grasped her long hair in one hand and pulled her head back so she had to look at him. "If you're not the most exasperating woman in the world, you're a strong contender! I want you so much I deserve a medal for self-control. The only reason I'm not undressing you right this minute is because I'm afraid of destroying the trust you're beginning to have in me. I care about you, damn it! I don't want to drive you away."

The ice that had formed around Kylie's heart melted as she looked into his angry face. She smiled enchantingly and started to unbutton his shirt.

"It seems to me that you're the one who's being argumentative now—not to mention repressed," she added.

He looked at her searchingly for a moment before his grim expression changed slowly to a lilting smile. What he whispered in Kylie's ear as he lifted her into his arms made her blush.

Chapter Five

Adam carried Kylie into the darkened bedroom. She had only an impression of a wide bed and stars shining in a black velvet sky. The glitter was reflected in Adam's eyes as he stood her gently on her feet.

"I've imagined this moment so often," he murmured as he slowly pulled her blouse out of her waistband.

Kylie lifted her arms so he could draw it over her head without stopping to unbutton it. She shivered slightly as his eyes caressed her body while he unclasped her bra. When his hands brushed against her breasts she made a startled movement.

"Don't be timid, darling. I want you to be free with me." He drew her to his chest, gently kissed her, then nuzzled her ear, sending tremors of sensation all the way to her toes. "Tell me what you want so I can please you," he said huskily.

"I can't," she whispered. Adam's caresses were lighting flames throughout her body, but the inhibitions of a lifetime weren't easily overcome.

"It's all right," he soothed. "We'll find out together."

His hands stroked her shoulders and arms before finally cupping her breasts. Kylie reached for him blindly as he bent his head to take one aching nipple in his mouth. Her fingers anchored in his thick hair while his kisses feathered over one breast, then the other. She thought she would die of pleasure.

Only dimly aware of Adam unfastening the waistband, she felt her skirt slide over her hips and slither to the floor. She drew a sharp breath as he knelt in front of her and slowly stroked the curving length of her legs from thigh to ankle.

"You don't know how difficult it's been not to touch you," he murmured. "I knew your skin would feel like warm velvet."

He leaned forward and kissed her navel before rubbing his cheek against the flat plane of her stomach. Kylie closed her eyes to savor the shockingly sensual feeling, which intensified when Adam eased her panties down. She lifted each foot in turn as he gently guided each ankle. But when he sat back on his heels to stare at her with glowing eyes, she uttered a tiny moan of protest and wrapped her arms around her nakedness.

"Let me look at you, sweetheart," he said huskily. "You're utter perfection."

"Please, Adam," she whispered, feeling her skin flush with color.

"My sweet, shy little darling." He grasped her wrists and lowered her hands to her sides, then drew her body close.

His intimate kisses both shocked and delighted her. Tiny flames licked at her midsection as his warm, moist mouth slid along her inner thigh. He released her hands and manacled her hips with his arms. She clutched at his shoulders to steady herself when the flames threatened to burn out of control.

He stared up at her drugged face, his eyes smoldering. "Do you know how it makes me feel to see you look like that? To know I bring you pleasure?"

"I never knew there could be this much pleasure." She sank down next to him and put her arms around his neck.

Kylie's mouth sought Adam's this time, with passion and urgency. To her amazement, her inhibitions had been burned away in the hot flame of desire. Her fingers dug into the bunched muscles of his back, raked through his hair. She fumbled with the buttons on his shirt, frantic with the need to touch him, to feel his body against hers without any barrier.

When his shirt was open to the waist, she moved against him, her sensitive nipples stiffening to diamond-hard points.

A shudder rippled through Adam's solid body. "Beautiful lady, you're driving me wild."

Her eyes were the color of a turbulent sea. "Show me how wild," she murmured.

He lifted her into his arms in a convulsive movement and carried her to the bed. Kylie watched in fascination as he removed his clothes swiftly. Her breath caught in her throat at the magnificence of his male form.

He returned to kneel over her for a heart-stopping instant, rampantly masculine. "This is how wild," he said thickly. Then he lowered himself onto her and began to fulfill her need to feel all of him.

Adam's possession was masterful, filling her with limitless joy. In spite of his assertion of wildness, he was in complete control, guiding her in ways that would ensure her pleasure.

She arched her body against his as he skillfully, tantalizingly led her to a distant peak where ecstasy awaited. The spiraling ascent finally climaxed in a burst of throbbing sensation that penetrated every part of her body.

She was still gripping Adam tightly when she finally floated back to earth. His close embrace was a wonderful postscript to passion. She didn't want to let go.

When their heartbeats returned to normal, he kissed her tenderly. "Didn't I tell you it would be like this?"

She smiled blissfully. "I'll never doubt you again."

"You will, but it's all right." He chuckled. "I've cleared up our most important difference of opinion."

"Don't be so pleased with yourself. *I* was the one who had to convince *you*. You're the one who wanted to go home."

"You'll have to admit I changed my mind rapidly." His laughter died as he smoothed the damp hair off her forehead. "No second thoughts, darling?"

"Only regret at the time I wasted," she answered softly.

His eyes kindled as he stroked her bare back. "We have the next twenty or thirty years to make up for it."

Supreme happiness filled Kylie as Adam's mouth closed over hers. If that wasn't a commitment, it would certainly do for now.

After that weekend, Kylie's life was so ideal that it almost scared her. Adam was not only a marvelous lover, he was a wonderful companion and friend. They didn't need anyone else. They had each other.

The one thing that would have made life perfect was a marriage proposal. It was too soon to expect that, Kylie knew, but she had hopes for the future. Adam was so possessive. Surely he'd want some assurance that they would remain together.

Still, that was rushing things. Adam hadn't even said he loved her—not in so many words. She brushed aside the slight disquiet that caused. Hadn't he shown her over and over again?

Kylie bloomed like a hothouse rose. She had always been attractive and competent; now she was also confident. The divorce cases she was forced to litigate were still a thorn in her side, but she was determined to get her own way on public assistance work. It was simply a question of proper timing.

Opportunity came in the form of a very large fee won from a famous rock star. Kylie felt no compunction about plucking this rooster's feathers. He'd taken infidelity out of motel rooms and elevated it to a media event.

Maxwell Cunningham stopped by Kylie's office to congratulate her the day after the trial. This was an event in itself. He usually held audiences in his own office.

"Capital job, Kylie." The senior partner's face was wreathed in smiles. "We're all proud of you."

"I guess we won't have to worry about the rent for a while," she answered dryly.

"You're invaluable to the firm," he admitted in a rare burst of candor. "We'll have to start thinking about a junior partnership for you one of these days."

"In the near future?" she asked directly.

"I can't tell you exactly. The partners have to meet and discuss it." He chuckled. "You know how it is when a group of attorneys get together."

"It could be a long time then," she said evenly.

"I wouldn't say that." He edged toward the door.

"There's something that would please me almost as much."

"We certainly want you to be happy, my dear."

"You know how I feel about pro bono work, Mr. Cunningham. After the fee we just collected, I think we have an obligation to give something back to the community."

"Your high moral code is very commendable," he answered suavely.

Kylie moved swiftly between her boss and the door. "Then let me donate some of my time. It would be good publicity for the firm," she added craftily. "Articles have been appearing lately criticizing our profession for being self-serving."

"It's certainly something to think about." He changed the subject abruptly. "Have I told you how much I like your new wardrobe? You really brighten up the office. Keep up the good work, Kylie."

She let him go, satisfied that she was gaining clout. Before Adam had come into her life she hadn't realized her own worth.

Marcia brought in some folders a few minutes later. "What did you do to the boss? He went out of here like he was jet propelled. Did you make advances to the old boy?"

"The only thing I advanced on was his wallet," Kylie said with satisfaction.

"Do you want to give him a heart attack?" Marcia exclaimed.

"Relax. Granite doesn't shatter easily."

Susan phoned unexpectedly at noon. "It's such a beautiful day, I'd like to get out of the house. Is there any chance you're free to meet Tommy and me for lunch?" she asked.

Kylie groaned. "I'll be lucky if I get through here in time for dinner. I have a deposition to take and two new clients to meet with this afternoon."

"You do sound busy."

"Everyone in Los Angeles seems to be getting a divorce."

"The ones who can afford it, anyway."

Something in Susan's voice disturbed Kylie.

"It's like the old joke," her sister continued. "Money can't buy happiness, but it's useful for paying alimony."

"That's not much of a joke," Kylie said sharply.

"Okay, so it lost something in the translation." Now Susan's voice was sharp.

Kylie was silent for a moment. She hadn't imagined it. Susan wasn't her usual sunny self. "I wish I could get away for lunch," she said slowly. "I miss you."

"I can't expect to compete with Adam," Susan replied, with no resentment in her voice. "Is he still lighting up your life?"

"I never knew it could be like this," Kylie said softly.

"Good for you! It's time you came out of your cocoon."

"I've been neglecting you, though."

"We're sisters, Kylie. You don't owe me anything but love—and then only if I deserve it." Susan laughed.

"I could win that case in any court," Kylie answered fondly. "I only wish we saw more of each other. There never seems to be enough time lately."

"That's great. It means you're enjoying life."

"I don't want to leave you out of it, though. Why don't you and Neal come for dinner Wednesday night? I'll get away from the office early for once so we can have a long visit. Bring Thomas, of course."

"It would be super, but Neal doesn't get home until late these nights." The gaiety had gone out of Susan's voice.

"That's too bad. But it sounds as though they're giving him more responsibility at the store," Kylie remarked casually.

"I suppose so. Well, I won't keep you. I know you're busy."

"Susan, wait!" Kylie thought rapidly. "I'd like to have Thomas this Sunday, if that's all right with you."

"Don't you usually spend weekends with Adam?"

"It isn't carved in stone. Besides, if he's free, we can spend the day at home for a change."

"That isn't exactly his kind of day, is it?"

"It's time he got a little taste of domesticity. Who knows, it might even give him ideas. You'd really be doing me a favor," Kylie added shrewdly.

Susan's voice regained its former lift. "Well, if you're sure. Neal's been dying to go to the tennis matches."

"Make a day of it, and have dinner out, too. I want to unload my supply of strained spinach and tapioca on Thomas before he gets old enough to rebel."

Susan was on Kylie's mind all day. Adam could tell she was troubled as soon as he walked in her door that night. His ardent kiss didn't quite elicit the usual response.

"What's wrong, Kylie? Are your battling spouses wearing you down?" he asked.

"In a way."

"I advised you to get into another line of work. How about belly dancing?" he teased. "You have the world's most beautiful navel," he added huskily. When she didn't respond, he tipped her chin up. "Tell me what's troubling you, sweetheart."

"It's Susan. I'm afraid she and Neal are having problems."

Adam raised an eyebrow, but he didn't look surprised. "What makes you think so?"

"Neal's working late at the store every night."

"That's not much evidence. Maybe they're taking inventory, or getting ready for a sale. Any number of things could explain it."

Kylie shook her head. "I know my sister. She didn't sound right."

"Stop acting like a mother hen. Susan is a grown woman."

"You're not being very sympathetic," Kylie said coldly.

"I've learned not to get in the crossfire between husbands and wives. Don't you get enough of that at the office?"

"This is family!"

"All the more reason to stay out of it."

Kylie was torn between annoyance at Adam and concern for her sister. Concern won out. "You think they really do have a problem, don't you?" she asked soberly. "You saw it coming weeks ago."

Adam hesitated. "I formed some opinions, but they're not necessarily valid."

"I trust your impressions. As an outsider, you could pick up signals I missed."

His smile was devoid of humor. "Thanks for putting me out like the cat."

"You know what I mean," she said impatiently. "The problem now is what to do about them."

"I already told you—stay out of it."

"How can I when it's partially my fault?"

"Where did you get an idea like that?"

"I let them down. They used to be able to do fun things together the way they did before the baby came. But since I met you, I haven't taken Thomas for a single weekend."

Adam's gray eyes were stormy. "*Our* time wasn't important?"

"Of course it was! But I should have been able to spare some for Susan and Neal."

"You can't take care of the whole world, Kylie," he growled. "Marriages last just so long, whether you're willing to admit it or not."

"I'm not! And I'm tired of your cynicism!"

"I'm not responsible for your sister's problems," he answered evenly.

She set her chin stubbornly. "You are, in a way."

Kylie knew that was preposterous, but she was worried and tired, and she wanted to lash back at Adam for his hateful views on marriage. Especially since he seemed to be right.

"I'm sorry if I diverted your attention from the really important things in your life," he answered sardonically. "It was foolish of me to think I was one of them. I guess I got carried away by all those impassioned things you whispered in my ear at appropriate moments."

Her color rose. "I might have known the only important part of our relationship to you was sex."

A muscle bunched in his strong jaw. "Are you trying to tell me you didn't enjoy it?"

Kylie had a slightly sick feeling. How had a simple difference of opinion escalated into such a bitter argument? She desperately wanted to smooth things over, but Adam had turned into a cold-eyed stranger.

He jerked her chin up. "Look straight at me and tell me it wasn't good for you, too."

Anger mixed with Kylie's misery. He knew perfectly well he'd brought her such ecstasy that she'd begged for his possession. It wasn't fair to use those stirring moments against her.

"I don't place the importance on it that you do," she said coolly.

"Oh, really?"

He snaked an arm around her waist and jerked her against his body. Every remembered muscle raised her pulse rate. Yet Kylie knew that if she allowed him to subjugate her this way, it could mark a turning point in their relationship. Adam would realize how much he meant to her, and that could be dangerous. But suddenly, as she felt his heat and hardness against her, that fear no longer seemed to matter. She began to melt in his arms.

"I could teach you the difference between a lie and the truth." His face was taut as he released her. "But it isn't worth the effort."

Kylie's heart fractured into a million pieces as she watched him leave. She sank down onto the couch, trying to figure out how matters had reached this point. She'd said some foolish, wounding things, yet if Adam really cared about her, he'd have stayed and shouted back instead of walking out. Had he been waiting for an opportunity like this?

After asking herself unanswerable questions for nearly an hour, Kylie went into the bedroom and undressed. It was still early, but the traumatic day had taken its toll. She got into bed, too exhausted to think anymore. A short time later her eyelids drooped and her breathing became regular.

The doorbell woke Kylie out of a deep sleep. She went to the door, not fully awake.

"Who's there?" she faltered.

"Adam." His deep voice was unmistakable.

"What time is it?" she asked vaguely.

"It's ten o'clock. Let me in," he said urgently.

The mists of sleep vanished when she opened the door. His collar was rumpled and his face was haggard, but he looked wonderful! Before she could say anything, he gathered her fiercely in his arms and besieged her with frantic kisses.

"I'm sorry, darling," he muttered. "Can you forgive me?"

"I'm sorry, too." She smoothed the lines in his face lovingly. "Oh, Adam, I was so miserable after you left!"

"I don't know how I could have been such a jerk," he said disgustedly.

"I was as much to blame as you were."

"No, I acted like an insensitive clod."

Kylie started to laugh a little giddily. "I think we're having another argument."

"Never!" Adam's arms tightened. "I couldn't go through this agony again."

His kiss was draining in its intensity. She clung to him, making unintelligible sounds of happiness. Their reunion seemed like a miracle. Their restless hands moved over each other's bodies as though for reassurance. Finally he swung her into his arms and carried her to the couch.

Kylie turned her head to press her lips against his throat. "I thought I'd lost you," she said softly.

He buried his face in her tumbled hair. "What would I do without you? From now on I'll take whatever you're willing to give. Just don't shut me out, sweetheart."

"How could I possibly? You're the most..." Some residual fear made her hesitate. "You're an important part of my life."

"I hope so." He kissed her tenderly, but his voice carried an undertone of doubt.

"You must know it by now. The way I feel about Susan doesn't take anything away from you. She's my sister—she'll always have a special place in my heart. I'll always love her, and I'll probably continue to worry about her, but that doesn't affect my feelings for you."

Adam groaned. "I'm surprised you have any feeling left after the way I stormed out of here. Imagine a grown man being jealous of two kids and a baby!"

"Is that what this was all about?" she asked doubtfully.

"I'm not excusing myself, but try to consider how I felt when you seemed to be regretting the time we spent together."

"I didn't mean it that way!"

"That's how it sounded—especially when you called me an outsider. That reduced our relationship to a pleasant diversion."

"It was merely an unfortunate choice of words. I meant you could see things more clearly because you weren't personally involved."

"I'm involved with *you*, Kylie. That makes everything about you important to me."

"I tried to ask your advice, and look what happened."

"I regret it bitterly, darling. Will you give me another chance?"

"Perhaps we'd better not discuss it," she said cautiously. "You and I have some pretty basic differences of opinion."

"We agree on all the things that count," he said huskily.

When his hand moved slowly over her breast, Kylie was abruptly reminded that she wore only a thin nightgown. Her body was exquisitely vulnerable to his touch, and it came to life instantly under his ardent caresses.

Adam slipped her shoulder strap down to free one rounded breast. She shivered with pleasure as his tongue circled the sensitive tip while his hand slipped under her gown to stroke her bare thighs.

"How did I think I could ever do without you, my love?" he murmured against her heated skin.

"Don't ever leave me, Adam." His intimate probing destroyed Kylie's inhibitions and allowed her to voice her secret fear.

"Not in a hundred years."

He lifted her slightly to pull the nightgown over her head, then cradled her nude body in his arms. His blazing eyes and sensuously stroking hands were almost unbearably erotic. She turned on his lap and crushed her body against his, begging for the ultimate embrace.

"You do need me, don't you, angel?"

"In so many ways," she whispered.

He stood up with her in his arms and clasped her legs around his waist. The close contact drove Kylie's passion higher. She vibrated like a bow as his mouth devoured hers and his hands explored her rounded contours.

"Love me, darling," she finally gasped.

"I do," he murmured deeply.

Adam's need was as great as Kylie's, and their joining was swift and fevered. They danced to remembered music, their bodies moving in perfect harmony. The frantic rhythm ended in fulfillment so complete that they clung together in awe.

Kylie stroked his back languidly afterward. "That was almost worth the argument. You were inspired."

He bit her shoulder gently. "I don't need an incentive."

"I'll have to agree with you there." She laughed. "You're like those batteries they tout so highly."

His face didn't reflect her amusement as he raised up on one elbow to look down at her. "You don't really think that's all I want from you, do you?"

"Of course not," she answered quickly. No matter what her reservations, she was determined that nothing was going to spoil their blissful reunion.

Adam wasn't completely satisfied. "I love you, Kylie. You can't doubt that."

Her eyes widened as she stared up at him. She was almost afraid she'd imagined what she wanted to hear. "You . . . you love me?"

"Haven't I told you so?" he demanded.

"Not until now."

"That's not true. I distinctly remember telling you as I carried you into the bedroom."

"But that was only because . . . I mean, it's something you say . . ." Her voice trailed off.

"In the heat of passion?" He pulled her into his arms. "Darling Kylie, sex is part of love, but it's *only* a part. If I never told you I loved you when we were riding in the car or eating a hot dog, that's only because I assumed you knew."

She put her arms around his neck, gazing at him with shining eyes. "I wouldn't mind a little direct testimony now and then."

"You've got it. I'll hire a skywriter to write in giant letters, Adam loves Kylie."

She was afraid he might do it. "I'd prefer a more private declaration," she said hastily.

"I thought we'd gotten rid of your inhibitions," he teased.

"The important ones, anyway." She snuggled closer with a contented sigh. "I can't believe such a disastrous day could end like this."

"Everything will work out for your sister," he soothed.

"I suspect you don't really believe that, but thanks for saying so."

He hesitated. "I'm no oracle, Kylie. You're right about my marriage warping me. It was a bad scene, and maybe it did leave me cynical, but Susan and Neal are an entirely different equation."

"They do love each other," Kylie said eagerly.

"Then they'll weather the storm."

"I'd feel better if they were arguing. But Neal's staying out nights, and Susan sounds bitter."

"Do you think there's another woman?" Adam asked quietly.

"It could be, but I sort of think it's money. Neal feels trapped by his responsibilities, and he doesn't know what to do about it. I realize this was his choice," she said before Adam could point out the fact. "But Neal is immature. You spotted it immediately. He's really a good kid, but he's floundering."

"That must be hard on Susan."

"Yes, but she doesn't mind making sacrifices. She's his biggest booster—or used to be. Why can't he see that he already *has* all the important things?"

"He doesn't believe the best things in life are free. At his age they all carry price tags," Adam said dryly.

"Including a divorce," Kylie replied grimly. "A little matter of child support would clip his wings even more."

"Don't jump the gun, honey."

"I feel so helpless! That's where my guilt comes in. At least when I was taking Thomas off their hands, they had the illusion of freedom. You do understand now, don't you?"

"That was only a stopgap. What Neal needs is a good jolt."

Kylie's eyes were shadowed. "I'm afraid he's about to get it."

Adam looked thoughtful. "I only met him that once. Tell me something about him. What would he be likely to do with his evenings if he isn't playing around?"

"Probably hanging out with Marshall Courtney at the Family Club." She laughed wryly. "That's an ironic name for a club made up of males. Women are only admitted as guests—at the pleasure of the men."

"I'm familiar with the place."

"You're not a member!" she gasped, outraged.

"No, I don't get my jollies hanging out with a bunch of overgrown adolescents who think it's macho to discriminate against women and minorities."

"That describes Marshall to a T."

Adam raised an eyebrow. "He's a friend of Neal's?"

"Not until recently. Neal couldn't stand him in college. Marshall was always the rich kid who tried to buy his way into things. Then, a couple of months ago, they ran into each other again, and for some reason, he looked better. Marshall took Neal to lunch at one of his 'good old boy' clubs and invited him and Susan to a party at his home in Bel Aire. Since then they've become friendly, although Susan isn't thrilled."

Adam's mouth twisted. "I suppose Neal is hoping affluence might rub off on him."

"It's hopelessly juvenile, but you're probably right. Plus the fact that Marshall still treats him like the big campus hero."

"Well, maybe it's better than having some new woman hang on his words."

"Not much. Neal is still running out on Susan. He's also getting ideas he can't afford."

They were silent for a few moments. Adam had his arm around Kylie, and her cheek was resting on his chest.

He stroked her long hair tenderly. "I wish I could be of some help."

"You have been," she assured him. "Just by letting me talk it out. I've been the big sister for so long. I feel as though I finally have a big brother to share the burden."

Adam scissored his legs around hers and positioned her hips against the juncture of his loins. "I'm more than happy to share any burden with you, but *not* as a brother."

Kylie's desire awakened in response to his. "It was only a figure of speech," she said demurely. "Would you rather be a kissing cousin?"

His eyes gleamed in the darkness as he shifted her body beneath his. "I intend to be a great deal more than that."

The next morning Adam was out of bed before Kylie awoke. It was the first time he'd stayed overnight, and he'd forgotten about the crib. His howls of outrage roused Kylie. She opened her eyes to see him hopping around on one foot.

"Do you always do Indian ceremonial dances first thing in the morning?" she asked innocently.

"It's a good thing I don't have a tomahawk! I'd make kindling out of that damn crib," he exclaimed indignantly. "It's carrying out a vendetta against my big toe."

"Poor baby." Her tone was sympathetic, but her eyes were brimming with mirth.

"I'm going to burn that booby trap in the fireplace," he threatened.

"I don't have a fireplace."

"Then get out the marshmallows. You're about to see one hell of a bonfire."

When he stalked out of the room, Kylie thought he'd gone to take a shower, but he returned a few minutes later with some tools in his hand.

The sight of Adam wandering around unself-consciously naked with a screwdriver and a hammer was so ludicrous that Kylie started to laugh.

"Aren't carpenters supposed to wear overalls?" she asked.

"It depends on what they're fixing."

When he started to unfasten the bolts on the crib, Kylie jumped out of bed. "What on earth are you doing?"

"I told you."

"Surely you weren't serious!"

He laughed at the incredulous look on her face. "Not about burning it. I'm just going to dismantle it and store it in the garage."

"But I need it for Tommy," she protested.

"You also need some room to move around in. I'll put it up again the next time he comes to visit," Adam promised.

"He's coming this Sunday," Kylie said slowly.

She wondered how Adam would take the news. Their delicious interlude hadn't changed his belief that she was being taken advantage of. Would he also feel excluded once more? As usual, Adam surprised her.

"Okay, I'll take it down Sunday night after he leaves," he said casually.

"You're going to spend the day here, too?"

"Don't you want me to?"

"Of course I do, but I know how you feel about children."

"How do I feel?"

"You go home when they start to get fussy," she said succinctly.

"Does Thomas fuss much?"

"No, he's a very happy child."

Adam grinned. "Then what's the problem?"

Kylie could only think of one as she gazed at his handsome, laughing face and magnificent nude body. She wanted to marry this man and live with him the rest of her life. The chances were slim at this point, but he *had* said he loved her. That alone was a miracle; maybe lightning would strike twice.

She smiled enchantingly. "I guess we don't have any problems."

Chapter Six

Their blissful night together had to satisfy Kylie and Adam for the rest of the week. One or the other of them was working every evening, and Adam was scheduled to go out of town on Saturday. Phone calls were their only contact, which was unutterably frustrating.

"I can't believe we're only a few miles apart and we haven't found some way to see each other," he complained. "Couldn't you get out of whatever you're doing tonight?"

"It's the Bar Association awards dinner. One of our partners is out of town, so I have to pick up his award for him."

"Let them mail it to him," Adam growled.

"Somebody has to say how thrilled he is to receive another plaque, and how great it's going to look on the shelf in his closet," she joked.

"That isn't worth wasting an entire evening on. Why can't somebody else do it?"

"Because I've been selected for the honor. Can't you get out of your thing tomorrow night?" she asked hopefully.

"Unfortunately not. Several of my editors are coming into town. All male," he added. "The object is to talk about future assignments, but they like to do it in restaurants and nightclubs. I'd ask you to join us, but one of them would be bound to make a play for you."

"I wouldn't mind a little admiration," she teased, even though she reveled in his sentiment. Possessiveness was a good sign, wasn't it?

"I can supply all the admiration you'll ever need. Besides, I'm the jealous type. I'd be sure to deck the guy, and it would be bad for your image."

"*My* image?"

"Sure. The tabloids would read: Lady Lawyer's Lover Lays Out Lustful Lout."

"You're right. Bradley, Cunningham & Smythe would have a collective panic attack. I guess we'll just have to wait until Sunday."

"Unless you reconsider about tonight."

"I can't."

Kylie was slightly annoyed. Her engagement was clearly work related, while his boiled down to a night out with the boys. Yet he expected her to meekly adapt her schedule to his.

"You don't know what you're missing, but I'll give you a clue on Sunday." His voice was deep and liquid.

"We're baby-sitting," Kylie reminded him.

"I'd forgotten," Adam groaned. "I suppose Susan's already made plans?"

"She and Neal are going to the tennis matches."

"Well, maybe they'll end early."

"I told them to stay out for dinner," Kylie said hesitantly.

"Is this some sort of stress test?" he asked, only half-joking.

"I didn't know we were going to have conflicting schedules this week," she answered defensively.

"Of course you didn't," he soothed. "I'm acting like a schoolboy, but only because I miss you so. Does young Thomas take long naps?" he asked hopefully.

"Not always," she admitted.

He started to laugh. "I knew that kid was going to beat me at my own game."

Kylie was relieved that he was taking it so well. "He goes to bed at eight o'clock," she said delicately.

Adam chuckled. "That's a coincidence. I was planning on turning in soon after that."

Susan and Neal were already there when Adam arrived at Kylie's on Sunday.

Susan's greeting was tinged with defensiveness. "Kylie insisted on having Thomas today. I hope that doesn't interfere with any plans you made."

"Not at all. We weren't going to do a thing today." He shot a mischievous glance at Kylie.

She frowned at him. "It isn't the end of the world. Loafing at home for one day," she added hastily.

"Not when you can do what you feel like the rest of the week," Neal agreed.

"Some people think that's their privilege all the time." Susan's face looked pinched.

The barbed remark was so uncharacteristic of her sister that Kylie was stunned. Her eyes met Adam's in dismay.

"I haven't been to a tennis match in a long time." He changed the subject smoothly. "I guess I was more interested when I used to play."

"I'll bet you were good at it." Neal appraised the taller man's broad-shouldered, lean-hipped frame.

Adam smiled. "In my youth, you mean?"

Neal reddened. "You always think I'm taking potshots at you, but I'm not. As a matter of fact, I'd like to be just like you."

"That's very flattering, but I'm not sure you really know what I'm like."

"You've got it made. You're rich and successful. You can do whatever you want, whenever you want."

"Is that your definition of success?"

"What else?"

Adam looked at him for a long moment. "This is a very interesting conversation, but hadn't you better be going? Parking is murder at these events."

"That's for sure. Let's go, Sue."

"In a minute." She lifted Tommy out of the playpen. "Be a good boy, sweetie. Mommy will be back later."

Neal leaned over and nuzzled the little boy's neck. "Try not to give Aunt Kylie a bad time. She thinks you're almost as big a deal as we do."

After they left, Kylie sank down onto a chaise. "At least he loves his son. Maybe that will keep them together."

She regretted the incautious words as soon as they were out of her mouth. They echoed Adam's cynical remarks about children and marriage. Why had she made his case for him?

"Don't say anything!" Her voice was sharp.

"I wasn't going to," he answered quietly.

Kylie sprang up and walked to the edge of the patio.

After watching her tense back for a moment, Adam said, "Let's take Tommy to the playground."

"He has to have lunch soon."

"We'll have a hamburger in the mall."

She turned and smiled reluctantly. "He doesn't eat that kind of food."

"What does he eat?"

"Pureed liver and chopped peas, things like that."

"Good God, convicts riot over a better diet than that! It's a wonder the kid hasn't run away from home." He walked over and picked up the little boy. "Come on, champ, I'm going to show you what real food should look like."

Adam's behavior with Tommy was somewhat unexpected. When they got to the park he took charge. He was the one who held the toddler's hand as he lurched unevenly across the grass. And he was the one who took him on the swings.

Kylie had to laugh as she watched him hunch up his long legs to keep his feet from scuffing the ground. The child on his lap squealed with delight, displaying complete confidence in the big man.

Adam also took pictures, for all the world like a proud father. His photographic equipment was awesome, and it was obvious that he was a master at his craft.

Kylie was fascinated by his technique. It was the first time she'd seen Adam in his professional guise. He moved unobtrusively, taking numerous shots from different angles. The shutter clicked so rapidly she couldn't count the exposures.

"How can you focus so fast?" she asked. "I have an excellent camera, but I have to center a needle inside a little bracket to be sure I'm focused correctly. You could shoot a whole roll before I'm ready to take one snap-shot."

"I have different equipment." He laughed wickedly. "For which I give constant thanks."

"I'm serious, Adam!"

"You think I'm not?" When she made a face at him he said, "I'll give you a crash course when you come down to the studio. Here, hold the camera while I take Tommy on the slide."

After several trips down the slide he deposited the little boy in a large sandbox before coming back to sink down next to Kylie. "This is almost as strenuous as handball," he announced.

"Tommy is certainly enjoying himself. Have you had a lot of experience with children?"

"I've hardly been on a first-name basis with one."

"No nephews or nieces or little cousins?"

He shook his head. "I was an only child, and my entire family consists of a couple of maiden aunts. My parents died some years ago."

"Mine, too. It's sad to be all alone, isn't it?"

"I'm not alone. I have you." He put his arm around her shoulders and gazed into her eyes. "Don't I?"

"You know the answer to that," she said softly.

"When you look at me that way, I want to hold you very close. I don't suppose you'd let me make love to you under that tree?" he asked in a melting voice.

"All the other women in the park would be jealous. They might demand equal time."

"I couldn't oblige them. You're the only woman for me." He kissed her gently, moving his lips over hers with savoring pleasure.

Kylie moaned before drawing away reluctantly. "That feels good enough to be illegal. I wonder if it's a misdemeanor to kiss in public places."

"It's the *private* places that get you arrested, but I'm game if you are." He dipped a forefinger inside the round neck of her T-shirt and circled the knit band suggestively.

"Behave yourself," she admonished. "You're setting a bad example for Thomas."

Adam glanced at the toddler and began to laugh. Tommy was transfixed by a small girl who had climbed into the sandbox with him. His soft little mouth hung open as he stared at her.

"I think we're seeing a case of love at first sight." He chuckled.

"I didn't realize he was so precocious. I'll bet even *you* didn't start at such an early age."

"Not that I remember."

"How old were you when you discovered girls?"

"I don't remember that, either."

"That young, huh?" Kylie asked cynically.

He smiled. "My mother was a very wise lady who taught me not to kiss and tell."

"What was your mother like? You've never mentioned her before today. Or anything else about your past, for that matter."

"It isn't lurid. I had a very happy home life, I liked school, and my parents were firm but not too strict."

"Sounds ideal. What did your father do for a living?"

"He was a commercial airline pilot. He'd flown fighter planes during the war, so it was a natural transition."

"And your mother? Was she a stewardess? I hear that's often the case."

"No, she was a Southern belle." He smiled reminiscently.

"Is that an occupation?" Kylie asked cautiously.

"It was for my mother. She devoted herself to her home and family. She was also a fantastic hostess. People always felt welcome in our house." He spoke with great warmth.

"I see." Kylie suspected this was a significant revelation. "You admired your mother, didn't you?"

"Very much. Everyone did. She had more friends than anyone I've ever known."

"So that's why you're a male chauvinist," she said lightly.

Adam's eyes narrowed. "How did you arrive at that conclusion? I've never considered myself one."

"Men never do," she observed mildly.

"That doesn't answer my question. What have I ever done to give you that impression?"

"It's just your general attitude," she said vaguely.

"Can you be more specific?"

"As a matter of fact, I can. You think your work is more important than mine."

"Because I'm not a fan of the legal profession? My feelings about that include females *and* males. I still respect you as a person."

"But not my work," she insisted. "Take the other night, for instance. You were miffed that I didn't walk out on a business dinner I was committed to."

"I wasn't miffed," he answered evenly. "I was disappointed. I wanted to be with you."

"Not enough to cancel your date with the boys the next night."

"That was business, whether you choose to believe it or not. *You* were simply being used by a *real* chauvinist who didn't want to sit through a boring evening. He dumped it on you instead."

"It's something you have to put up with when you're low person on the totem pole."

"If you say so."

"I just did! You're obviously conditioned by your background, but I'm not a Southern belle."

Adam's jaw set dangerously. "You're suggesting I have an Oedipal complex?"

"Not at all," she said hastily. "It's natural for a man to think the way his mother did things was the right way. I was merely pointing out that certain women want different things out of life."

"And you think they have a right to them?"

"You bet I do!"

"Thanks for making my case for me," he said with satisfaction.

"In what way?"

"True liberation means the right to choose. My mother—and many women like her—preferred to stay at home and be that much-maligned individual, a housewife. That doesn't make her stupid, or a second-class citizen."

"I wasn't implying as much," Kylie murmured.

Adam brushed that aside impatiently. "In case you think my father pressured her into staying home, he didn't. Actually he wouldn't have had a chance. She was an intelligent, free-spirited woman who knew her options and exercised the one she preferred."

"I wasn't criticizing your mother," Kylie protested.

"Nor was I criticizing you. I'm full of admiration for working women. I consider it totally unfair when they're paid less than a man in an equal position. I hope that will change soon, and I believe any man who practices sexual harassment should be hung up by more than his thumbs.

... be tempted!

See inside for special
4 FREE BOOKS offer

Silhouette Special Edition ®

Discover deliciously different romance with 4 Free Novels from

Silhouette Special Edition®

Sit back and enjoy four exciting romances—yours **FREE** from Silhouette Books! But wait . . . there's *even more* to this great offer! You'll also get . . .

A USEFUL, PRACTICAL DIGITAL CLOCK/ CALENDAR—FREE! As a free gift simply to thank you for accepting four free books we'll send you a stylish digital quartz clock/calendar—a handsome addition to any decor! The changeable, month-at-a-glance calendar pops out, and may be replaced with a favorite photograph.

PLUS A FREE MYSTERY GIFT—A surprise bonus that will delight you!

You can get all this just for trying Silhouette Special Edition®!

MONEY-SAVING HOME DELIVERY!

Once you receive your 4 FREE books and gifts, you'll be able to preview more great romance reading in the convenience of your own home. Every month we'll deliver 6 brand-new Silhouette Special Edition® novels right to your door months before they appear at retail. If you decide to keep them, they'll be yours for only $2.49 each!* That's 26¢ less per book than the retail price—with no additional charges for home delivery!

SPECIAL EXTRAS—FREE

You'll also get our monthly newsletter, packed with news of your favorite authors and upcoming books—FREE! And as a valued reader, when you join our Reader Service, we'll be sending you additional free gifts from time to time—as a token of our appreciation.

BE TEMPTED! COMPLETE, DETACH AND MAIL YOUR POSTPAID ORDER CARD TODAY AND RECEIVE 4 FREE BOOKS, A DIGITAL CLOCK/CALENDAR AND A MYSTERY GIFT—PLUS LOTS MORE WHEN YOU JOIN OUR READER SERVICE!
* Terms and prices subject to change.

A FREE DIGITAL CLOCK/ CALENDAR

and Mystery Gift await you, too!

Clip and mail this postpaid card today!

Silhouette Special Edition®

Silhouette Books®
901 Fuhrmann Blvd., P.O. Box 1867, Buffalo, NY 14240-9952

☐ **YES!** Please rush me my four Silhouette Special Edition® novels with my FREE Digital Clock/Calendar and Mystery Gift, as explained on the opposite page. I understand that I am under no obligation to purchase any books. The free books and gifts remain mine to keep. If I choose to continue in the Reader Service, I'll receive 6 books each month as explained on the opposite page. I can cancel at any time by dropping you a line or returning a shipment at your cost.

235 CIL R1XP

NAME _____
(please print)

ADDRESS _____ APT. _____

CITY _____ STATE _____ ZIP _____

Offer limited to one per household and not valid to current Silhouette Special Edition subscribers. Prices subject to change.

Clip and mail this postpaid card today!

BUSINESS REPLY CARD

First Class   Permit No. 717   Buffalo, NY

Postage will be paid by addressee

SILHOUETTE BOOKS
901 Fuhrmann Blvd.
P.O. Box 1867
Buffalo, NY 14240-9952

NO POSTAGE
NECESSARY
IF MAILED
IN THE
UNITED STATES

Now tell me which of my beliefs makes me a male chauvinist.''

Kylie realized that she'd misjudged Adam once more. What had gotten into her? Was she so afraid of losing him that she was deliberately trying to find fault to soften the ultimate blow?

Before she could try to make amends, however, a riot occurred in the sandbox. Love's first bloom withered prematurely when the little girl dumped a pail of sand over Tommy's head. He responded with a loud roar of anger, accompanied by a push that sent her sprawling. Kylie, Adam and the girl's mother converged on the sandbox at the same time.

"You should do something about your son's antisocial behavior," the woman said disapprovingly.

"How about your daughter's behavior?" Kylie asked indignantly. "Who was her ancestor, Attila the Hun?"

Adam was having trouble containing his laughter. "Ladies, please."

They ignored him. The woman's face was very red as she said, "I'll have you know my Diane never has any trouble with other children."

"What does she do, beat them into submission?" Kylie demanded.

Adam had tucked Tommy under one arm and the small girl under the other. Both were protesting vociferously. "I believe one of these is yours," he said to the irate woman. "I'd give you your choice, but his mother would never forgive me."

The woman snatched her child away and stalked off with an outraged expression.

"Whose side are you on?" Kylie muttered to Adam, staring balefully after the retreating woman.

"I was only trying to avert a lawsuit. You wouldn't have to hire an attorney, but litigation is so time-consuming."

Kylie smiled reluctantly. "You think I overreacted?"

He put his arm around her. "Absolutely not. It's exactly the way any mother tiger would react if her cub was threatened."

She frowned. "The nerve of that woman, blaming Thomas when he was only defending himself."

"You'll both feel better after you've had some lunch," Adam soothed. "Next stop, the mall."

"Maybe we'd better go home," Kylie said doubtfully. "I'll make sandwiches for us, and Thomas can have what he's used to."

"That pulverized pap? The kid needs red meat to stay in shape for his next bout."

Adam drove to the shopping center over Kylie's halfhearted objections.

The section devoted to food stands was crowded with young families eating hamburgers and chili dogs. Tommy was wide-eyed at all the noise and activity.

The center of the large area was filled with tables and chairs, mostly occupied, but Adam managed to find a vacant table. He seated Kylie and secured Tommy in a highchair provided by the management.

"You two wait here while I get lunch. Are hamburgers okay?"

"What are you going to get for Tommy?" Kylie asked.

"How about a pepperoni pizza with anchovies?" Adam teased. "And a beer to wash it down."

"They don't serve beer here."

"No problem. We'll stop at a bar on the way home."

Kylie honestly didn't know what Adam would find for the child to eat, but her worries proved to be for nothing. He returned with a large baked potato brimming with melted cheese, a glass of milk and a dish of Jell-o topped with whipped cream.

She smiled. "I see they were out of pepperoni pizza."

"A kid in a stroller beat me to the last piece. Speedy little devil." Adam put Tommy's lunch on the tray of his highchair. "Does he feed himself?"

"More or less."

While Adam transferred their hamburgers and french fries from the tray he was carrying to the table, Tommy stuck his fingers into the baked potato. Kylie gently removed them and handed him a plastic spoon. The toddler made a few tries with the implement before throwing it on the floor and reverting to his fingers.

"Were you being optimistic?" Adam asked. "Or is he an admirer of Henry the Eighth?"

"He's used to a smaller spoon," she said defensively.

"Okay, champ, I'll rescue you this once, but I don't believe this helpless act for a minute."

Adam transferred his hamburger to his left hand and fed the boy with a clean spoon. Tommy opened his mouth like a hungry bird as Adam alternated between bites of potato and sips of milk.

Kylie watched with mixed emotions. Thomas had always depended on her for everything, even turning to her many times in preference to his mother and father. Suddenly, on the briefest acquaintance, he'd transferred his affections to someone who wasn't even a relative.

Adam glanced over at her. "You're not eating. Is something wrong with your hamburger?"

"No, it's fine." She took a bite and chewed slowly.

"This youngster will need a bath when he's finished," Adam commented. "I missed his mouth completely a couple of times, but I'm getting the hang of it."

"You're doing fine," she answered a little curtly.

He assessed her tone of voice. "Would you like to take over?"

"No, I couldn't do any better."

Adam's expression was enigmatic as he gazed at her. "That proves nobody's indispensable, doesn't it?"

He smiled then, to show he'd been joking, but Kylie wasn't so sure. Had Adam's conduct all day been designed to demonstrate that Thomas didn't really need her? That would mean his obvious enjoyment had been merely a pretense. Could he be that devious to prove a point? Or was she once again desperately searching for faults where none existed?

While she was mulling over her dismaying thoughts, an elderly couple stopped at their table. Their faces were wreathed in smiles as they gazed at Tommy.

"How old is your little boy?" the woman asked.

"He isn't—" Kylie decided the misconception didn't matter. "He's almost a year."

"I told you!" the woman remarked triumphantly to her husband. "Our youngest grandchild is that age. They live back in Connecticut, and we sure do miss them."

"I can imagine," Kylie murmured politely.

"Your young fellow is really a daddy's boy, isn't he?"

Adam gave the older woman a wide grin. "Won't let me out of his sight."

"I can tell." She beamed at all three of them. "Such a nice family." Her gaze lit on Adam's camera. "Would you like my Sam to take a picture of you?"

As she reached for the camera on the table, Kylie said, "No, don't! I mean, we don't want to trouble you."

"No trouble at all. I know how it is with our son. He takes all the pictures, so he's never in any of them."

"But that camera is very...complicated," Kylie finished lamely. The woman obviously didn't know how expensive it was.

"Don't worry, Sam's almost a professional photographer. You should see the pictures he took in Hawaii last winter. Better than anything in those travel brochures."

"Well, maybe Sarah's exaggerating a wee bit." Her husband looked as though he agreed with her despite his modesty. "I do know a thing or two about cameras, though."

"Sit on the other side of the little one, so he can get you all together," Sarah instructed Kylie.

"Do as the lady says, dear." Adam's eyes were sparkling with amusement.

Sam took snapshots the way Kylie did. Her smile congealed as he squinted through the lens, then lifted his head to group them closer together. After another lengthy period of focusing, he finally pressed the shutter.

"Thank you," Adam said when the older man returned his camera. "I really appreciate your kindness." His voice held no trace of mockery.

"You'll have a picture you can frame," Sarah told him, patting his arm.

After the couple walked away, Kylie said, "I was more worried about your camera than you were."

He shrugged. "I don't get bent out of shape about possessions. They were a sweet old couple."

"They really did mean well. And who knows?" She laughed. "Sam might be as good as Sarah says he is."

"I wouldn't go out and buy a frame," Adam warned. She looked at him quizzically. "He forgot to remove the lens cap."

Kylie's mouth dropped open. "Why didn't you tell him?"

Adam grinned. "How could I embarrass a fellow professional?"

"You're really a nice man," she said slowly, wondering how she could have had any doubt about it.

Once they got back to Kylie's, Adam read the Sunday paper on the patio while she bathed Tommy and put him down for a nap.

When she rejoined Adam a short time later, he moved over to make room for her on the chaise.

"Come lie down next to me." He gave her a second look. "You changed clothes."

She had exchanged her jeans for a softly feminine pink sundress and matching sandals. "I had to. Thomas is a splasher."

Adam put his arm around her and cuddled her close, burying his nose in her hair. "Mmm, you smell good, too."

"So do you." She rubbed her cheek against his shirt-front. "You smell like sunshine and fresh air."

They shared a companionable silence for a while before he said, "Today was fun. We ought to do it more often."

"Do you really mean it?"

"No, I'm just saying it to make Brownie points." When she looked up at him sharply, he hugged her and chuckled. "Of course I mean it. Why else would I say so?"

"You're not exactly the domestic type," she said hesitantly.

"That's where you're wrong. I don't know where I got my image as a playboy. I'm really a one-woman man."

"One at a time, you mean," she said dryly.

"No. I was never interested in one-night stands."

"Is that why you got married?" Kylie asked in a muted voice.

"I made a mistake, but that's a long story. You're the woman I've been waiting for all my life."

Adam's kiss was deep and convincing. Kylie felt as though she'd died and gone to heaven. Her lips parted from his reluctantly.

"I've been thinking about us a lot," he said, stroking her hair lovingly. "I think we should make it more permanent. How about you?"

Kylie's breath caught in her throat. At the most important moment in her life, she couldn't utter a word.

Adam was looking around consideringly. "We'll have to get a larger place, but don't worry, we'll find one with a yard. I know how much you like to garden."

She finally found her voice. "We wouldn't have to move right away."

"We need a guest room for Thomas," he said firmly. "I'm not dragging that crib in and out of the garage forever."

"He'll be sleeping in a regular bed soon."

"Not in our bedroom, he won't!"

Kylie stared at Adam through a pink haze of happiness. Had it really been this easy? Had one day of domesticity converted him? And to think she'd only used that as an excuse to make Susan feel better!

"I never dreamed... I mean... are you *sure*, Adam?" She couldn't bear it if he had second thoughts before their wedding day.

"Very sure, sweetheart. You're the one I was worried about." He kissed her tenderly. "I thought your scruples might be a problem."

"Scruples?" The pink haze started to dissipate.

"When two people love each other, there's no stigma attached to their living together these days. But I was afraid you might worry about appearances."

Kylie struggled to her feet in spite of Adam's restraining arm. The collapse of her dream had been like a physical blow, but she couldn't let him see her desolation.

"What's wrong, Kylie?" he asked in concern.

"Nothing!" She called up every ounce of pride. "You just brought up a point I hadn't thought about. The firm might take a dim view of what they'd consider unconventional living arrangements."

"They can't dictate a life-style to you," Adam said sharply.

"In a way, they can. An attorney is supposed to be circumspect."

"I could name you a couple of notable examples who weren't."

"Please, Adam! I don't want to get into a discussion of legal ethics." She was near the breaking point without that.

"We have to talk about it. You're letting those people control your life!"

"You mean I have a choice?" she asked bitterly. "Them or you?"

He put his hands on her rigid shoulders and turned her to face him. "I don't want to run your life, honey. I just want to be part of it." When she didn't answer, he said, "I know it's a big step for you to take, but I love you. And I thought you loved me," he continued after a slight pause.

"I do," she whispered. God help her, she did.

"Then why worry about what people will think? It's nobody's business. If we feel good about our relationship, that's all that matters."

"I'm not as indifferent to public opinion as you are," she answered.

He cradled her chin in his hand and looked deeply into her eyes. "It would be so wonderful, sweetheart. We'd have time together every day, even when our schedules conflicted. I miss you when I don't see you. I want to share my life with you.''

But not his name, Kylie thought bitterly. If he loved her more than superficially, he'd want to be sure their relationship couldn't be tossed aside easily. But Adam wanted it both ways—the pleasures of marriage and the freedom to walk out if he felt like it. Kylie knew she couldn't handle such an arrangement. If they broke up now, she'd survive somehow, but once they'd lived together, she could never give Adam up.

She drew away. "I need time to make a decision."

His eyes narrowed slightly. "That wasn't your first reaction."

"Well, I . . . I wasn't thinking clearly then." He mustn't guess the conclusion she'd leaped to.

"You think too much—that's your trouble."

"It's difficult to change the habits of a lifetime." She tried to speak lightly, but her voice had a catch in it.

Adam's dissatisfied expression changed to concern as he noticed her drawn face. "I didn't mean to crowd you, Kylie. If the idea upsets you this much, we'll drop it."

"Maybe that would be best for now," she mumbled.

He rubbed his knuckles gently over her cheek. "Hey, don't look so tragic. Nothing's changed between us."

"I know. I—I have a headache. Too much sun, I guess."

"Why didn't you say so? Lie down, and I'll bring you some aspirin."

He made her comfortable on the couch before going into the bathroom for aspirin and a glass of water.

"Take a little nap, and you'll feel better."

"I don't want to leave you alone," she protested.

"I'm a big boy. I promise not to turn on the stove or run out into the street." He leaned down to kiss her. "I love you, funny face."

It was ten o'clock, and Susan and Neal still hadn't returned. Tommy had been fed, dressed in his pajamas and put to sleep in his crib.

"I'm really getting worried," Kylie remarked. She and Adam were playing backgammon, but Kylie couldn't keep her mind on the game. "Susan usually picks Thomas up around eight."

"Did she say anything about leaving him overnight?"

"No, she knows I have to work tomorrow. It would be too much of a hassle in the morning."

"Well, relax. They're probably enjoying themselves so much they forgot about the time. Wasn't that the idea?"

"I guess so," she answered doubtfully.

"I know so. Lie down, and I'll take your mind off them," he teased.

When the young couple finally did arrive, Adam was proved right. They were both in high spirits.

"I'm sorry we were so late," Susan apologized. "I hope you weren't worried."

"Oh, no," Kylie lied. "Did you have a good time?"

"We had a fabulous time!"

"Where did you go?"

"Well, we happened to meet Tammy and Bruce Patterson at the tennis matches. They were with a lot of the old crowd that we hadn't seen in ages."

"Is that Tammy Weldon, your old sorority sister?" Kylie asked.

Susan nodded. "And Bruce was in Zeta Chi with Neal."

"He still knows how to throw a great party," Neal said.

"They were having a little get-together after the matches," Susan explained. "So we went to their house. Then everybody decided to go over to the Conovers' and have an impromptu barbecue. They have a gorgeous house with a swimming pool. The guys were bragging about what great chefs they were, so the girls went swimming while the men burned the steaks.''

"We were looking out for your health.'' Neal grinned. "Red meat isn't supposed to be good for you.''

"Lumps of charcoal aren't, either. You should have seen what they did to those beautiful steaks!'' Susan laughed. "We all wound up eating peanut butter sandwiches.''

Neal put his arm around her. "They weren't bad with the red wine. Admit it.''

She giggled. "All I can remember is the wine.''

"How about some coffee before you take off?'' Adam asked casually. "I could do with a cup myself.''

"We have to get Thomas home,'' Susan said.

"He's already asleep,'' Kylie told her. "Another half hour won't be a big deal.''

She went into the kitchen before Susan could argue the point. Kylie knew why Adam had suggested coffee, and she agreed with him. She wasn't sure if the young couple's hilarity was due to wine or simply an enjoyable evening, but it was safer not to play a guessing game.

Susan followed her into the kitchen and watched Kylie fill a plate with cookies. "I wish you wouldn't go to all this bother.''

"It's no bother. Besides, it will give us time to visit. Tell me some more about your evening. It must have been fun seeing all your old friends again.''

"Oh, it was! None of us could understand how we'd grown apart that way.''

"It happens when you graduate from college,'' Kylie remarked. "Unless you live near each other or you're in the same line of work.''

"That's a bit of a problem.'' Susan looked thoughtful. "A lot of the guys became professional men, and some went into family businesses. They're a lot more affluent than we are.''

"Did you feel you were being patronized?"

"Not at all! It was just like the old days. We're going to stay in touch from now on. Neal and I can't entertain on the scale they do, but I don't think money matters when people really like each other," Susan said earnestly.

"It certainly shouldn't." Kylie hesitated. "Neal seemed to have enjoyed himself, too."

"He was the life of the party." Susan laughed self-consciously, slanting a glance at her sister. "I guess you noticed that we were on less than cordial terms when we left here today."

"Well, you seemed a little, uh, tense."

"It was a lot more than that. We'd been battling for weeks."

"I'm sorry," Kylie murmured.

"I am, too, because we made each other miserable for nothing. Everything's wonderful again!"

"I'm so happy for you," Kylie said sincerely.

"How about you? How's everything going with Adam?"

"Just fine." Kylie suddenly became very busy setting out cups and saucers.

"What did you do today?"

"Devoted ourselves to your son, mostly."

"Did he have the desired effect? Did Adam beg you to marry him and have six children exactly like Thomas?" Susan laughed.

Kylie kept her head bent. "No, he criticized his table manners. I'm afraid children are out."

"Well, maybe you can raise puppies instead. You can feed those in the garage."

Kylie was grateful when Neal appeared in the doorway, clamoring for his coffee. He carried the tray into the living room for her.

"We have to drink this and run. We're in a hurry to get Thomas home, aren't we, Suzy-Q?"

It was Neal's pet name for her. As she murmured agreement, their exchanged glances spoke volumes.

After they left, Kylie turned to Adam with shining eyes. "I knew they could straighten out their problems if they had some time alone. Did you see how happy they were?"

"They certainly seemed to be," he answered noncommittally.

"You don't know how relieved I am!"

"I can imagine."

She frowned suddenly. "You sound sort of negative."

"Why would you think that?" He picked up the tray and carried it toward the kitchen. "I'll help you clean up so you can go to bed."

That didn't sound as though he planned to share it. "Are you leaving?" she asked slowly.

"It's been a long day, and you look tired," he said quietly.

Although she *was* tired—emotionally drained, actually—Kylie knew it was a convenient excuse. Adam was punishing her for not letting him have his own way. But if he thought she was going to beg him to stay, he was mistaken.

Raising her chin, she said coolly, "You must be tired, too. You needn't bother to help with the dishes."

Adam hesitated. "I honestly think it would be better all around if I left, but I'll stay if you want me to."

"I don't." When that sounded too harsh, she added, "We're both half asleep already."

He looked at her searchingly for a moment. "Get some rest, Kylie."

She nodded. "You, too."

He put his arms loosely around her and bent his head to kiss her good-night. When their bodies touched and their lips met, his arms tightened. For an instant it was the same as it always was between them. Then Adam dragged his mouth away.

With a final farewell, he left.

Chapter Seven

Kylie's eyes were shadowed the next morning after her restless night. Just when Susan's problems were solved, her own life seemed to be falling apart.

Had Adam's farewell signaled the beginning of the end? It certainly looked that way. Why else would he leave before midnight when they hadn't had any time alone together in a week? She sighed and reached for a thick manila folder on her desk.

"Did you have a good weekend?" Marcia asked when she came in a little later.

"It was all right," Kylie answered tepidly.

"You must be hard to please." Comprehension dawned in Marcia's eyes. "Or weren't you with Adam?"

For once Kylie regretted the easy camaraderie she had developed over the years with her secretary. Marcia's interest was becoming increasingly personal. Kylie knew the young woman's concern was genuine and her loyalty unquestioned, but her worthy sentiments proved inconvenient at times. Like now.

"I spent yesterday with Adam," she admitted grudgingly.

"Lucky you!" Marcia tilted her head, gazing at Kylie admiringly. "He's made you into a whole new woman."

A neurotic and insecure one, Kylie thought bitterly.

"You used to dress so, uh, severely," Marcia was continuing. "I really like your new image."

Kylie had shortened all her skirts and bought silk blouses in pretty colors to soften the somberness of her suits. She also wore separates and classic dresses to the office on occasion.

The telephone rang before she had to respond to Marcia's comment. Adam's voice caught Kylie off guard for a moment. "Adam?" she said breathlessly.

Marcia grinned. "I'm out of here."

"Are you busy?" he asked.

"No more than usual."

"Do you feel better this morning?"

"I felt fine yesterday," she replied in a clipped tone.

"You had a headache," he reminded her.

"Oh, yes... well... it's gone."

Kylie wondered when he was going to get around to suggesting it would be better not to see each other again. At least he had the decency to call, she thought drearily.

"You're still angry at me, aren't you?" he asked quietly.

"I was never angry," she answered stiffly. "Actually, I welcomed an early night."

"I didn't mean that. I was referring to our earlier...discussion." He swore softly. "I wish now I'd never brought it up, but I had no idea you'd get so upset."

"And I had no idea you'd retaliate the way you did," she flared, forgetting her vow to stay cool.

"Darling Kylie, do you think I wanted to leave you? I'd looked forward to that night all week."

"Then why did you leave?"

He sighed. "My proposal had disturbed you. You were a bundle of nerves, ready to pick on anything I said. I realized that when you challenged me over Susan and Neal."

"I just wondered why you weren't more enthusiastic about their reconciliation," she said defensively.

"I don't want to talk about them. I want to talk about us! The hardest thing I ever did was leave you last night. I wanted to hold you in my arms until the sun came up. But I couldn't jeopardize our relationship over some chance word I might say or omit saying. You mean too much to me, sweetheart."

Kylie's misery evaporated like dewdrops in the sun. "You're implying I was spoiling for a fight."

He couldn't see her smile. "I'm asking for your understanding and your love," he said soberly.

Tears clogged her throat. "Adam, darling, I don't deserve you."

Relief was evident in his voice. "Just try to get away!"

"I'll say the same thing to you tonight," she answered softly.

He groaned. "I don't know how to tell you this, but I'm catching a plane to Tucson at four o'clock."

"Oh, no!"

"That's the way I feel, but I just received an okay to photograph a natural wildlife habitat there."

"How long will you be gone?"

"Several days," he said reluctantly. "Maybe even longer. It's hard to predict when you're photographing animals. You can't exactly ask them to pose."

"I want to see you before you go," Kylie said urgently. It was suddenly important to erase the image of their last time together.

"I feel the same way, sweetheart, but what can we do about it?"

She thought rapidly. "I can juggle things around and get away for lunch. How about you?"

He hesitated. "I have some photos to develop before I go." His voice firmed. "The hell with them! Where shall I meet you?"

"I'll come down to your studio to save time. I've been wanting to see it anyway."

"If I take those pictures of you we discussed, I'll never get to Tucson," he said huskily.

Kylie laughed out of sheer exuberance. "I wouldn't do that to you. I only have lunch in mind."

"I wish I did," he muttered.

Kylie had never known time to pass so slowly. She became a clock watcher for the first time in her life. At eleven o'clock she declared her independence. Who decreed you couldn't go out to lunch before noon?

Adam was surprised and delighted to see her. "I didn't expect you for at least another hour."

"That will teach you to take my behavior for granted. I have a few tricks up *my* sleeve, too."

"I can't wait to see them." As he took her in his arms and she raised her face to his, a bell sounded in an inner room. He released her reluctantly. "I have to take some prints out of the developer. Hold that pose."

"Can I come with you?" she asked.

"Sure."

The darkroom was filled with a bewildering array of equipment. Kylie had no idea what any of it was used for, but it was very impressive. So was Adam's expertise. The large photographs he removed from the developing solution were sharp and clear.

She gazed with admiration at the pictures he deftly attached to something that looked like a clothesline. "They're magnificent! I can almost feel the wind in his face."

Adam followed her gaze, staring critically at the rider jumping his horse over a hurdle. "The composition is wrong on that one."

"How can you say that? I can make out every separate hair in the horse's tail."

He smiled. "I'm a professional. I'm supposed to take clear pictures. But look at this next shot. See how much more interesting it is?" The doorbell rang, cutting short his demonstration. "That must be the messenger service. I'm sending some prints to New York."

The phone rang while he was gone. "Will you answer it?" Adam called.

Kylie was impressed by the person at the other end. She hurried out to the anteroom. "It's Washington, D.C.," she told him, giving the caller's name.

"Tell him to hang on."

"But, Adam, he's an important man!"

"Everybody's important," he said indifferently as he continued to fill out a shipping label. "Tell him I'll be there in a minute."

Kylie was surprised when the man meekly agreed to wait. She listened with growing respect a few moments later while Adam discussed a pictorial story he had done on world hunger.

Subsequent phone calls were from a magazine associated with the Smithsonian Institute and from a famous Hollywood mogul.

"I had no idea you moved in such rarefied circles," she said slowly. "Your work takes you into a lot of different worlds."

"So does yours," he reminded her. "That's one of the reasons we enjoy each other's company so much. We each have more interesting things to contribute than small talk."

Kylie sighed. "I hope one day I'll have more to contribute than what some husband did to his wife."

"Or vice versa," he commented dryly. When the phone rang again, Adam muttered impatiently, "Let's get out of here or we'll never have lunch."

As they left the studio he said, "Would you mind if we stopped by my apartment for a minute? I planned on leaving from the studio, but I forgot my suitcase."

"You're not very organized for a man who hops all over the world," she scolded mildly as they climbed into his Jaguar. "I don't know how you manage."

"I keep a spare toothbrush and a clean pair of shorts in my camera case. People make too big a deal about things," he said negligently. "You can usually send someone out to buy anything you forgot."

"Not all of us stay in plush accommodations that supply those services."

"Is that what you think all my travels are like? You should have been along on my trip to Africa when I came out of the john in the middle of the night and found a rhino camped outside."

"What did you do?"

"Closed the door rapidly." He laughed and turned his attention to driving.

Adam's apartment was in an unfashionable part of Hollywood—not at all what Kylie would have expected.

"Do you want to wait here?" he asked after pulling up in front of an old pink stucco building. "It will only take me a minute."

"I'd like to come up. I've never seen your apartment." The occasion had never arisen.

"It isn't very grand," he warned.

"Not like the apartment in Beverly Hills?" she asked soberly, feeling guilty.

His expensive condominium had gone to Donna in the divorce settlement. His wife had claimed it, and he hadn't argued the point, although it was unfair.

"Good Lord, no!" he exclaimed in answer to Kylie's question. "I always hated that place. Glass and chrome and chairs you can't sit down on belong in a store window, not a home."

Adam's present apartment was obviously furnished with comfort in mind. A reading lamp was positioned next to a large comfy chair with a foot stool, and the couch facing the fireplace had big squishy cushions at either end. It was long enough for him to stretch out on.

"This is nice," Kylie said, glancing around at the profusion of books piled on built-in shelves. "It looks lived in. I wish I had a fireplace."

"I'll invite you over next time it's cool enough for a fire," he promised.

"Not before?"

His eyes kindled. "Anytime you like."

"Tonight would be nice," she answered wistfully. "I wish you didn't have to leave."

He sighed, pulling her into his arms. "I feel like chucking the whole thing, but I can't."

"I know you can't. I wasn't suggesting it."

"I wish you could come with me," he said. When she tensed slightly and started to draw away, he pulled her back. "It was just an observation. I'm not asking you to."

She turned her face up to his pleadingly. "You know I want to, don't you?"

"That's all that matters."

He kissed her, gently at first, then with increasing urgency. A week of being apart had sharpened the desire that was ever present between them. Their bodies strained closer, demanding what the other had to give.

"We shouldn't have come here," he muttered, burying his face in her neck.

She raked her nails through the hair at his nape. "It was my fault for coming in with you. I should have known better."

"We both should have." His hands curved under her buttocks, lifting her slightly so she was burningly aware of him. "How can I be expected to resist you when it's been so long since I've held you like this?"

"We really have to go, Adam."

"Why?"

It was difficult to remember when his body was singing a siren song and his warm, wet tongue was exploring the cavity of her ear.

"You have a plane to catch," she managed finally.

"Not till this afternoon." He slid her jacket off her shoulders.

"I have to go back to work," she said weakly.

"How soon?" He tugged her blouse out of her skirt.

Kylie could hardly think when his hands slipped inside the waistband of her pantyhose and kneaded the firmness of her bottom. "I have an hour before my next appointment," she gasped.

Adam's eyes blazed like the heat of his body. "We can get to heaven and back in that time."

They undressed each other hastily, their fingers fumbling with eagerness. When their clothes lay in a tumbled heap, they came together in a close embrace, prolonging the exquisite anticipation.

Then he guided her down to the thick carpet and covered her body with his. She received him with a cry of joy. Their passion had escalated so swiftly neither could hold back. They arched their bodies again and again in a relentless attempt to reach nirvana.

Throbbing pleasure put a satisfying end to the tantalizing torment, spreading contentment as warm as a soothing bath.

Adam rolled over on his side, carrying Kylie with him. His breath feathered her cheek as he said, "Thank you, sweetheart. I'll remember this while I'm gone."

"You gave me a going away present, too, and I'm not even leaving," she said mischievously.

A slow smile curved his mouth. "Wait till you see what I bring you back."

After they were dressed there was still a short time to spare. When Kylie pointed it out, Adam snapped his fingers.

"Damn! I could have tried out a few innovations."

"I didn't have any complaints," she answered softly.

"Not even about missing lunch? I wasn't much of a big spender."

"I'm prepared to overlook that in light of your other good qualities," she answered demurely.

"Sometimes I think all you want is my body," he teased.

"I respectfully refuse to answer that on the grounds that it might tend to incriminate me."

Adam's laughter died as he took her in his arms. "I want more than *your* body, sweetheart. I hope you know that."

Kylie's heart soared as she lifted her face for his kiss.

A stack of phone messages awaited Kylie at her office. Most of the callers were predictable, but one name wasn't.

She buzzed Marcia on the intercom. "Did Linda Dorset leave a message? I only see a phone number."

"No, she just asked that you return her call when you have a chance."

Kylie sat back, pensive. She and Linda had gone to law school together. They'd been part of a group that knew all the answers to the world's problems. During bull sessions in the dorm, they'd spent hours talking about how much better they were going to handle things than the power-mongers in charge were. Everything had seemed so simple in college.

Kylie had seen Linda a few times after graduation, but then they'd drifted apart. She'd heard the other woman had joined a public advocate firm, part of a group sometimes termed storefront lawyers.

Linda personally answered the phone when Kylie returned her call. "It's been a long time, Kylie. I'm glad you remembered me. You do, don't you?" she asked with a laugh.

"Of course I do! How's it going, Linda?"

"Not bad. I hear you've done all right for yourself. Bradley, Cunningham & Smythe is a very prestigious firm."

"It's a living," Kylie said offhandedly.

"You're lucky. It's a red-letter day around here when we can pay the rent on time. But that's not what I called about."

"What can I do for you?" Kylie asked.

"We're putting together a class action suit against a major slumlord. You wouldn't believe the condition of his buildings. No repairs are ever made, the places are rat- and roach-infested. His apartments aren't merely substandard, they're subhuman."

"If conditions are that bad, why hasn't the city health board investigated?"

"Would you like a short lesson in the time-consuming qualities of red tape?" Linda asked cynically.

"No, I've run up against it myself."

"But probably not when people's physical and mental health are at stake. The thing that really burns me is that this creep lives in a mansion," Linda said angrily. "He's got his, and he couldn't care less about the other guy."

"Unfortunately there are a lot of people like that in the world."

"Well, this one's going to be held accountable if I have anything to do with it."

"Good for you!" Kylie exclaimed. "I hope you nail his hide to the wall—or lighten his wallet, which will undoubtedly hurt more."

"You're so right. But being on the side of angels doesn't insure success. The devil holds a couple of aces, too—namely, power and money."

"If you want a contribution, you've got it," Kylie said.

"I want more than that. I'm asking you to work with us on a pro bono basis."

"I'd like nothing better," Kylie said slowly. "I've been pushing our senior partner to let me donate some time, but I haven't been able to pin him down."

"Now's your chance. This case will be splashed all over the papers—I guarantee it. We have promises of media support."

"Then why do you need me? I don't want to come in at the last minute. You people deserve the credit," Kylie protested.

"It's one thing to try a case in the newspapers. It's another thing to win in court. A sad fact of life is that a lot of judges regard us as wild-eyed liberals, out to get the system. We need the legitimacy of a stuffy law firm like yours." Linda laughed. "Sorry about that, pal, but I'm laying it all out for you."

"I appreciate that, and you're right in some ways, even if you're biased in others. Bradley, Cunningham & Smythe is an ethical firm. I wouldn't be with them otherwise. The fact that we get paid for our services isn't wrong. Our clients can afford it, and they deserve representation, too. Everyone does.'

"I guess that means you're turning me down," Linda said.

"No way! I was only presenting my defense. We're entitled to make a profit like anyone else, but we're commensurately responsible to give some of it back. That's what I intend to tell Mr. Cunningham."

"All right!" Linda exclaimed.

"Don't cheer too soon," Kylie warned. "He's practiced law a lot longer than I have. This case could go either way."

"My money's on you. As I remember, you were very convincing in college. Let me know when the verdict is in."

Kylie was exhilarated after her conversation with Linda. All in all, it had been quite a day. Adam's disclosure that he loved her for herself alone had touched her deeply. She must be doing something right if a man like that saw special qualities in her. And he must have been telling the truth; he certainly wasn't hard up for sex.

Linda's request had also boosted her ego. While it was true that her law firm was an important factor, Linda wouldn't have asked her to participate if she hadn't thought Kylie's expertise would be an asset.

The public advocacy case seemed like a sign. It was a chance to follow her conscience and justify the confidence of the people who believed in her. Kylie set her chin firmly as she walked down the hall to the senior partner's office.

Maxwell Cunningham's greeting was slightly tepid. "I was on my way out. Can I talk to you later, Kylie?"

"Could you tell me when? This is rather important."

He looked at her set jaw warily. "I see. Well, I have a board meeting at my club. I don't have much time."

"I can wait till this afternoon when you get back."

"I'm not quite sure when that will be."

"Tomorrow morning will be all right," she said adamantly.

He suppressed a sigh. "If it's truly urgent, I suppose we can go into it now. What's on your mind?"

Kylie gave him an account of her conversation with Linda Dorset. "I'd really like to be part of their team. This case means a great deal to me," she concluded.

His face was carefully sympathetic. "While I think your concern is admirable—indeed, I'm concerned about these people, too—there are a lot of factors to be considered."

She waited, saving her ammunition until he'd backed himself into a corner.

"You have a very heavy case load—which is a tribute to you," he emphasized. "You're making quite a name for yourself."

"I could be making a name for the firm. This case will generate a lot of publicity."

"We leave that to the more flamboyant members of our profession," he said disapprovingly. "Here at Bradley, Cunningham & Smythe, we tend to frown on that sort of thing."

Kylie barely restrained a snort. His dignity hadn't been ruffled by her recent client's widely publicized settlement from the famous rock star.

"I'm afraid I used the wrong word," she said. "I meant it would be good for our image."

"I can't agree with you there. Our clients are substantial citizens. They come to us because we're a dignified firm."

Kylie's eyes glinted blue fire. "If you'll excuse me for saying so, they come to us because we have a great track record for getting big settlements—especially in the divorce field."

"Exactly, my dear." He wore the satisfied expression of a hunter hearing the trap close. "Your reputation is spreading. When you're on a wave, you must ride it."

Kylie smiled, forcing down her anger. "If I'm that good, maybe I should open my own office."

The older man's eyes narrowed slightly, but his answering smile was genial. "There are thousands of young attorneys struggling to make ends meet. They'd jump at the chance to have your security."

"I'm not exactly in their class anymore. I've had wide exposure, as you so kindly pointed out."

Cunningham's geniality fled, leaving his face hard. "I don't appreciate being threatened, Kylie. Are you prepared to tender your resignation if I turn down your request?"

Kylie had a moment's pause. She hadn't expected things to go this far. Yet she had no intention of retreating in panic. If she couldn't win a minor concession, what were her chances of ever becoming a partner?

She met his gaze squarely. "That wasn't my intention. I came to see you because I thought my request was a valid one, but I evidently overestimated my standing with the firm."

They stared at each other for long seconds. Then the older man's eyes shifted. "I'd hate to oppose you in court, my dear." He chuckled. "If this case means that much to you, by all means pursue it. Bradley, Cunningham & Smythe is behind you all the way."

Kylie walked back to her own office, almost floating on air.

"I did it!" she exclaimed to her secretary. "I got an okay to work pro bono on a class-action case."

Marcia's eyebrows climbed. "I thought you'd been made a partner, at the very least."

"That comes next," Kylie said confidently. "I never realized how easy it is when you take the bull by the horns."

"You must have twisted his tail a little, too," Marcia commented dryly.

"I hope Adam hasn't left yet. I can't wait to tell him!" Kylie rushed into her office.

There was no answer at the studio, however. She was forced to wait until he telephoned that evening.

His voice sounded wickedly masculine. "Do you still have a smile on your face?"

"I'm grinning from ear to ear. Today was absolutely unbelievable!"

"For me, too," he murmured.

Kylie barely heard him. "Mr. Cunningham agreed to let me work on a pro bono case."

After an instant of silence, Adam said, "Congratulations."

"The whole thing sort of fell into my lap." She told him about Linda's phone call. "I knew this was something I had to do, so I stormed right into the old man's office."

"It's nice that he agreed with you." Adam's voice had a peculiarly flat tone.

"It would have been, but he didn't. We had a real confrontation. That's the exciting part—I stood up to him, and I won!"

"I can see where that would make you happy."

"The best part is, I owe it all to you."

"In what way?"

"You've given me confidence in myself," she said softly. "I never had a sense of my own worth until I met you."

"That's very sweet, honey," he said huskily. "But you don't need me or anyone else. You're a wonderful person in your own right."

"I do need you, darling. I'll always need you." Her voice was filled with love.

"I hope so, but I don't deserve you." His own voice was muted. "Would you believe my nose was out of joint because you were more excited about your new case than our hour together?"

"Is that what you thought?" Her laughter bubbled over. "What do you think made me feel invincible?"

"I'll be glad to stroke your ego anytime," he purred.

"I'm counting on it. When are you coming home?"

"I just got here." He laughed.

"I know, but I miss you already."

"That's what I wanted to hear. I'll get through in record time," he promised.

Adam's intentions were good, but the weather didn't cooperate.

"It's raining here," he reported the next night when he phoned.

"I thought the desert was supposed to be dry."

"It is, most of the time. Unfortunately, I can't locate a complaint department."

"Did you get any work done at all?" she asked.

"I took some indoor shots. You really must see this place, Kylie. They have a wonderful reptile and insect collection. The diamondback rattlers and gila monsters are a marvel of natural design. They're almost like mosaics."

"I'm not too fond of things that hide under rocks," she said.

"Then I suppose you wouldn't be interested in the tarantulas," he teased. "Some are as big as the palm of your hand."

"Don't they have anything more attractive?" she asked plaintively.

He chuckled. "Stop worrying, I won't bring you home a pet. When it stops raining I'll be able to photograph the mountain lions and bobcats."

"Don't bring me home one of those, either," she warned.

Adam had to remain in Tucson for almost a week, due to the vagaries of both weather and wildlife. Just when Kylie was resigned to spending a lonely weekend, as well, he phoned on Friday to say he was coming home that evening.

"My plane is due in at eight," he told her. "We can have a late dinner if you don't mind waiting."

"Mind? I'll be counting the hours!"

"Me, too, sweetheart. I'll hop in a cab and come directly to your house."

"I have a better idea. I'll pick you up so we can see each other an hour sooner."

"Have I mentioned that I love you very much?" he asked tenderly.

"I'll expect more than mere words when you get here," she answered with a breathless laugh.

His answer was so explicit that she blushed.

On the ride home from the airport Kylie asked, "Did you have a good time with your furry friends?"

"I'd have had a better time if you'd been there," he said fondly. "You would have enjoyed it, too. The museum is located on the edge of the desert, with mountains in the background. The scenery is unsurpassed, and the plant life is fascinating."

"What is there besides cactus?"

"A great deal, from tiny flowering plants to big trees. The grounds serve as a plant museum. All the paths are lined with native desert plants, labeled so you'll know what you're looking at."

"I always thought of a desert as a barren place, except for cactus, of course."

"Don't turn up your nose at cacti. They come in all shapes and sizes, and some have blooms that would walk off with first prize at any flower show."

"You certainly did your homework," Kylie commented admiringly.

He laughed. "You'll get used to it. I come home from every trip filled with enthusiasm. You just have to find a way to turn me off."

"I don't want to. I'm getting a liberal education. Tell me more."

"Later. Right now I want to hear about your case."

"Nothing's happened since I talked to you. The legal process will take a while."

"What else is new?" he teased good-naturedly. "How are Susan and Neal getting along?"

"Just great. They went to the boat show Wednesday night with their newfound old friends, and tomorrow night they're invited to a black-tie dinner-dance at the yacht club. Tammy and her husband are members."

"Don't tell me we're baby-sitting!"

"No, they hired someone," Kylie said hastily, hoping Adam wouldn't ask questions.

She didn't want him to know she'd given Susan a check as an advance birthday present. He didn't approve of her interfering in her sister's life. She wanted to be truthful with him and justify herself, but not enough to chance spoiling the evening.

"I hope you like pot roast," she remarked, changing the subject abruptly. "After eating in restaurants all week, I thought you'd prefer to have dinner at home."

"That was very thoughtful of you," he answered pleasantly.

But from the expression on his face, Kylie gathered she wasn't fooling him. He suspected something.

"I chose pot roast because it wouldn't have gotten overcooked if your plane was late," she explained hurriedly.

"Since it wasn't, we'll have time for a drink." He smiled, tacitly agreeing to avoid any subject that might provoke an argument.

When they arrived at her house, Kylie went into the kitchen to check on dinner while Adam fixed them each a drink.

She returned a short time later to join him in the living room. Adam's long legs were stretched out, and his head was resting on the back of the couch.

"This is nice," he said with a contented sigh. "It's good to be home."

"When will you have to leave again?"

"Not for a few weeks." He lifted her hand to his lips and kissed each fingertip. "I need some time with you."

"Do you know where you'll be going next?"

"Maybe up north to Gilroy for the garlic festival."

"You're kidding! A garlic festival?"

"It's a big event," he assured her. "They had over twenty-five thousand people last year. Gilroy is the garlic capital of the world."

"What do you do when you get there?"

"Eat, mostly. Various booths sell things like garlic soup, roasted garlic on toast, even garlic ice cream."

"I'd love to have the breath mint concession," Kylie observed.

"I gather it's not your kind of event." He chuckled.

"I'd prefer someplace a little less . . . aromatic," she admitted. "Where will you go if you don't go there?"

"Maybe Las Vegas. I've been kicking around an idea for a backstage pictorial on the casino nightclub shows—the sweat and tears under all the glamour."

"How long would you be gone?"

"Only a few days." He turned his head to look at her. "Why all the questions? Are you checking up on me?"

"I . . . I was thinking perhaps I could go with you next time," she said hesitantly. "If you were planning a short trip."

"That would be wonderful!" He squeezed her hand. "I'd almost given up hope of convincing you."

She smiled ruefully. "It takes me a little while to see the light."

"You must have missed me," he said fondly. "Is that what changed your mind?"

"That has something to do with it, but partly it was hearing you talk about Tucson and all the things it has to offer. You soak up local color like a sponge."

"I'm a photographer. I've trained my eyes to really *see* things."

"It's more than that. You get the most fun out of every experience because you're intelligent and curious. I want to tag along and see people and places the way you do."

"That's a lovely compliment." He kissed her tenderly.

She laughed self-consciously. "Especially from a repressed spinster who thought she knew all the answers."

His gray eyes began to smolder as he gazed at her. "No one could call you that."

"Not anymore. You've changed my whole life," she said softly.

"For the better, I hope."

"For the best."

He lifted her onto his lap and curved his hand around her breast. With his lips grazing hers, he said, "You did say pot roast could stand a delay, didn't you?"

"It gets more tender the longer it waits," she murmured.

Deep laughter rumbled in his chest. "A most provocative statement," he said just before his lips claimed hers.

Chapter Eight

The weeks that followed were idyllic. Kylie and Adam's relationship was unmarred by even a whisper of an argument, and Susan and Neal also seemed to be getting along famously.

Kylie didn't speak to her sister as often as she would have liked, because her workload at the office was so heavy. The public advocacy case was finally gaining momentum, so she had to spend a lot of time on that in addition to her own cases. Adam tried to conceal his impatience with her frantic juggling act, but she was aware of it nonetheless.

"It will all be over shortly," she said placatingly one night when they were at her house and she was having trouble staying awake.

"I hate to see you so tired." He frowned.

"I'm doing double duty right now, but as soon as the tenants' case is settled, I'll have more free time."

"You shouldn't be handling so many other cases. You're not superwoman, you know."

She smiled. "I was hoping *you* thought so."

"Be serious, Kylie. Go to Cunningham and tell him you can't do it all."

"That's exactly what he's hoping for. I'd never have a prayer of picking my own cases again."

"What good is the privilege if you're missing all the fun in life?"

She slowly unknotted his tie. "I wouldn't be if you'd think of something to do besides scold me."

In the days that followed she continued to divert his attention either that way or by teasing him out of his concern—until something came up that defied either method.

Adam called her at the law firm one day when she'd just finished with a difficult client and was rushing to get to Linda Dorset's office.

"Great news, honey!" His voice was vibrant. "We're going to Las Vegas next week."

"We, who?" she asked cautiously.

"Us," he answered succinctly. "*Entertainment* magazine wants to buy my pictorial."

"That's wonderful, darling."

"I'm giving you a week's notice so you can arrange things."

Kylie groaned. "You know how much I'd love to, but I can't possibly get away now."

"It isn't tomorrow, it's next week," he said evenly.

"But our case against the slumlord goes to trial in a few days."

"Why do you have to be there? You've put in your time preparing the case."

"I committed myself to seeing it through. I put my job on the line for this opportunity. What would Mr. Cunningham think if I simply took off on a whim?"

"Thanks for reducing our relationship to a whim," Adam said icily.

"That was a stupid choice of words," she replied penitently. "You know what I mean."

"Unfortunately, I do. Your loyalties belong to the great god of profit, the lesser god of the underprivileged, and assorted people in between. Unluckily for me, I don't fit into any slot."

"You're being unreasonable, Adam. I'd shift things around if I could."

"The chances of our schedules ever coinciding are remote. I should have realized you knew that when you said you wanted to go with me."

"I *do* want to! But I can't right now."

"Okay, then we have nothing more to discuss."

"You're being selfish and insensitive," she flared.

"Men tend to become unreasonable when they're rejected," he answered sarcastically.

"You might try to understand. I can only divide myself into so many parts."

"I'll make it easier for you," he said curtly. "You can assign my part to someone else." The click of the phone at his end had a sound of finality.

Kylie was as furious as Adam at first. She mentally enumerated his least desirable qualities. He was impulsive, intractable, selfish and uncaring. She slammed drawers, swore under her breath and got it out of her system.

Assuming Adam was doing the same thing, she waited for him to call and apologize. When the days passed and he didn't phone, she became irate all over again. But underneath her anger was a feeling of desolation. Surely he wouldn't let it end like this?

Kylie spent a wretched weekend. She raced to the phone every time it rang, only to be disappointed. On Saturday night she called Susan to offer her services as baby-sitter. Someone might as well benefit from this miserable fiasco.

Kylie made an effort to sound cheerful when her sister answered. "How's everything over there? I haven't talked to you in ages."

"Yes, I guess it has been a while," Susan replied. "I figured you were busy."

"That doesn't begin to describe it! My pro bono suit finally got on the calendar, and I've been in court every day."

"How is it going?"

"Extremely well. I think we'll win in a breeze."

"That's nice."

Kylie assumed from her sister's lukewarm responses that Susan felt neglected. "I called partly to tell you to bring Thomas over tomorrow," she said hurriedly. "I know it's last minute, but I hope you and Neal can still make plans."

"Thanks, but I don't think so," Susan answered politely.

Kylie's frayed nerves snapped. "I know you're annoyed with me, but don't cut off your nose to spite your face," she said impatiently. "Go out with your husband and enjoy yourself."

"That's very funny," Susan said bitterly.

Kylie abruptly realized that her sister's coldness wasn't directed at her. "What's wrong?" she asked sharply.

"Nothing."

"Don't try to pretend with me."

"I've dumped on you long enough," Susan insisted.

"Will you kindly tell me before I imagine all kinds of things?" Kylie demanded.

"It isn't anything, really. Neal and I . . . well, we've had a couple of arguments, that's all."

"I thought that was all straightened out."

Susan sighed. "So did I."

"But you were having such a good time with your old gang," Kylie said helplessly.

"That's what started it up again. We *were* enjoying ourselves—until Neal began comparing our living standard with theirs."

"He saw right away that they were better off financially. You said it didn't bother him," Kylie reminded her.

"It didn't at first, especially since they were so tactful about saying they had extra tickets and things like that. But then Neal started picking up restaurant and bar checks he couldn't afford. When we argued about it, he said he was tired of being a charity case. I told him we could entertain at home to pay off our social obligations, but he wouldn't hear of it." Susan's voice broke. "He's ashamed to have our friends see how we live."

"*Ashamed* is a pretty strong word," Kylie said haltingly. "Neal is just a trifle insecure. Maybe he feels they wouldn't enjoy themselves at a simple little get-together. He's wrong, of course," she added hastily.

"I know he's wrong, but I can't talk to him anymore."

"You have to try," Kylie said urgently.

"When?" Susan's voice was sardonic. "In the morning before he rushes off to work, or late at night when he comes home after I'm in bed?"

Kylie was appalled. All she could do was whisper, "I'm so sorry."

"So am I, but I guess statistics just caught up with us. We're in the high percentage of marriages that fail."

"Don't talk like that! You're simply going through a rough period. Neal will come to his senses."

"I'm not so sure I'll be here when he does."

"You don't mean that, Susan!"

"Probably not. Anyway, it isn't your problem. How's that gorgeous Adam? Now there's a man in a million."

"He certainly is," Kylie agreed weakly. Susan had enough woes without someone weeping on her shoulder. They made small talk for a while on safer subjects until Susan had to hang up to tend to Tommy.

Kylie was shaken and depressed after talking to her sister. Didn't *any* romance have a happy ending? She wandered restlessly through the house, wishing she could discuss her troubles with Adam, even though she already knew his views.

What she really wanted was his comforting embrace, Kylie finally admitted to herself. She'd grown so dependent on his strength.

Without stopping to think about it, she went to the telephone. What difference did it make who was right and who was wrong? She couldn't let a wall build between them.

Adam's answering machine clicked on, and his clipped voice sounded. She hung up without leaving a message.

Kylie looked at the clock. Nine o'clock on a Saturday night. The last time they spoke, he was feeling unloved. Who was assuring him that he was desirable? It didn't bear thinking about.

The following week was probably the worst of Kylie's life. The only bright spot was that on Monday morning before court convened, the slumlord caved in and offered to settle. They won a resounding victory, complete with press coverage, but it was a hollow victory for Kylie. She could have gone to Las Vegas with Adam after all.

Things didn't get any better for Susan, either. Thomas caught a cold that settled in his ear. He was fretful, and neither she nor Neal were getting any sleep.

Kylie had gone over to help out one night after work, but Neal was so hostile that she thought it better to stay away. Although she was careful not to appear judgmental, he couldn't help knowing she was on Susan's side.

By the end of the week Kylie was emotionally drained. She came home, took off her clothes and soaked in a steaming tub for a long time. Then she put on a night-gown and got into bed, too dispirited to bother about dinner.

The doorbell rang while she was trying to read. Swift hope quickened her pulse rate, then died. Adam hadn't called all week; why would she expect him now?

When she opened the door a moment later, the incredible fact of his presence kept her silent. Neither spoke for what seemed an eternity.

"You're still angry with me, aren't you?" he asked finally.

"No, I . . . not anymore."

"I came to apologize," he said gravely.

"Why didn't you phone?"

"I was afraid you'd hang up on me."

"I wouldn't do that," she protested.

"You'd have had every right. I was all the things you called me—a selfish, unreasonable, insensitive jackass."

"We both got a little carried away," she murmured, crossing her arms over her breasts.

Kylie felt strangely constrained. He was being so formal. The old Adam would have swept her into his arms by now. She didn't know how to break down his unnatural reserve.

"How is your case going?" he asked, still in a restrained manner.

"It's all over. We won."

"I'm happy for you," he remarked politely.

"Thank you."

After a nerve-racking pause he said, "Do you want me to leave, Kylie?"

"No! I mean ... not unless you want to."

His taut body relaxed. "You know I don't. I've been thinking about you all week, remembering how you felt in my arms." He walked slowly toward her, a dawning smile softening the harsh planes of his face. "But recollection is no substitute for reality."

His kiss was so torrid that Kylie's legs felt weak. She clung to him as he caressed her through the thin silk nightgown, feeling golden sparks ignite in her midsection.

"So beautiful," he murmured, feathering kisses over her neck and shoulders.

When his warm tongue dipped into the valley between her breasts she uttered a breathy moan. Adam lifted his head and stared down at her face with glistening eyes.

"You're mine, aren't you?" he demanded exultantly.

"All yours," she whispered.

"That's the only thing that matters. Nothing will ever come between us again." His promise was sealed with a deep, passionate kiss that sent her senses reeling.

Adam's lovemaking was both tender and ardent that night. They turned to each other over and over again, renewing their vow of love with every throbbing encounter.

During a quiet period of sated pleasure they talked softly, smoothing out their differences.

"I'm going with you on your next trip," Kylie told him.

"Don't worry about it, honey." He smoothed her tumbled hair gently. "As long as I know you love me, that's all that matters."

"You can't have any doubt about that, but I *want* to go with you, Adam. You've been right about so many things. I've been so busy cultivating the garden that I haven't taken time to smell the roses. No more, though. You're my top priority from now on," she said firmly.

He gave her an amused look. "I'm flattered, but you do have a tendency to go overboard. You still have a career to pursue."

"I'm going to manage it better. You were right about that, too. I'm not superwoman, and the office will have to realize that. The workhorse just rebelled."

His smiling eyes held a golden glow. "I can't take credit I don't deserve. I'm not always right."

"You don't think I should lighten my caseload?" she asked in surprise.

"I was referring to another statement I once made." His hand wandered erotically over her body. "You definitely *are* superwoman."

If it hadn't been for Susan, Kylie would have been in seventh heaven. It finally seemed as though she and Adam had thrashed out their problems once and for all.

But Susan's problems only increased. Tommy caught one cold after another, and his mother was getting worn down. She and Neal were nervous and on edge, which led to a final argument. The result was that he moved out of the house.

Kylie couldn't very well keep the news from Adam, much as she wanted to. He was sympathetic, yet not overly surprised. They tacitly avoided the subject, but he knew she was worried about her sister. It became a faint shadow between them.

Most of the time, though, she and Adam were blissfully happy. They had picnics in the park, went to the theater and did offbeat things like driving into the country to pick oranges.

"We ought to be getting paid for this instead of having to pay the grower," Kylie complained, although she loved the smell of orange blossoms and the fresh country air.

"You get to keep the oranges," Adam pointed out.

"I can do that in a supermarket, and they put them in a bag for me."

"This is better exercise than wheeling a wobbly cart down an aisle," he replied, climbing higher on the ladder. "Here's a consolation prize." He handed her a cluster of orange blossoms.

"I feel like a bride," she said lightly.

He laughed, tucking a floral sprig into her hair. "I can see it in the society column now: 'The bride wore blue jeans and carried a tasteful bouquet.'"

"At least you've heard of the custom," she muttered, burying her face in the fragrant flowers.

"What? I didn't hear you," he called down.

"I said these oranges better be sweet, or you'll never hear the end of it," she answered sadly.

They had come home from a late dinner one night and were feeling pleasantly languid. The stereo was playing softly; Adam was stretched out on the couch, his head in Kylie's lap.

"I don't know which I like best," he pondered. "Taking you out and making every other man jealous, or having you all to myself like this. Which do you prefer?"

Kylie stroked his brow gently. "I'd have to hear more about those other men," she teased.

He captured her hand and held it against his cheek. "They all have warts and smoke big black cigars."

"Is that the only kind of man you think I can attract?" she asked indignantly.

Adam smiled meltingly. "If Anthony had seen you, he'd have sent Cleopatra back to Julius Caesar gift-wrapped."

"You're just trying to get on my good side."

"You don't have a bad one." He reached up and grasped her long hair, pulling her face down to his.

After a moment Kylie raised her head. "Kissing upside down is weird. Everything's in the wrong place."

"I can remedy that."

Adam swung his long legs to the floor, eased her flat on the couch, then stretched out beside her. In the close confines of the narrow sofa, his lithe body molded to hers at every point.

"Is that better?" he asked in a deep, velvet voice.

"Much better." She moved against him, fueling their mounting desire.

As Adam's tongue slipped between her willing lips, the telephone rang.

"Let it ring," he growled.

A premonition chilled Kylie's passion. "I can't."

"Sure you can," he murmured, locking his legs around hers. "I'll show you how easy it is."

"Please, Adam, I have to answer it."

When she began to struggle, he released her. "Okay, but your priorities still leave something to be desired."

Susan's voice greeted her, as she'd somehow known it would. "Is anything wrong?" she asked anxiously.

"It's Thomas." Susan sounded overwrought. "His temperature is sky high, and I'm terrified!"

"Have you called the doctor?"

"Just before I phoned you. He said he'd be over as soon as possible, but who knows how long that could be? Maybe I should take Tommy to the emergency room."

"You can't drive him there by yourself. Hang on. I'll be over in ten minutes. If the doctor isn't there by then, I'll take you to the hospital."

Adam had gathered enough from Kylie's end of the conversation. When she started to tell him the rest of it as she ran into the bedroom for her purse, he stopped her.

"The details can wait."

"My car keys!" She stared at him distractedly. "Where did I put them?"

"I'll drive you." He took her arm and hurried her out the door.

The doctor was already at the house when Kylie and Adam arrived. He was a competent man who inspired confidence. Susan calmed down once he assured her that Tommy wasn't seriously ill.

"A high temperature can be frightening, but antibiotics will lower it quickly," the doctor said.

Susan twisted her fingers nervously. "His eyes were so glazed. I didn't know what to do."

"You did exactly the right thing," the physician said soothingly. "I'm going to give you some pills. You and your husband can spell each other, because Tommy has to have one of these every four hours through the night."

"I'll stay with you," Kylie told her sister swiftly.

"That might be best," the doctor said after a concerned glance at Susan. "You look as though you've been through more than your son has."

"I'll be fine as long as he's all right." She managed a weak smile.

"He will be. Try not to worry." He turned to Adam with a chuckle. "You'd think I'd know better by now. Telling a mother not to worry is like trying to empty the ocean with a teaspoon."

While the doctor was rummaging in his bag for the pills and giving Susan last-minute instructions, Kylie and Adam went into the other room.

"Never a dull moment when you have a baby," he remarked ruefully.

"I wouldn't say this was the norm," she answered sharply.

"Of course not." He slanted a glance at her drawn face. "Did Susan get in touch with Neal?"

"I doubt it. She had more pressing things on her mind."

"I think she should call him now," Adam said quietly.

"If he'd been here in the first place, he might have been of some use," Kylie answered bitterly. "Susan doesn't need him now."

Adam started to say something, then reconsidered. "I'd better run along."

"Don't go!" She put her arms around his waist and rested her forehead on his chest. "I'm sorry for snapping at you. Reaction, I guess. I was so worried."

"I know, and it's all right." He hugged her and kissed the top of her head. "I have broad shoulders."

"I don't know what I'd do without you," she said. "Poor Susan."

"She's stronger than you think," he soothed.

Kylie sighed. "I guess she'll have to be."

Adam raised an eyebrow. "Don't tell me you're throwing in the towel?"

"What else can I do?"

"You can keep on believing in true love," he told her tenderly. "Look at us. Aren't we living proof?"

But we aren't married, she thought silently, and we won't ever be. Kylie had never felt the impermanence of their relationship more strongly. Adam had been sweet and understanding tonight. But how many more incidents would it take before he became restless? He wasn't interested in becoming part of a family.

"Keep a good thought." His advice broke in on her troubled thoughts. "You aren't Susan's only hope for salvation."

"I wish somebody was."

"Will you listen to the doctor and stop worrying?"

She tried to smile. "You heard him admit how silly that advice is."

"Only for mothers."

Kylie turned away to hide her sudden pain. "I think I'll make some coffee," she mumbled.

"Not for me." He kissed her cheek. "I'm going to take off. Say good-bye to Susan for me."

Kylie was so hurt that she didn't try to dissuade him.

Adam didn't go home. He drove to a stately brick building in a fashionable part of the city. The lawn in front was carefully tended, and lights shone from most of the windows.

The large dining room on the left of the entryway was darkened at this hour, but the bar was filled with raucous voices. The bigger common room was quiet by comparison. Several men were watching television in a corner, while a few other groups played bridge and gin rummy.

Adam glanced around the room before entering the bar. He nodded at a few familiar faces as he stood in the doorway, scanning the scene.

A waiter came up to him. "Can I get you a drink, sir?"

"Not right now. I'm looking for someone. Would you happen to know Neal Parker?"

"Yes, sir. He's a frequent guest of Mr. Courtney's."

"Is he here tonight?"

"He was earlier, but I haven't seen him in the last hour. Maybe they're downstairs in the billiard room."

Adam thanked the man and walked down a wide marble staircase.

The billiard room took up fully half of the lower floor. Two beautifully carved tables occupied one end of the vast room, their vivid green felt surfaces glowing like patches of grass under the bright lamps overhead.

In contrast, the other side of the room was softly lit. A long bar ran along one wall, and round tables filled the central area. The atmosphere spoke of money and privilege.

Neal was sitting at the bar with another man his age, although age was all they seemed to have in common. His friend was more than a little overweight. His expensively tailored suit camouflaged many of the extra pounds, but his face was already developing jowls, and his hands were pudgy.

Neal, on the other hand, looked almost scrawny. He'd lost weight since Adam had seen him, and his face was haggard.

Adam approached the two men. "Hello, Neal," he said casually.

"Adam!" Neal's rather sullen expression became animated. "I didn't know you were a member here."

"I'm not. What was it Groucho Marx once said? I wouldn't join any club that would have me as a member."

Neal laughed a little uneasily. "I'd like you to meet my friend, Marshall Courtney."

After the two men shook hands, Marshall invited Adam to have a drink. "You're ready for another one, too, aren't you, Neal?"

Neal slanted a glance at Adam. "No, this one's fine," he said.

"I'm sure you could use another," Adam said genially. "Come on, be one of the boys."

"I like your friend's style," Marshall remarked. "What do you do for a living?"

"I make lots of money," Adam answered, most uncharacteristically.

"I can see that." Marshall gazed admiringly at Adam's cashmere sport jacket and Italian shoes. "Do you do it legitimately or at something you don't want the I.R.S. to know about?"

"What difference does that make?" Adam's eyes had a steely glint. "Money is the bottom line. The one who has it is king of the mountain."

"You've got that right!"

"Okay, Adam, you've made your point." A dull flush stained Neal's cheekbones. "Now buzz off!"

"What's the matter with you?" Marshall looked puzzled.

"Neal has indigestion." Adam's steady eyes held the younger man's. "He can't stomach what he's become."

"Is this some of that existentialist stuff?" Marshall asked plaintively. "I never could figure out that junk in college."

"It gets even harder in the real world," Adam assured him. "Would you excuse us while Neal and I have a little talk?"

"I don't have to listen to you." Neal's jaw was rigidly set. "Your view of life is skewed by your own success. How can you possibly understand the trauma of frustration?"

Marshall shook his head. "Man, I'm out of here! Just sign my name to the check."

Adam waited until the chubby man had gone before saying, "He's quite a role model—if you want to learn to be stupid."

"All right, so he's not Mr. High I.Q., but he's a good friend."

"What's your criteria for a good friend? Someone who picks up the bar tab?"

"Marshall and I are buddies," Neal said defensively. "He knows I don't make a lot of money, but it doesn't matter to him."

"Your fraternity brothers feel the same way," Adam observed mildly.

"A fat lot you know," Neal muttered. "Do you have any idea what it feels like to be patronized? Oh, they were really clever about it! All that garbage about having extra tickets to the theater that their uncle couldn't use, and picking up the check at the country club because they had to spend their minimum. I'm not stupid!"

"You're giving a good imitation of it."

"I wouldn't expect you to understand," Neal said bitterly.

"You're right, I don't understand. Why is it acceptable to freeload off Marshall, yet not to accept the hospitality of friends who genuinely like you?"

"Because he...I mean, they... Oh, hell, I can't explain it to you."

"Is it because you value the respect of your friends, and you don't give a damn about Marshall?"

"I was on an equal plane with them in college," Neal said in a low voice. "I don't want them to feel sorry for me now."

"They already know you're a failure, and it doesn't bother them," Adam said calmly.

Neal's face paled. "Who the devil do you think you are, writing me off like that? You don't know what you're talking about! I'm only twenty-three. I have my whole life ahead of me!"

"Then I suggest you get on with it," Adam said crisply. "While you're wallowing in self-pity, have you ever considered what you're doing to your wife? Or your sister-in-law, for that matter. She's been very good to you."

"Kylie is on Susan's side," Neal muttered.

"Which doesn't leave you in an enviable position. The only one in your corner is Marshall."

Neal looked at Adam with shamefaced comprehension. "I've been acting like a real jerk, haven't I?"

"The world's champion," Adam assured him.

"Do you think Susan will take me back?"

"You have some ground to make up." Adam told him about Tommy.

"My God, why didn't you tell me sooner?" Neal stood up so abruptly he knocked over the bar stool. "I have to go home right away."

"Calm down, Tommy's fine now."

"Poor Suzy, going through this all alone. I wouldn't blame her if she never forgave me."

"Humility is the key," Adam said dryly.

"I didn't realize what I was doing to both of them. But if she'll only take me back, I'll make it up to her. I swear it!"

"Tell her, not me."

"Will you give me a lift?" Neal asked eagerly. "Marshall picked me up tonight."

When they got to the house he begged Adam to come in with him.

"You don't need me," Adam declined.

"I can't face Susan alone."

"You won't be alone. Kylie's there. Any more people and it will turn into a circus," Adam said impatiently.

"Kylie's as angry at me as Susan is. I need somebody on my side."

"This isn't mixed doubles! Go in there and apologize like a man. I do it regularly," Adam said wryly. "It builds character."

When it appeared that Neal wouldn't, or couldn't, go through with it on his own, Adam agreed reluctantly to accompany him.

Susan had gone to bed for some much-needed sleep, and Kylie was reading on the couch. Her greeting to Neal was lukewarm.

"How is Tommy?" he asked.

"His temperature is down, and he's breathing a lot better."

"Can I see him?" Neal asked humbly.

Kylie's coolness dissolved in a warm rush of pity. "Of course you can. Just be careful not to wake him. He needs his sleep, the poor baby."

Adam had been hovering by the front door. When Neal left the room he started to slip out, but Kylie stopped him.

"You went to find Neal," she marveled, deeply moved. "That's why you said you had to leave."

He gave her a lopsided smile. "I guess meddling in other people's business is catching."

"Did he come home to stay?"

"I imagine that's up to Susan."

Kylie bit her lip. "I'm sure she'll take him back, but what if he only returned because he felt guilty? I hope their problems don't start up again as soon as Tommy gets well."

"I think Neal grew up a lot tonight."

"Did you tell him to act his age instead of behaving like a spoiled child?"

"I don't believe in giving advice. No one ever takes it anyway."

"You give me advice all the time," she said.

He smiled. "That proves my point."

Neal rejoined them, looking chastened. "I wish I could have picked him up and held him."

Kylie glanced at her watch. "You'll get your wish in about two hours. He's due for his medicine then."

Susan appeared in the doorway. "I heard voices. Is anything—" She stopped when she saw Neal.

He looked at her longingly but was afraid to go to her. They remained like statues, neither saying a word.

After a comprehensive glance, Adam took charge. "You'll have to fill Neal in on what the doctor said," he told Susan, as though her husband had just come home from work. "I tried, but I don't know anything about these childhood upsets."

"He said it was an infection that lodged in the inner ear," she repeated obediently, staring at Neal in a daze.

"You've had a rough time, and it's all my fault." Neal's expression was agonized.

"You weren't responsible for Thomas getting sick," she protested faintly.

"But I should have been here. I'm sorry, Suzy-Q."

They rushed toward each other at the same time. He crushed her in his arms, raining frantic kisses over her eyelids, her cheeks, her mouth.

"I'm sorry! Forgive me. Please forgive me!" he kept repeating.

"I'm sorry, too," she murmured, clinging tightly to him.

Adam beckoned to Kylie. "I don't think our presence is required here anymore."

On the drive back to her house, she reached for his hand. "I don't know how to thank you for what you did tonight," she said softly.

"I only gave them a nudge in the right direction."

Kylie gazed up at his chiseled profile, silhouetted by the dash lights.

He smiled down into her dazzled eyes. "And now everyone's going to live happily ever after."

"Amen." She murmured it like a prayer.

Chapter Nine

Adam's prediction was justified. Susan and Neal were like a pair of newlyweds. The manner in which Neal had learned his lesson was painful for both of them, but it brought them closer together.

Kylie was finally free to devote more attention to Adam as she'd vowed. Her other promise, to lighten her caseload, was easier than anticipated.

"I was spoiling for a fight that never materialized." She laughed, telling Adam about it. "I felt like a heavyweight who trained hard and then had his bout cancelled."

"What happened?"

"I went into Mr. Cunningham's office and told him I needed either another law clerk or fewer cases."

"And he agreed without one of his pompous, long-winded speeches?"

"Well, no, nothing's *that* easy." She grinned. "But I couldn't complain, because this time his speech was about the excellent quality of my work and what a promising future I have.''

"Sounds as if it would have been a good time to hit him up for a partnership.''

"In the old days I would have, but you're looking at the new me.''

"I didn't find anything wrong with the old one," Adam said fondly.

"She was one-dimensional. I want to be a whole woman.''

"You're certainly that." After kissing her in a very satisfactory manner he said, "How would the *new* woman like to go on a vacation with a man who's crazy about her?''

She gazed at him, wide-eyed. "Anyone I know?''

"For that I ought to withdraw the invitation, but I won't. How about it?''

"What did you have in mind?" she asked.

"I decided it would be interesting to photograph the mating habits of centipedes and scorpions. I thought we'd go camping in the desert.''

She looked at him searchingly, but his face was quite serious. "Camping," she said woodenly. "In the desert. With bugs.''

"*Insects* is the proper term." He frowned slightly. "You did say you'd go along on my next trip.''

"Yes, I did, didn't I?" She sighed. "Okay, it's a deal.''

Adam dissolved into gales of laughter. "If you could see your expression!''

"I can't help it if I don't share your enthusiasm for creepy-crawly things. I said I'd go.''

"Yes, you did." He wiped his eyes.

"Greater love hath no woman," she muttered.

"I appreciate that, angel." He took her in his arms. "Would you really do that for me?"

She smiled. "I guess it won't be so bad. But if one of your mating couples gets into the tent, I'm going to zap them with bug spray. Excuse me, *insect* spray."

"All the world is supposed to love a lover," he teased.

"I'll try, but I can't promise. For some strange reason I'm prejudiced against anything with a hundred legs."

"In that case, how would you like to go to the Caribbean instead?"

She looked at him warily. "Is this a trick question?"

He chuckled. "You don't actually think I'd take you out where the tarantulas and the millipedes roam?"

"It was only a joke? You rat!" She picked up a pillow and thumped him repeatedly. "Regular flights to Mars will be scheduled before I agree to go anywhere with you again."

He fended her off, laughing. "Not even the Caribbean?"

"I would have enjoyed *that*."

"Okay, get out your bikini."

"Do you mean it?" she asked uncertainly.

He nodded. "I have an assignment on St. John in the Virgin Islands."

"Oh, Adam, that's fabulous!" She threw her arms around his neck. "When are we leaving?"

"Not for three weeks. I'm giving you plenty of notice this time, so I don't expect to hear any excuses," he warned.

"You won't get any. All my current cases will be settled by then."

"You'd better alert Cunningham, too. I don't want any last-minute foul-ups."

"He won't be a problem. The slumlord case produced unexpected benefits," Kylie said cynically. "Our Mr. Cunningham has been asked to speak before the Metropolitan League on the humanitarian responsibilities of the legal profession in today's society."

"His opinion ought to make for the shortest speech on record," Adam commented dryly.

"Don't knock it. That's why my stock is so high. The old boy might even buy me a going-away present."

When Kylie called to tell her sister the news, Susan was delighted.

"It's time you took a vacation. And *what* a vacation! Adam really does things in style."

"I'm so excited. I've never been to the Virgin Islands."

"Be sure you get out of the room and see them," Susan teased.

Kylie didn't respond with a joke. "I never thought I'd be doing something like this," she said soberly. "Going off with a man . . . in public."

"Don't be a dodo bird," her sister said fondly. "They're extinct, and you're alive. No one thinks anything about it today."

"I know."

"Besides, it isn't as though you're going off with any old guy. You and Adam are in love. Think of it as an advance honeymoon."

"He won't ever ask me to marry him," Kylie said sadly.

"You never know."

"Unfortunately, I do."

Susan hesitated. "Some of the most celebrated love affairs in history lasted a lifetime without marriage. Does it really matter that much?"

"It does to me."

"Well, maybe you should do something about it."

"Like what?" Kylie asked ironically. "Ask him to marry me?"

"No, silly. I know you'd never go *that* far. Make him jealous. Adam's crazy about you. If he thought some other man was, too, he might see the light."

"I'm not going to trap him into anything. He has to want to get married, or it wouldn't work."

"If you say so." Susan was clearly unconvinced. "Anyway, you're going to have a smashing time. Tammy and Bruce were there over the Christmas holidays, and she says it's gorgeous."

"Are you still seeing them?"

"They've gotten to be our best friends."

"Neal doesn't feel he has to compete?" Kylie asked cautiously.

"He's a changed man," Susan said happily. "I'll never stop being grateful to Adam."

"He's really wonderful, isn't he?" Kylie asked softly. "I'm glad whatever he said to Neal that night did the trick."

"He did more than that. I have big news, too, but I wanted to let you tell yours first. Adam got Neal a job in public relations—where he's always wanted to be."

"Adam never breathed a word of it to me!" Kylie exclaimed.

"I know. He's the dearest man. He didn't want Neal to mention it, either, but Neal wouldn't hear of it. He thinks Adam's the greatest."

"Tell me about the new position."

"It's an entry level job. It doesn't pay a great deal more than he was making, but he has a future. And he's finally doing something he loves. I don't know when either of us has been happier."

Adam was annoyed when Kylie told him about her conversation with Susan.

"It was no big deal," he said. "I heard of someone who was looking for a trainee, and I got them together. It isn't as though I recommended him for the president's job."

"Why don't you want to take credit for saving a marriage?" she asked quietly.

"Nobody can do that but the people involved. I just happen to like Susan and Neal." He squeezed her hand. "Maybe because they're related to you."

Kylie couldn't figure out why Adam had gone out of his way to save her sister and brother-in-law's marriage, when he probably thought it would fail sooner or later anyway. Was it really for her sake? Or did he secretly hope he was wrong about them?

Kylie was instantly impatient with herself for grasping at straws when she'd already supposedly accepted her situation. She would rather have Adam on his terms than any other man on her own.

Kylie was breathless with anticipation, her nose pressed against the plane window. Below was a chain of green islands, scattered like a broken emerald necklace on aquamarine silk.

As they glided lower, the small jewels became larger and more distinct. Peaks covered with dense vegetation rose out of a ribbon of white sand.

"I thought the islands would be flat," she exclaimed.

"No, most of them are hilly," Adam replied.

"It's so beautiful and exotic. I can't believe we don't need a passport. I thought all the Caribbean islands were English or French."

"Actually the Virgin Island we're going to was Danish originally. The United States didn't buy it—along with St. Thomas and St. Croix—until 1917."

"How do you remember things like that?"

He chuckled. "I deliberately file them away so I can answer all your questions. I'm trying to fool you into thinking I'm a very wise man."

Kylie turned away from the fascinating scenery outside. "I'm already convinced that you're perfect." She gazed at him with shining eyes. "Oh, Adam, this is going to be the best vacation I ever had."

"I hope so, sweetheart," he said fondly.

"I know so," she answered confidently. "Nothing bad ever happens in paradise."

They were met by a dark-skinned young man in khaki shorts. A chauffeur's cap sat on his shiny black hair.

"I'm Daniel," he introduced himself. "The hotel sent me to pick you up."

He led them to a luxurious car, then went to collect their luggage.

Daniel was their self-appointed guide on the scenic ride to the hotel. He pointed out Cinnamon Bay and Hurricane Hole, two scenic harbors that were havens for small sailboats. He also gave them a brief history of the islands.

"These were pirate waters in the early days. Blackbeard and Captain Kidd often put in at Charlotte Amalie. They were tolerated as long as they didn't break the rules."

Kylie was amused. "I didn't know pirates played by the rules."

"The guidelines were very strict," Daniel assured her. "Privateers could anchor in the harbor as long as they liked, but a pirate couldn't stay for more than twenty-four hours."

"What was the difference between them?"

"Privateers took the ship but spared the men. Pirates didn't."

"That's a delicate way of putting it," Kylie murmured to Adam.

He smiled. "Daniel is protecting your sensibilities. He agrees with you that nothing bad is supposed to happen in paradise."

The hotel was a restored plantation with added wings that were compatible with the original structure. Old World charm had been preserved without sacrificing modern convenience.

Their room was spacious and airy, with a balcony that overlooked the ocean. Kylie leaned on the railing, watching the waves break from far out. A narrow band of white foam rolled over and over, gaining momentum until it crashed on the white sand and was dragged back to sea.

"Aren't you going to unpack?" Adam called.

"In a minute. I can't tear myself away from this gorgeous view."

He came up behind her and put his arms around her waist. "It won't go away."

"But *I* will. I wish we could stay here forever," she said wistfully.

"How about Bradley, Cunningham & Smythe?"

She leaned her head back against his shoulder. "Let them get their own island."

"I think you've set a speed record for going native," he teased.

She turned and put her arms around his neck. "Would you like me in one of those flowered sarongs?"

"I'd like you better in nothing at all," he murmured.

Darkness had fallen and the tropical sky was spangled with a million stars before they dressed and went downstairs for dinner.

One end of the dining room overlooked the beach. Accordion doors were folded back, letting in a breeze scented with the salty tang of the sea and the perfume of island flowers. The ocean formed a rhythmic counterpart to the music of a small combo.

"Let's go swimming first thing in the morning," Kylie suggested. "I can't wait to get into that beautiful water."

"It will have to be a quick dip for me," Adam said. "I have an appointment at ten with the people at Peaceful Harbor."

"What's that?"

"It's one of the great houses I came to photograph. A great house is a plantation manor," he explained, anticipating her next question. "In the seventeen-hundreds they were stately homes occupied by planters who grew cotton and sugar cane."

"Like our Southern plantations?"

"Exactly. They represent a way of life that doesn't exist anymore. With the changing times, many of the houses fell into ruin, but a lot of them have been restored."

"Can I go with you tomorrow?" Kylie asked.

"Wouldn't you rather laze around on the beach?"

"No, I'd love to get a glimpse of history." She smiled. "Maybe I can absorb some of those facts and figures you're so famous for and impress my friends back home."

He returned her smile. "Like how the Virgin Islands got their name?"

"Do you really know, or do you plan to make it up? I've had my suspicions about you."

"Just for that, I don't think I'll tell you."

"Please, Adam, I didn't mean it."

He gave her a mock frown and sighed heavily. "Somehow, when you beg, I'm putty in your hands. So I'll tell you. When Columbus saw all the peaks on the horizon, they reminded him of the legend of Saint Ursula and her eleven thousand virgins. The story goes that she was a British princess and the forerunner of today's liberated woman." Adam laughed. "She convinced her father to let her go on a cruise before he gave her in marriage to a pagan king. So many other virgins asked to go along that eleven more ships were needed to accommodate them. They sailed around, living it up for three years before returning home. Columbus named the island Las Virgenes in their honor. He never was one to grasp the complete concept."

"Shame on you. He sounds like a very discreet man."

Adam grinned. "Maybe that's what Queen Isabella saw in him."

They had lingered over dinner until late that evening, but Kylie was up early. The sun was only a glowing semicircle on the horizon when she opened the French doors to the balcony.

Adam scrunched his eyes shut as a golden stream of sunlight bathed his face. "Turn off the light," he growled.

"It's morning," she announced. "The birds are up, and you should be, too."

"They *have* to get up early—I don't." He pulled a pillow over his head.

"Why do they have to get up early?"

"It has something to do with worms. Ask me later when I'm awake." His voice was muffled.

She tugged at the pillow. "You're awake now."

"No I'm not. I talk in my sleep."

She heaved a martyred sigh. "All right, I'll go swimming by myself. But if I swim out too far and drown because you weren't there to rescue me, you'll be sorry."

When there was no answer from the bed, she went into the bathroom, disappointed that Adam wasn't joining her.

But when she returned to the bedroom, he was pulling on a pair of swim trunks.

"You're coming with me!" she exclaimed happily.

"I couldn't let you drown." He smiled. "What would I do with your return ticket?"

The sand was like granulated sugar, and the water was just cool enough to be refreshing. It was so clear she could see seashells on the ocean floor and brilliantly colored fish swimming by her. They seemed fearless, even venturing close to investigate the human invaders, but when she reached out her hand, they darted away.

"Aren't they fascinating?" she asked, surfacing after a dive. "I wish we had snorkeling equipment."

"We'll rent some while we're here," Adam promised.

After an invigorating swim they strolled hand in hand up the beach, stopping now and then to pick up unusual shells.

Kylie would have been content to do nothing else all day, but Adam had to work. They had breakfast at the hotel's outdoor patio restaurant, then returned to their room to shower and dress.

The road to Peaceful Harbor wound through a tropical forest. Tall coconut palms grew in clusters surrounded by even taller trees, some with leaves several feet across. Punctuating the dense greenery were flashes of color where orchids or other native flowers trailed from branches.

"Do you know the people who own the estate?" Kylie asked.

"No, the arrangements were made by the magazine. All I know are their names, Lucille and Michael Goodwin."

Mr. Goodwin turned out to be a pleasant man in his early fifties, and his wife appeared to be in her late forties. They were both tanned and athletic-looking. They were also very friendly.

"Make that Lucy and Mike," their host said, shaking hands with Adam.

"And this is my assistant, Kylie O'Connor."

"Lucky you," Mike said with a frankly admiring glance at Kylie.

"I'm not really his assistant," she said, knowing he'd find out in short order. "I tagged along because I wanted to see your home. I hope you don't mind."

"On the contrary. We're delighted to show off the place," he assured her.

"You've certainly done an extensive restoration job," Adam remarked, looking around appreciatively.

"It took a lot of courage," Lucy said.

"Everyone thought we were crazy," Mike agreed. "The roof had fallen in, and the floors and woodwork had rotted away."

"I can scarcely believe it," Kylie marveled.

The charming living room they were standing in had polished parquet floors and tall windows that afforded a stunning view of the ocean and offshore islands. Unobtrusive cream-colored draperies and neutral upholstery fabrics set off the vivid colors outside.

"Let me show you the rest of the house," Mike offered.

The main rooms were gracious examples of modern living, but the basement was a step into the past.

Centuries of grime had been removed from the brick floor, but other than that the cellar remained the same as it had been in the 1700s, from the hand-hewn beams to the walls fashioned from blocks of native rock. Old rum casks were still stored on their sides in a niche built into the wall.

Adam's eyes gleamed at the sight. "I'd like to start shooting down here," he said.

They left him alone once it became clear they were in his way. Lucy gave Kylie a tour of the gardens, where flaming pinwheels of poinsettias rivaled the sun in brilliance.

When Adam was finished shooting, they all gathered on the patio for tall rum drinks flavored with the juices from locally grown fruit.

"You've done a magnificent job with this house," Adam said.

"It's been worth all the headaches," Mike answered with satisfaction.

"Did it take very long?" Kylie asked.

Mike exchanged a smile with his wife. "It seemed like it at the time, but we've lived here for five years now, and the pain has lessened."

"How did you happen to settle on St. John?" Adam inquired.

"I came here to recuperate after a heart attack, took one look and asked myself why I was beating my brains out in the big city. I had a seat on the stock exchange. Need I say more?"

"That's pretty stressful work," Adam agreed.

"Fortunately, Lucy felt the same way. We both swallowed the anchor, as they say down here, and we've never been sorry."

"You don't find retirement a little...quiet?" Kylie asked delicately. They both seemed too vital to sit around watching the grass grow.

"We've never been busier," Lucy assured her. "Only now we do the things we enjoy."

"The yacht club is having a regatta tomorrow," Mike said. "How would you like to join us on our boat?"

When Adam looked questioningly at Kylie, she nodded eagerly.

The cluster of sleek sailboats perched on the blue water like a flock of nervous birds. They surged forward at the starter's signal, white sails billowing in the breeze.

It was a day of exciting experiences. Kylie gasped every now and then when it seemed the trim craft would capsize, but Adam was in his element. He braced himself against the rolling motion of the boat on strong legs spread slightly apart, meeting the challenge of the sea with exhilaration.

Kylie watched him with pride. In his brief khaki shorts and chest-hugging T-shirt he was dashingly handsome. A kind of superman, at home in any situation. She still had moments of incredulity that he had chosen her.

When they returned to the marina in the late afternoon, sounds of revelry came from many of the boats already docked. As they walked down the pier, several invitations were called to come aboard for a drink, but Lucy wanted to show Adam and Kylie the yacht club.

The large bar was crowded with healthy, happy-looking men and women, all enjoying themselves after an invigorating day. Kylie was introduced to so many people that she eventually gave up hope of remembering all their names.

Everyone was very friendly and eager to tell her about places of interest when she revealed she'd never been to the Virgin Islands before. In the constantly shifting conversational groups, Kylie became separated from Adam.

When she finally glanced around to see where he was, she glimpsed him over in a corner talking to a beautiful blonde. Her face was animated, and his was smilingly indulgent. He was clearly enjoying himself.

Kylie felt a stab of jealousy. It was one thing to know intellectually that women found Adam attractive, and vice versa; it was another thing to see it with her own eyes. Her old insecurity blossomed like a poison plant.

Adam happened to glance over. He waved and beckoned to her, but she turned away. A few moments later he was by her side.

"Were you giving me the cold shoulder?" he teased.

"Not at all. You seemed to be having such a fascinating conversation that I didn't want to interrupt you."

"Were you jealous?" He grinned, thinking she was joking.

"No, just resigned. I'd always heard gentlemen preferred blondes." She tried for a light tone but failed miserably.

"You're serious!" He stared at her, incredulous. When she glanced nervously at the people surrounding them, Adam led her away from the group. "How could you be jealous of a young kid who isn't bright enough to carry your briefcase?"

"Thanks a lot for mentioning the fact that she's younger than I," Kylie answered tartly.

"What does age have to do with it? You'll still be a fascinating woman when you're eighty."

"But you won't be around to appreciate me," she muttered.

"I will unless you plan on putting arsenic in my morning coffee. That's the only way you can get rid of me." He framed her face in his palms and looked deeply into her eyes. "I expect to spend the rest of my life with you."

Her leaden heart turned to cotton candy. "Do you really mean it?"

"I thought I'd shown you in a thousand ways. What more proof do you want?" he asked tenderly.

Maybe Adam didn't realize how much marriage meant to her. The moment had never been more perfect to tell him. As Kylie paused to find precisely the right words, Mike joined them.

"It's time to get the show on the road," he said. "We're all going to Lobster Pete's for dinner."

Adam's slow smile spoke volumes to Kylie. "Thanks, but we have other plans."

The eventful week went by much too fast. The days were crammed with activity, and the nights were filled with romance.

Kylie went with Adam to photograph other great houses, finding fascinating differences in how the owners had restored them. Some were strictly modern; others preserved the graciousness of antiquity. All the people they met were cordial, and they made many new friends.

In their free time they explored the island and played on the beach. And one day Adam fulfilled his promise to take Kylie snorkeling. It was an experience beyond all her expectations.

The coral reef where they dived was another world, inhabited by brilliant fish of every hue in the rainbow. Even the plant life was bizarre. Sea fans waved their delicate fronds, and turtle grass looked like giant houseplants.

Some of the marine life was familiar to Kylie from visits to the aquarium. She'd seen the banded angel fish and the tiny neon tetras with their glowing stripe down an almost transparent body. But some of the sea life seemed like creatures dreamed up by a surrealist painter in collaboration with a science-fiction writer. Delicate, fluted flowers turned out to be tube worms, and a fragile collection of brittle sticks came to life as an arrow crab that scuttled away when she disturbed it.

Kylie was reluctant to leave the fascinating underwater world. "If I'd visited the islands sooner, I might have become a marine biologist instead of an attorney," she told Adam.

"In the interests of harmony, I'm not going to comment on that." He grinned.

One night they took Lucy and Mike out to dinner to repay them for their hospitality, letting their guests choose the restaurant. The Goodwins selected a place that served authentic native food. Everything was either highly spiced or cooked in an unconventional way.

"I hope you like it," Lucy remarked anxiously. "I told Mike that Caribbean cuisine is an acquired taste, but he wouldn't listen to me."

"They're too young to have problems with their digestion," her husband answered. "Besides, they can eat steak and potatoes at home."

"This is delicious," Kylie assured them. "I've seen plantains in specialty markets at home, but I assumed they were just like bananas."

"Even though they look like bananas, you can't eat them raw," Lucy said.

"They're great with the pompano," Adam commented, referring to the locally caught fish. "Just the right blandness to cool down the other dishes."

Dessert was a pudding made with coconut milk and rum, accompanied by large cups of strong coffee.

They lingered over dinner, then had snifters of brandy while they talked and looked out at the stunning vista.

"I wish we had time to go to St. Thomas," Kylie said wistfully.

"It's a shopper's paradise," Lucy assured her.

"I don't especially want to buy anything, I'd just like to see as much as I can while I'm here."

"Why don't you go over for a day or two?" Lucy asked.

"Adam won't thank you for that advice," Mike joked. "In spite of what she thinks, Kylie would turn into an instant shopper."

"Shall we take a look?" Adam asked Kylie.

"We only have two days left, and you still have work to do," she answered.

"We could stay for a few more days."

"I can't," she said regretfully. "I'm due back at the office."

"That sounds familiar." Mike exchanged a glance with his wife. "I used to be a slave to business, until I discovered there was more to life."

Adam smiled. "I hope I've already convinced Kylie of that."

"Besides, they're not ready to retire," Lucy said.

"I wasn't suggesting retirement, just flexibility. You're here now," Mike told them. "How do you know when you'll return again—or *if* you will?"

"We're not exactly in outer space," Lucy chided.

"No, but circumstances change. If my illness taught me one thing, it's to grab the brass ring when it comes by. Who knows what the future will bring?"

"We know." Adam's hand enclosed Kylie's firmly.

Kylie awoke the next morning feeling terrible. Her stomach was churning so violently that she barely made it to the bathroom.

Adam was extremely solicitous. He helped her back to bed and draped a cold cloth on her brow before going down to the hotel drugstore for some antacid medicine.

"The druggist said this ought to fix you up, sweetheart," he said, pouring something thick and pink into a glass.

Kylie barely got it down. "If I die, bury me under those beautiful poinsettia plants." She flopped back onto the pillows.

"You're not going to die, angel. Your stomach simply isn't accustomed to native cooking."

"That fish is getting its revenge, and I wasn't even responsible for its demise," she said weakly.

"Just lie still," he soothed. "You'll feel better soon."

"That's a safe bet, since I couldn't possibly feel worse." She closed her eyes and dozed off a short time later.

Adam had showered and dressed by the time she awoke for the second time. "Do you feel any better?" he asked.

"Lots better. That stuff you gave me really worked." She glanced at the clock. "You're going to be late for your appointment if you don't hurry."

"I don't like to leave you," he said uncertainly.

"I'm fine now. I'd even go with you if it weren't so late."

"You'd better stay in bed and take it easy."

"I'm not going to waste one of my last two days here."

"Well, you can go out and lie on the beach, but don't overdo it," he warned.

Kylie wasn't keeping up appearances for Adam's sake. She really did feel fine. She was even hungry, although she'd never expected to eat again. The sight of food a couple of hours previously would have sent her dashing for the bathroom once more. After ordering breakfast in the room, she put on her bathing suit.

Kylie spent the day on the beach as Adam had suggested. He returned early and joined her there. They swam and sat on the deck chairs, reading and sipping cool drinks.

That night they had dinner in the hotel after a lovely, relaxing day. The fresh air had given them both an appetite, but even though she felt fully recovered, Kylie ate lightly. She didn't want to take a chance on spoiling their remaining time in paradise.

"I can't believe this is our last night here," she remarked when they returned to their room. They were taking a plane for home the next evening.

Adam put his arms around her. "I think something special is called for."

She smiled bewitchingly. "We've been doing that regularly."

"I have a few new things in mind," he murmured, sliding her zipper down slowly.

It was a night of love that would live forever in Kylie's memory. Adam aroused her over and over again with intimate caresses that had her writhing in his arms. She cried out as his avid mouth trailed scorching kisses over the most vulnerable parts of her body, and she welcomed his possession hungrily when he finally took her.

The driving force of his hard body brought throbbing pleasure that went on and on until her taut limbs could take no more. The ecstasy Adam brought her that night was unequalled in her experience.

The next morning Kylie woke up in Adam's arms as usual. She opened her eyes when he nuzzled her neck, but something was different. Instead of her usual euphoria, she felt wretchedly ill. Scrambling hastily out of bed, she ran to the bathroom as before.

Adam was waiting for her with a worried expression. "I'm going to call a doctor," he stated.

"Don't do that. I'll take some more of that pink stuff. It worked like magic yesterday."

"I want to know why you're getting these stomach upsets," he fretted. "You didn't eat anything last night that should have disagreed with you."

Kylie groaned. "I know. I tried to be so careful."

"I hope you didn't pick up some kind of tropical bug."

"I don't see how that could be. I'm only—" She stopped abruptly.

Cold sweat broke out on her forehead at the implication of what she'd been about to say—*I'm only sick in the morning*. Swift mental arithmetic confirmed the possibility that raised. She could very well be pregnant!

The fact that she'd been late that month hadn't alarmed her unduly, because so many things could disturb a woman's cycle. Then she'd gotten so busy that she'd lost track of how long overdue she was. What would happen if her suspicions were correct?

The revelation made Kylie blanch. Adam was regarding her with increased concern. "It's foolish to stand here and speculate when you feel this rotten. I think we should find out what's wrong."

"No! I—I'm too sick to see a doctor." She smiled faintly to indicate it was a joke. "Just let me lie down for a while. Then if I don't feel any better, you can send for someone."

While Adam reluctantly went into the bathroom to shower, Kylie closed her eyes and tried to still her mounting panic. No birth control method was completely safe, but would Adam believe it had been an accident? She wasn't worried that he would run out on her. He was too fine a person to walk away from his responsibilities. Yet what good was that if he felt trapped and resentful? He knew how much she loved babies, and they'd argued enough over their divergent views on marriage. Would he think she'd taken this method as a last resort to convince him? Might he possibly suggest she terminate the pregnancy?

Kylie wound her arms protectively around her middle. She would never agree to that. She wanted this baby with all her heart and soul, even if it meant losing Adam. The prospect caused an actual physical pain in her breast.

She watched him through her lashes as he tiptoed around the bedroom, gathering his clothes. His lean, muscular body was as familiar to her as her own, and as necessary as breathing. How could she live without him? Yet how could she live *with* him and see his love turn to coldness and cynicism?

Kylie breathed a sigh of hopelessness as she renounced the love of her life and forced herself to make plans. Adam must never know about the baby or he'd feel compelled to "do the right thing." That meant she'd have to drive him away.

She fought back tears, aware of Adam standing over her waiting to ask how she felt. She simulated even breathing, and after a moment he moved away, convinced she was sleeping. When the nausea receded as it had the day before, she pretended to wake up.

He sat next to her on the bed and smoothed her hair tenderly. "Your color is back to normal. How do you feel?"

"Fantastic! I'm going to take home a case of that pink stuff."

He didn't share her enthusiasm. "That doesn't solve the basic problem. I want to know what's wrong with you."

She put her arms around his neck. "You once told me I was perfect."

"You are, and I want to keep you that way."

"Nobody's *completely* perfect," she answered, attempting a smile.

"Try convincing me of that," he replied in a husky voice.

"I could, but I don't want to." Kylie savored his kiss as never before.

Chapter Ten

The work that had piled up on Kylie's desk while she was gone proved to be a blessing in disguise. For the first few days she was too busy to dwell on her own problems. Adam was equally busy, so their contact was limited to phone calls, which didn't satisfy him.

"I miss you," he complained. "It's no fun waking up without you in my arms."

"But I'll bet you get an earlier start."

"Big deal! Mike had the right idea. There's more to life than work. How would you like to run away to a desert island with me? Just the two of us."

Her eyes were shadowed. "One of us has responsibilities to someone besides herself."

"Don't tell me the kids are battling again."

"No, everything's going smoothly there." Kylie was grateful for that, at least. "Neal is doing well at his job,

Thomas recovered completely from his ear infection, and all's right with their world."

"That's good news." Adam's voice deepened. "Our world is pretty special, too—or it could be. When am I going to see you?"

"Don't you need a breather? We were together night and day for a week."

"That proves how compatible we are. We're better than hot fudge and ice cream. So how about it?" he asked.

"I can't discuss it now. I'm meeting a client in ten minutes."

"Okay, but I warn you, I'm not giving up. We belong together, funny face."

She hung up the receiver slowly. Adam wasn't making this easy.

As the days went by, Kylie grew more and more tense. She knew she had to break up with Adam, but the prospect of life without him was so bleak that she kept putting it off.

As far as he knew, everything was the same between them. They went on whimsical outings when time permitted—to the aquarium to visit relatives of their St. John underwater friends, to the playground to ride the swings *without* Tommy—and spent wonderful weekends together. And they made glorious, fulfilling love. Adam was captivated by Kylie's ardor, not knowing it was partly because each time she vowed that this would be their last. But then she would weaken and grant herself one more week.

Kylie realized time had run out when they were in bed together one Friday night. Adam was stroking her nude body the way he often did after they made love.

He started to chuckle when his palm circled the formerly flat plane of her stomach. "Putting on a little weight, aren't we?"

She tightened her stomach muscles and grabbed for his hand. "I'm not . . . I don't think that's very chivalrous."

"Don't worry, honey. There's just more of you to love," he teased.

She eluded his embrace and sat up in bed, wrapping the sheet around herself. "It's all those big dinners we've been eating."

"I know." He patted his own flat middle. "I've gained a couple of pounds myself. Maybe we should start jogging."

"I suppose so," she answered mechanically, her thoughts on more important matters.

He assessed her somber expression. "I didn't mean to hurt your feelings, sweetheart. Come here." He threw back the sheet and pulled her into his arms. "Don't you know by now that I love more than just your beautiful face and figure? You're the most important person in my life. I don't know what I'd do without you."

She framed his face in her palms and stared at him as though for the last time. "I don't know what I'll do without you, either," she whispered.

He didn't catch the slight difference in phrasing. "We won't ever have to find out," he answered confidently.

They had a date to attend a formal dinner-dance at a local country club the next night. It was being given by a photographic association Adam belonged to.

Kylie dressed carefully, wanting to look her best for him on their final night together. The outfit she chose was her most glamorous. The dramatic white gown, with its satin skirt and crystal beading on the low-cut bodice, was a stunning foil for her long black hair and golden tan.

As she gazed in the mirror, Kylie thought it ironic that, although her heart was breaking, she'd never looked better.

Adam was lavish with his praise when he arrived to pick her up. "I don't think I want to take you out in public looking this gorgeous. I'll have to spend half the night fending off men you've driven crazy with lust."

"You look pretty smashing yourself," she answered lightly. "I might have the same problem with amorous women pursuing you shamelessly."

Adam always rated a second glance, but that night he was especially handsome. His sculpted features and commanding height were enhanced by an expertly tailored dinner jacket that emphasized the width of his shoulders and the narrowness of his hips. The total effect was one of sophistication and charm.

"Why would I want any other woman?" he asked fondly.

"You never can tell."

He tipped her chin up. "I wish I could be as sure of everything in life."

She turned away and picked up her purse. "We'd better go."

Kylie received all the attention Adam had predicted. Many of his friends flattered her extravagantly in front of him. She hoped he would show signs of jealousy—it would give her a reason to provoke an argument after the party— but Adam merely smiled indulgently.

Kylie got her excuse a little later—in a way that was somewhat more painful. Adam usually remained with a group of people when someone asked her to dance. But on one occasion she returned to find him deep in conversation with a stunning redhead. They had retreated to a more private corner of the room.

Adam greeted Kylie with a welcoming smile and introduced her to the other woman. "This is Jean Lightner, a really fine photographer."

She smiled at Kylie. "That's high praise, coming from Adam. He's the best."

"You're being modest. Those skyscraper photos you took were sheer poetry. It isn't easy to make a tower of glass and steel seem to float in the air."

"It is if you use an F-3.5 zoom and Panatomic-X film." She laughed, but her gratification was evident.

"It's interesting that you chose Panatomic," he said. "I've always gotten better results with the higher A.S.A. index."

Kylie drifted unobtrusively away. The fact that Adam didn't even notice was very revealing. Would Jean be her successor? Not that it should matter, she thought drearily.

Kylie was very quiet on the way home from the dance.

"Are you tired?" Adam asked.

"Not especially."

He turned his head to look at her. "Is anything wrong?"

"Why would you think that?" she asked evenly.

"Because you don't usually give me the silent treatment for no good reason."

"I've *never* given you the silent treatment."

"That's true." He grinned as he parked in front of her house. "You usually lash out when you're angry."

"Are you intimating that I'm a shrew?" she asked, deliberately antagonistic.

His face sobered as he looked at her set expression. "It was only a joke."

She opened the car door. "Sorry, I guess I don't find you amusing tonight."

He followed her up the path and into the house. When they were inside he said, "Okay, suppose you tell me what this is all about. What did I do?"

"You have a right to do whatever you please," she replied distantly.

He ran a hand through his thick, dark hair. "If you want to argue, I'll be happy to oblige you, but I'd like to know what we're arguing *about*."

"That innocent act isn't very convincing. If *I'd* spent the evening letting another man fawn all over me, I'd never have heard the end of it!"

"What are you talking about?" His bewilderment was real.

"It's a shame you didn't go to the party alone. Then you could have spent all night with your red-headed friend."

"You're jealous because I had a conversation with Jean?" he asked incredulously. "I can't believe it! She's a fellow photographer."

"Oh, really? She doesn't look like any fellow *I* ever saw," Kylie commented waspishly.

Adam smiled and tried to take her in his arms. "My silly love. Why would I want her when I have you?"

She pulled away from him. "All of the reasons are visible to the naked eye."

"You're being overly emotional, sweetheart. Jean is attractive, I suppose, but I've never even thought of her as a woman. She's a brilliant photographer. I'm sorry if I neglected you, but we were just indulging in shop talk."

Kylie didn't want him to apologize; she wanted him to get angry. "You weren't that animated with your male photographer friends. Maybe you should spend some time with Jean and see what develops, as it were.''

"You don't mean that," he said quietly.

"Yes, I do. It's obvious that monogamy is starting to wear thin for you, so I'm giving you my blessing."

Adam's jaw was starting to set. "I'm a big boy now. I don't need your permission."

"Then by all means, get out your little black book. Just don't expect to be welcome around here anymore."

"I can't believe you're making this much out of an innocent conversation with an old friend," he said helplessly.

"How many more 'old friends' do you have who look like that? Are they the ones you go out on the town with every now and then? I'm beginning to wonder about a lot of things. How do I really know who you're with when you're not with me?"

Adam's eyes narrowed. "You're beginning to sound remarkably like a wife."

"That's your ultimate insult, isn't it?" she asked scornfully.

"Do you expect compliments on your present behavior?"

"At least it proves not only married people have arguments," she flared.

"I don't believe I ever suggested that," he answered evenly.

"You implied it. Your least endearing quality is the way you're always denigrating marriage."

He looked at her searchingly, his anger draining away. "Do you want to get married, Kylie? Is that what's at the bottom of this?"

Her heart started to beat faster. It was the first time Adam had indicated even the slightest willingness. Could it possibly work?

"If that's what you want, we'll get married." He didn't look like a man proposing to the woman of his dreams. In fact, his expression was grim. "I only hope you won't resort to trickery to get what you want after you're my wife. I've had enough of that."

Kylie's hope died as suddenly as it was born. She *had* tricked him. Not the way he thought, but after he found out about the baby, he'd never believe she had actually intended to send him away. Their marriage would be doomed from the beginning.

She willed herself to sound convincing. "Thank you for your gracious offer. I don't know when I've heard a more tender proposal. But you can uncross your fingers. If I did want to get married, you wouldn't even be on the list of candidates."

"This is getting out of hand," he said impatiently. "Tell me what you want, and I'll do it."

"Great! I want you to go home and stay there!"

"I suppose I might as well, since you insist on acting so irrationally. I'll call you tomorrow."

"You're not getting my message. I don't want to see you anymore."

His eyes were a stormy gray. "At the moment I have a strong inclination to take you up on that."

"I hope you do, because I don't know how to make it any plainer."

As the front door banged violently behind him, Kylie's tense body wilted. The tears she'd held back welled up in her eyes.

"Goodbye, my love," she whispered brokenly.

* * *

Kylie had dark circles under her eyes the next morning, a testament to her sleepless night.

"Do you feel all right?" Marcia asked anxiously.

"I'm fine. Bring me the Strawbridge file, and get George Franck on the phone for me," Kylie said crisply.

Work was her antidote that day, a wall she built between herself and pain. But the wall crumbled when Marcia informed her that Adam was on the phone. Kylie hadn't expected him to call, so she hadn't left instructions to say she was out—which would have necessitated explanations to her secretary. In her euphoria over Adam's love, she had allowed Marcia to become too personally involved in her affairs.

Kylie lifted the receiver reluctantly. "Yes, Adam?" Her inquiry had a clipped tone.

"How are you feeling this morning?" he asked cautiously.

"The same as I felt last night—fine."

"You're still angry." He sighed. "I was hoping by today you'd have realized how silly your accusations were."

"What I realized was how naively trusting I've been."

"I don't understand any of this, Kylie," he said plaintively. "Everything was wonderful between us. What happened?"

"You got a little indiscreet," she answered woodenly.

"That's nonsense, and you know it! I love you."

"I'm very busy, Adam." It was an effort to keep her voice steady. She was reaching the breaking point.

"I'm not going to put up with this," he warned. "I apologized for neglecting you last night, although it's my personal opinion that you overreacted."

"You're entitled to your opinion, and I'm entitled to mine."

"Yours is all wet! You're behaving like a hysterical woman."

"Thanks a lot. It's nice to know what you really think of me."

"I'm sorry. I didn't mean that. I just want to make up."

"You have a strange way of going about it."

"What the hell do you want me to do?" he shouted.

"I've already told you. It's over, Adam. Finished. Through. I don't ever want to see you again." Kylie's nails bit into her palms as she tried to maintain control.

"Okay, you've got it, lady!" Adam was having trouble with his own control. "If that's the way you want it, I won't bother you anymore."

Kylie was trembling when she put down the receiver. If only it could have ended without his bitterness ringing in her ears. But there was no other way.

A week went by, and then two, with no word from Adam. Kylie was grateful that he'd accepted her ultimatum, yet it hurt, too. If he really loved her, he wouldn't have given up that easily.

Work became her salvation. She came into the office early and didn't leave until late. Her life had come full circle. She was back where she started from, only much more miserable.

Marcia voiced her disapproval of Kylie's hours after a couple of days. "If I had a gorgeous guy like Adam waiting in the wings, I wouldn't spend all my time hanging around here."

Kylie tried to discourage her by ignoring the remark. "Did you type those depositions I left for you last night?"

"They're almost finished. You must have worked really late. When do you and Adam get to see each other?"

"We don't." Kylie took a thick manila folder from a drawer and pointedly started to read the contents.

Marcia couldn't help getting the message, but curiosity overrode her better judgment. She hesitated for a moment, then said, "Did you two have a fight?"

"It really doesn't concern you, but yes, we had a disagreement. He won't be calling anymore, and I don't wish to discuss it."

"Everybody has lovers' quarrels," Marcia told her reassuringly. "You'll make up."

Kylie's deadly calm was more daunting than anger. "Perhaps I didn't make myself quite clear. I said I didn't want to discuss it." Each word was a tiny cube of ice.

"Well, sure. I didn't mean to..." Marcia backed toward the door. "I'll go finish my typing."

Kylie wasn't proud of herself. She stood up and walked to the window, staring out without seeing anything. Marcia was a good friend, and she meant well, but every reference to Adam was like touching an exposed nerve. Would it be more bearable in time? Kylie was afraid she knew the answer to that.

Although Marcia wouldn't be a problem any longer, Kylie's torment wasn't over. Susan had to be told, and she wouldn't be as easily intimidated. The subject surfaced a few days later when her sister phoned the office.

"Sorry to bother you at work," she said. "I tried calling you at home last night and the night before, but you and Adam must have been out to dinner. You two are on a perpetual merry-go-round."

Kylie had been working those nights, but she couldn't bring herself to tell Susan the reason. She changed the subject instead. "How's everything going?"

"Just great! I haven't talked to you in a week. Tell me about all the exciting places you've been."

Kylie took refuge in an excuse. "I'm a little busy right now."

"Okay, but before you rush off, I have something to ask you. Can you and Adam come over for dinner next Saturday night?"

"Oh . . . well, I don't . . . he won't be here."

"He's working on the weekend? Too bad. You're welcome, of course, but I want to pick another date when Adam can come, too. We owe him so much, and we've never invited him over."

"I'm sure he doesn't feel you're obligated." Why didn't she just tell her and get it over with? Kylie thought despairingly.

"I know he doesn't. That's what makes him such a great guy," Susan said. "But Neal and I really want to do this. It doesn't have to be on a weekend. When would be a good night for both of you?"

Kylie bit the bullet. "I can't make any dates for Adam. We aren't seeing each other anymore," she said quietly.

"You're kidding!"

"No, I'm not."

"But what happened?"

Kylie gripped the receiver tightly. "It isn't important."

"How can you say that? You were crazy about each other!"

"Haven't you ever heard Adam's opinion on the durability of love?"

"Did he walk out on you?" Susan demanded.

"It was mutual."

"There must have been a reason. People don't break up over nothing. Did you have an argument?"

"Almost all relationships end with an argument," Kylie said wearily.

"It needn't be final, though," Susan said earnestly. "Look at Neal and me."

"You're married, and you have a child. That's different."

Susan hesitated for a moment. "Did you quarrel about getting married? That was foolish, Kylie. It isn't worth losing him over a piece of paper."

"Actually, Adam asked me to marry him."

"And you turned him down?" Susan was incredulous.

"It wasn't much of a proposal," Kylie said bitterly.

"There's no such thing as a halfhearted proposal," Susan said impatiently. "That's like being a little bit pregnant. You should have grabbed him."

Kylie's hand went to her swelling abdomen. "Adam doesn't really want to get married, and I don't want a reluctant bridegroom."

"Then why couldn't you simply have gone on the way you were?"

"Because I didn't want to. It's my decision, and I don't care to talk about it anymore."

As predicted, Susan wasn't as easily cowed as Marcia. "Maybe Neal could talk to him."

"No! You're to stay out of this, Susan. It doesn't concern you."

"Where would Neal and I be if Adam had felt that way?"

"Mine is an entirely different situation," Kylie said desperately. "I honestly don't want to see Adam again."

"I can tell by your voice that you don't mean it."

"It's the truth. I want you to promise neither you nor Neal will so much as mention my name to Adam."

"We would only—"

"Promise," Kylie repeated adamantly.

"Well...all right, but you're making a terrible mistake."

"It won't be the first one," Kylie replied ironically.

"Will you come for dinner on Saturday?"

"Maybe some other time." Kylie didn't entirely trust her sister's intentions.

"I won't invite Adam." Susan had recognized the reason for her reluctance. "I just thought you'd like to see Thomas."

"You know I would," Kylie said. "As long as we understand each other, I'll be there."

Every day seemed to present another problem. Kylie had always been so slim that she worried about people in the office noticing her thickening waistline. Luckily, the current fashions played into her hands. The bulky sweaters everyone was wearing made any figure shapeless. She started wearing them to work over short skirts, which were another blessing. Since her legs were excellent, they drew attention away from her midsection.

Marcia was very complimentary about her *new* new look. They'd had a short period of awkwardness, but Kylie had gone out of her way since then to make amends, and things had gradually returned to normal.

"I love your clothes," Marcia said one day. "You bought a whole new wardrobe, didn't you?"

"I thought it was time for a change," Kylie answered carelessly.

"I wish I could afford to throw out everything in my closet. The styles they're showing are great for women like me who don't have a waistline." Marcia looked critically at Kylie's middle. "You have such a tiny waist, though. Why don't you pull that sweater down over your hips and wear it with a belt?"

"I ... It's an idea. Maybe I'll try it." Kylie went hastily back to her own office.

She pulled her desk calendar forward and studied it. How much time was left? She'd made her plans carefully. Before her pregnancy became apparent she would take a leave of absence and go to La Jolla, a beachtown nearby, to await the birth of the baby.

It would be a lonely time, but no one must know her secret. Not because she felt any shame. The baby was the only bright spot in Kylie's life. The sole reason for secrecy was so Adam didn't find out. Her baby wasn't going to be a burden to anyone. It would know only love.

Adam's phone call came as a shock. His behavior was even more jolting. He acted as though nothing had happened between them.

"Did you miss me?" he asked in that deep, rich voice Kylie would never forget.

"I ... I didn't expect to hear from you again," she faltered when she could catch her breath.

"Silly little Kylie. You could never get rid of me."

A spark of anger penetrated her dazed state. "Did it take you two weeks to decide that?"

"I've been out of town."

"In outer space, no doubt. That's the only place I know of that doesn't have telephones."

"Try the wilds of Alaska."

"What were you doing there?" she asked, her curiosity getting the better of her.

"Photographing the most beautiful scenery you could imagine. I'll have to take you there sometime."

Kylie had a feeling of unreality. How could she be having a normal conversation with a man she'd parted from so bitterly? She couldn't go through the whole terrible thing again!

"Why are you calling, Adam?" she asked desperately.

"That's a foolish question." He laughed softly. "Do you know how long it's been since I held you in my arms? I figured it out down to the last second."

"That's all over with," she said tautly.

His exuberance was dampened slightly. "You're not still angry?"

"No, our differences no longer matter," she answered in a low voice.

"You can't be serious, Kylie. You're making a federal case out of nothing."

"I don't want to argue with you, Adam. What's the point in going over the same ground? Why won't you accept the fact that we're finished?"

"I'm beginning to see the light. You're trying to punish me for not sending roses and begging your forgiveness for something I didn't do in the first place. That's what this is all about, isn't it?" He sounded angry.

"I didn't expect anything from you," she said bitterly. "I never have."

"Are you saying I was the only one who got anything out of our relationship?" he demanded. "You didn't seem to feel that way when you were lying in my arms."

She couldn't bear to be reminded of those tender moments. How could he bring them up so callously?

"I'm waiting for you to deny we were good together," he said bitingly.

Kylie was rapidly coming to the end of her rope. "That's all that matters to you, isn't it? Satisfying sex. Well, there's more to life than physical gratification, and it's time you grew up and realized it!"

"You're the one who's acting like a child." Adam was coldly furious now. "I also told you I loved you, but you still never trusted me. You think I was cheating on you? Okay, I'll try to live up to my image. See you around, pal."

Kylie was shaken to the core as she replaced the receiver. This had been even worse than the last time. She'd never heard such venom in his voice. It brought shudders to think what he'd say if he ever found out about the baby.

Adam was true to his word. The gossip columns reported his dates with a television actress, a singer and a top model. His picture also appeared in the papers occasionally, taken at glittering openings of various events or at Hollywood parties. He was leading the life he'd led with Donna.

Adam seemed like a stranger in the photos. Kylie couldn't believe this ultra sophisticate was the same man who had taken her on picnics in the country and gathered bouquets of wild flowers for her. His anger at their breakup must have been merely wounded male pride. Adam had slipped back into the fast lane easily enough.

Kylie was sleeping badly, and the slightest effort tired her. She knew it was time to leave town, but sheer lethargy prevented her from setting an actual date. A final call from Adam made the decision for her.

"What do you want this time?" she asked brusquely when he phoned her unexpectedly at the office. "If you called to tell me about your glamorous social life, I'm not interested."

"I don't blame you for being angry," he said quietly. "My behavior hasn't been very adult."

"You don't have to explain yourself to me."

He overrode her stiff protest. "I was trying to make you jealous. It was a stupid thing to do, but I was angry that you had so little faith in me. You're probably convinced more than ever now that I can't be trusted."

"It no longer matters one way or the other. You're free to do whatever you like."

"I didn't *do* anything—at least, not the way you mean."

Kylie was shaken out of her studied detachment. "Don't insult my intelligence!" she said furiously. "Do you expect me to believe you were interested in all those women for their minds?"

"No, I didn't take them out for that reason," he admitted candidly. "But it was an exercise in futility. You're the only woman I want to make love to."

Kylie didn't allow herself to believe him. "You're just out of practice. But hang in there," she advised. "It will all come back to you."

"Why are you so determined to end our relationship, Kylie? We've had arguments before, but we always shouted at each other and cleared the air. What's really behind this?" He sounded puzzled.

Her mouth was suddenly dry. If Adam started analyzing all the events that led to their breakup, he might arrive at the truth. "You've just answered your own question," she said hastily. "We argue about the slightest thing. I'm simply tired of it."

Her answer didn't satisfy him. "Actually, we hadn't had a serious disagreement in weeks until all this blew up."

"Our conversations since then have more than made up for our earlier compatibility."

"We can't keep hashing this out on the phone," he said impatiently. "I want you to look me in the eye and tell me you don't want to see me anymore."

"No!" Her reply was panicked.

"Are you afraid you can't do it?" he asked softly.

"Of course I... It's just that..." She took a deep breath to steady herself. "It wouldn't change anything, Adam."

"I intend to see you, Kylie." His voice was adamant. "You can agree to have dinner with me so we can discuss this privately, or I'll come to your office."

Her mind was working frantically. Adam mustn't be allowed to force a meeting. She could never keep up this feigned indifference face to face. And if he ever tried to take her in his arms, he'd discover the truth instantly! She pulled at her baggy sweater with nervous fingers.

"Which is it going to be?" he demanded when she didn't reply immediately. "I'm only fifteen minutes away."

"Don't come here," she said swiftly. "I—I'd rather not start a lot of office gossip."

"Tonight, then. Where would you like to meet?"

"Not tonight, either. I have a business dinner."

"Giving me the runaround won't work. I'll be over shortly, and if you're not there, I'll wait for you," he added firmly.

Kylie considered her alternatives desperately. "All right, you win. I'll meet you. But I can't make it tonight or tomorrow night."

"That brings us to Saturday," he said ominously.

"The weekend is really a better idea anyway. I never know when I'll get off work these nights. And it's only two days away." Her voice was placating.

"You evidently don't know how long even an hour is lately," he said grimly.

"Please, Adam."

He sighed in resignation. "Okay, I'll see you Saturday morning."

"Not in the morning! Come for a drink around five."

"What are you going to be doing all day? Is this some kind of trick?" he asked suspiciously. "Are you planning to be out when I get there?"

Kylie moistened her dry lips. "I agreed to see you, Adam. The least you can do is meet me halfway. I've been working very hard, and I'd like to sleep late on Saturday. I also want to wash my hair and do my laundry. I don't think I'm setting unreasonable conditions."

Kylie was drained when she hung up after receiving Adam's grudging acceptance. The prospect of all she had to do before the weekend was daunting.

The first order of business was cramming weeks of work into two days. She had to go over all her cases and brief the attorney who would inherit them. Besides the long hours involved was the very real danger that she wouldn't have a job to return to. Mr. Cunningham took her news badly.

"This is unconscionable, Kylie." He frowned. "A responsible person doesn't just take off without notice."

"I'm really terribly sorry, Mr. Cunningham. It's a family emergency. I wouldn't consider it otherwise."

"I don't understand any of this. Can't you hire someone to take care of the problem?"

"It concerns my... my sister. She needs me." She almost choked on the lie, but she could see no other way out.

"For how long?"

"I... It's difficult to say." She swallowed hard. "I might be gone for months."

"You expect us to keep your position open here?" he demanded.

"I'm hoping you will. I think I've proved my worth to the firm in the past, and I'll be just as productive in the future."

The older man tried to pin her down as to the length of her absence and the specific reason for it. Drawing on every ounce of her legal experience, she was skillfully evasive, parrying all of his questions but never really satisfying him.

It wasn't a pleasant interview. Kylie left the senior partner's office without a guarantee that she could return. What would she do then? She had only herself to depend on, and soon she'd be responsible for someone else. She forced down her rising panic. If this firm didn't take her back, she'd find a place with another. One thing was certain: her baby was going to have the best of everything.

Marcia was a different problem. She couldn't tell her the same story about Susan needing her, because Marcia would phone to find out how everything was going. After searching fruitlessly for an alternative excuse, Kylie finally told her she was taking an indefinite leave of absence because she was fed up with working so hard. Her tightly wound nerves gave credibility to the story.

Kylie was ready to leave by noon on Saturday. All the endless items on the lists she'd made were checked off. The daily newspaper had been canceled, the gas, electricity and telephone ordered turned off on Monday. The refrigerator had been emptied and cleaned, and the draperies were drawn. The house already had a deserted feeling. Only one thing remained to be done—the hardest one. She dialed the phone.

Her younger sister reacted badly to her news. "You can't just go off without telling me where you're going!"

"It's the only way, Susan. I know how you feel about Adam, and you wouldn't be able to lie to him." Kylie had admitted partially why she was leaving—that she needed to avoid Adam.

"I adore him, and I think you're making a huge mistake, but you're my sister! I wouldn't tell him where you were if you didn't want me to."

"He can be very persuasive. This way, if you genuinely don't know, you can't be swayed into telling him."

"That's insulting, Kylie!"

"I'm sorry. I've always put your interests first, but this is one time I have to think of myself."

"But you're not! If you care that much about him, and you know he'll come after you, why are you running away?"

"I don't care about him," Kylie said evenly. "It's all over, but he won't accept that fact. He's been harassing me, and I can't take it anymore. I simply want to get away."

"You can't run from the problem. He'll only be waiting for you when you return."

"No, by then he'll have found a new interest." Kylie knew, sadly, that it was true.

"How long do you expect to be gone?" Susan was clearly stunned.

"I don't know. I'm just going to wander around enjoying myself. I think I deserve some time off."

"For good behavior? It sounds to me like you're sentencing yourself to exile!" Susan exclaimed angrily.

"Believe whatever you like." Kylie only wanted to end the discussion.

"Don't you care anything about *us*? What happens if we have to get in touch with you?"

"I'll call you regularly. And if you need me, I—I'll see that any crisis is taken care of."

"I'm hurt that you'd think I was talking about money," Susan said stiffly.

"I wasn't!" Kylie had never felt more wretched. "You know how I feel about the three of you. Just go along with me this once, even though you don't approve. I need your support now."

"You have it." Susan was almost in tears. "I can't help saying I think what you're doing is wrong, but I'm on your side all the way. Just promise you'll call often. I'm going to miss you like crazy."

"That goes double," Kylie whispered.

Chapter Eleven

Kylie had made her plans weeks before. She'd chosen to have her baby in La Jolla because it was far enough from Los Angeles that she wasn't likely to run into anyone she knew and close enough that the trip wouldn't be burdensome. The little town was an artist colony, which was another point in its favor. The people were liberal-minded and wouldn't ask questions.

She rented a small apartment that had been added onto a house on a bluff overlooking the ocean. Her landlords were a young couple, Joe and Heidi Singleton. He was an artist, and she was a potter. They were both very friendly, although not intrusive. They told her to drop by if she felt lonesome, but they didn't pressure her with invitations. Best of all, they didn't seem curious about her pregnant yet seemingly single state.

Kylie's jangled nerves unwound once she settled in. The beautiful surroundings and the lessening of tension were like a tonic. She wasn't as tired any longer, and her eyes lost their haunted look.

The weeks slipped by surprisingly fast. She took long walks on the beach and read books she'd never had time for before. It was a relaxing sort of existence, like living in a kind of time warp, removed from everyday cares—except when she phoned Susan.

Kylie called her sister once a week. She needed to hear that everything was all right at home, but it took a lot out of her. For that short period on the telephone she was plunged back into intrigue, forced to pretend she was simply enjoying a vacation.

Most of the conversations followed the same pattern. "Won't you tell me where you are?" Susan always pleaded at the beginning.

"Someplace totally different from Los Angeles." Kylie would change the subject swiftly. "How's everything there? Is Thomas okay?"

"We're all fine. Are you okay?"

"Couldn't be better," Kylie always answered brightly.

One day Susan gave her some unwelcome news. "Adam came to the house," she said. "He told us you had a date with him the Saturday night you left."

Kylie sighed. "I'm really sorry about that, but he left me no choice. I suppose he was angry."

"That's putting it mildly. He wouldn't believe I didn't know where you'd gone."

"He'd have gotten it out of you if you did."

"I suppose so, but doesn't that tell you how much he cares?"

"Only his ego is bruised. He'll get over it."

Susan had neglected to tell her that Adam kept in constant touch with them, but one Sunday when Kylie called, she found out. He took over the phone. Her heart started to beat alarmingly at the sound of his deep, husky voice. It evoked a mental image of the man, tall, powerfully built, darkly handsome. Sudden longing gripped her like a vise, destroying all her hard-won tranquility.

"Do you know what you're doing to everybody?" he demanded.

"I don't want to talk to you. Put my sister back on the line."

"You were never a coward before, Kylie. Why are you so afraid to face me?" His voice was a mixture of frustration and anger.

"Why won't you leave me alone?" she countered drearily.

"I will if you'll come back and talk to me one last time. Or tell me where you are, and I'll come to you."

"Tell Susan I'll call her some other time." She hung up quickly.

Kylie was shaken by both Adam's voice and her sister's doubtless well-intentioned betrayal. She'd been calling Susan at approximately the same time every Sunday morning, but now she vowed to place future calls on different days at random hours.

Outside of those nerve-rending contacts with home, nothing happened to disturb her. She made regular visits to the gynecologist she'd selected, then shopped for baby things in the village after her check-up. The adorable little garments delighted her. She even bought some yarn and knitted a tiny sweater, although it required many trips to the yarn shop to correct her mistakes.

On her first return trip, the woman who ran the shop shook her head indulgently as she ripped out a couple of rows. "I can tell you don't make a living with your hands."

Kylie smiled. "No, I'm afraid I'm all thumbs."

"You're new around here, aren't you? Is your husband an artist?"

Kylie's smile wavered a little. "In a way. He's a photographer."

"Will anything of his be on exhibit at the show in the mall this weekend?"

"This is the first I've heard of it," Kylie said.

"They've had notices up all over town. A lot of local artists and photographers are showing their work. It might be worthwhile for your husband to enter something if it isn't too late. Some well-known people are coming from L.A. to award the prizes."

Kylie felt the hair on her nape prickle. "Do you know who they are?"

The woman shook her head. "I can never remember names."

Joe and Heidi were on the patio when Kylie returned home. She was spinning a clay pot on a wheel, while he basked in the sun, wearing only paint-splattered shorts.

He waved as Kylie got out of her car. "You're awfully energetic on this warm day."

Kylie held up her knitting ruefully. "I had to go into town for my latest lesson in humility. I worked hours on this, and the lady at the yarn shop ripped it apart in seconds."

Heidi glanced up and smiled. "Sit down and drown your sorrows in lemonade."

Kylie eased herself into a chair and took the glass Joe poured for her. "Aren't you working today?" she asked him.

"Just taking a breather." He grinned. "As you can see, my wife is the industrious one in the family."

"Are you entering anything in the art show this weekend?" Kylie asked casually. "The woman at the yarn shop was telling me about it."

"I sent a couple of things over."

"Do you know who the judges are going to be?" she asked, trying to show only mild interest.

He shrugged. "A couple of gallery owners who probably don't know oils from greasepaint."

"How about the photography division?"

Joe squinted at the ocean. "I heard the guy's name, but I can't think of it."

"It wouldn't be Adam Ridgeway by any chance, would it?" Kylie waited breathlessly.

"No, he's too big a fish for our little pond."

"You've heard of him?"

"Who hasn't? He's a real talent," Joe said admiringly.

Heidi had removed her pot from the wheel and was regarding Kylie curiously. "Do you know him?"

"No, I—well, slightly."

Kylie took a big gulp of lemonade that went down the wrong way. By the time Joe had patted her on the back and she'd stopped coughing, the subject of Adam Ridgeway was forgotten.

A few days later Joe stopped by with a newspaper folded open to an inside page. "Did you see this article on your friend?" he asked.

"Who's that?" Kylie took the paper with no premonition. When Adam's picture leaped out at her, she experienced a familiar weakness in her lower limbs.

"The guy's really got it made. I'm thinking of trading my paintbrushes for a camera."

Kylie didn't hear him. She was staring at Adam's picture, drinking in every line of the grainy photo. His expression was remote, with no trace of his usual charm, but he still looked wonderful to her.

The article reported that he'd won first place in an international competition of photographers from all over the world. He was flying to Paris to accept the award. But the part that chilled her was the news that he intended to live there permanently.

She read that part again: "When asked why he was moving to Europe, Ridgeway would only say, 'Why not?'"

Meaning he had nothing to keep him here, Kylie thought somberly. The knowledge that she would probably never see him again caused her actual pain. That was what she'd professed to want, but in the deep recesses of her brain had been the hope that someday, somewhere, their paths would cross once more.

That hope was gone now, and Kylie tried to view it as a blessing. At least she didn't have to worry about bumping into him accidentally.

Adam Michael O'Connor was born early on a Sunday morning. He had a soft fuzz of dark hair, navy-blue eyes and skin like cream. The nurses all exclaimed over how beautiful he was. To Kylie he was a small miracle. She couldn't wait to return home so she could take care of him herself.

It was a great convenience having all the baby equipment already in place. Everything was top quality, so it would have been foolish to replace it, yet Kylie suffered a small pang. She was reluctant to have her son use hand-me-downs, even her beloved Thomas's.

The reunion with her sister was joyous, although Susan went through the gamut of emotions from incredulous delight to anger at not being told.

"When I think of you going through this all alone, I could cry!" she scolded fiercely.

"It was a very easy pregnancy," Kylie said, gazing lovingly at the sleeping infant in her arms.

"That's not the point. I should have been there for you. You were there for *me*."

"I'm afraid we're in for a rough time with Thomas." Neal laughed. "He won't take kindly to sharing Kylie's affections."

"The boys will be good buddies in no time," Susan predicted. She threw her arms impulsively around her sister. "It will be such fun! We'll take them everywhere together."

"Maybe on the weekends." Kylie gently checked her sister's enthusiasm. "I have to go back to work shortly."

Susan looked dismayed. "What do you plan to do about Michael?"

Although she'd named him Adam, Kylie found that too painful. She used his middle name instead. "I'm going to hire someone reliable to take care of him while I'm at the office."

"A baby needs his mother during the first year at least," Susan said earnestly.

"You've been reading too many earth-mother magazine articles," Neal joked after a look at Kylie's face.

"Even if it's not true, you don't want to miss all the little stages they go through. You wouldn't believe how babies change from day to day."

Kylie smiled gallantly. "I'll see him before and after work. He can't do anything that radical in eight hours."

"Kylie has to work," Neal said quietly to forestall his wife's further objections.

"I know, but so soon?" Susan asked wistfully.

"The past months of living expenses and medical bills have eaten up most of my savings," Kylie answered matter-of-factly. "I'm cutting it rather close now."

"I'd help if I could." Neal looked unhappy.

She put her hand on his arm affectionately. "I know you would, but it isn't necessary. I'll be fine once I start receiving regular paychecks again."

"It isn't fair for you to have to shoulder everything yourself!" Susan burst out. "I'm sure Adam would support his son if he knew about him."

Kylie tensed. "You're not to tell him, either of you." Her face was deadly serious. "I know he was at your house that Sunday because you told him when I was going to call. You thought you were doing the right thing, so I never said anything about it, but this is different. If you contact Adam in any way, I'll take it as a deliberate betrayal."

Susan was clearly shaken by her intensity. "We won't, Kylie. This time I'll keep my promise."

Maxwell Cunningham was still annoyed with Kylie for leaving so abruptly. He wasn't receptive when she called to say she'd returned. At first she thought he wasn't going to take her back, but it didn't really trouble her. She'd gained confidence in her own ability. When he saw she wasn't going to plead for her job, he grudgingly gave it back to her.

Everyone else in the office was glad to see her, especially Marcia. "You look fantastic!" she exclaimed. "Where did you get that gorgeous tan?"

"Lying on the beach," Kylie answered evasively.

"Not any of the ones around here. Old man Cunningham had me call you about some of the cases you were working on, and your phone was disconnected."

"That's exactly why I had it cut off," Kylie said dryly.

"Were you in the L.A. area?"

"No, I . . . I traveled a little."

Marcia grinned. "They say travel is broadening, but in your case it's becoming. Those couple of extra pounds look great on you. I never thought I'd say this about anyone, but you were too thin before."

Kylie was grateful that she'd fooled the other woman so completely. It was no longer as urgent to keep Michael a secret, now that Adam was gone, but she'd decided it was still a good idea. Bradley, Cunningham & Smythe was a conservative firm, so why make waves? If the news happened to get out, she'd deal with it, but the possibility was remote. She didn't socialize with anyone in the office except for an occasional dinner or movie.

"What's it like to goof off for months?" Marcia was like a bulldog, unwilling to let go of a subject.

"It was very restful," Kylie replied evenly. "I needed some time to myself."

Marcia slanted a glance at her. "Is that why you didn't tell anyone where you were going?"

"I wasn't sure myself at the time." Kylie turned toward her own office, but Marcia's next words stopped her in her tracks.

"Adam Ridgeway phoned every day that first week after you left. I had a terrible time convincing him I didn't know how to get in touch with you."

"I hope he wasn't abusive. He can be quite difficult."

Evidently Marcia hadn't found him that way. "I enjoyed talking to him. We got to be good friends. After that he called regularly, every couple of weeks."

"Are you pen pals now that he's moved to Europe?" Kylie asked warily.

"He didn't move there permanently. He just took off for a while, like you did. It must be catching."

Kylie turned pale. "But the newspaper said . . . I mean, I happened to see an article about him."

"Those reporters never get anything straight," Marcia said scornfully. "Adam's been home for two months."

"Does he still call here?" Kylie asked nervously.

"He hasn't in some time. He should be about due." Marcia looked hopeful.

"If he phones, you're not to tell him I'm back," Kylie said urgently.

"I can't *lie* to him," Marcia protested.

"Which one of us are you working for?" The grim set of Kylie's jaw was challenging.

"Well, if you choose to put it that way." Marcia knew better than to argue the point, but her annoyance was evident.

"I do." Kylie went into her office and closed the door.

The knowledge that Adam was only a few miles away panicked Kylie. She'd thought this wild yearning for him had been replaced by resignation, but the urge to pick up the phone and hear his voice was almost overpowering. It would subside, she assured herself resolutely. She had to be strong for Michael's sake. She drew a shuddering breath. At least she had Adam's son.

Michael was the focal point of her life. She got up an hour earlier to play with him before Mrs. Banachek—the competent woman she'd hired as a nursemaid—arrived. Kylie also tried to leave the office promptly at five, although that necessitated bringing work home. After the baby was bathed and fed, she often reviewed cases until midnight.

Adam was always present in her subconscious, but her grueling schedule didn't leave much conscious time for dwelling on him. Michael rarely slept through the night, so she was functioning on five or six hours' sleep. The extra pounds she'd gained soon melted away.

Nothing was tranquil at the office, either. Her latest client, a wealthy socialite, was suing her husband for divorce on the grounds of adultery with the downstairs maid. He was countersuing, alleging that his wife had been unfaithful with the golf pro at their country club.

One of the more irreverent newspapers captioned an article: "Husband Teed Off By Golf Pro's Score." The next day they followed up with: "Wife Accuses Mate of Labor Relations with Maid."

Mr. Cunningham called Kylie into his office to express his displeasure at the tasteless publicity the firm was receiving. But she pointed out that the couple responsible for talking to the press were members of his own club. That's how Bradley, Cunningham & Smythe had gotten the case.

Kylie was back at her desk when Marcia buzzed her on the intercom.

"Someone to see you." She clicked off without saying who it was.

Kylie frowned. That was unusual. She glanced up as the door opened—and then froze. Her visitor was Adam.

They stared at each other silently, both absorbing every detail of the other. Kylie noticed new lines in his face. He looked thinner, too, his lean body pared down to solid muscle and sinew.

He broke the spell by walking up to her desk. "When did you get back?"

"A few weeks ago," she murmured. "Who told you?"

A brief smile glimmered on his face. "Nobody had to. Your name is beginning to appear in the papers more often than mine."

She should have realized all the publicity about her case would have bad side effects for *her*, too.

"I'm still stuck with messy divorce cases," she said ruefully. "Nothing's changed much, has it?"

"I'd say quite a lot has changed." He looked at her searchingly. "You've gotten thinner."

"I was thinking the same thing about you. We're both right in style," she remarked brightly. "Marcia always says you can never be too rich or too thin."

Adam ignored her nervous babbling. "Why did you come back, Kylie?" he asked quietly.

"I always intended to after... when I was ready."

"Did you find what you were looking for?"

"I wasn't looking for anything," she said defensively. "I just needed some space."

"Did I crowd you? You could have told me to back off. You didn't need to accuse me of things you knew I hadn't done."

She pushed her chair back and stood up, feeling trapped behind her desk. Adam seemed even bigger than she remembered.

"What difference does it make after all this time?" she pleaded.

"I have to know what happened. Otherwise it's like putting down a mystery without finding out the ending." His smile was a mere tic of facial muscles.

Kylie stared down at her twisting fingers. "You know the ending." When she looked up, he was standing over her.

"Not until you tell me what drove you away."

She knew he wouldn't give up until he got an answer. If he refused to believe their argument was the reason, she could think of only one other.

"You won't like hearing the truth," she said in a muted voice. "I hoped it wouldn't come to this, but you leave me no choice. I wanted out of our relationship, and I decided you'd feel better if you thought it was because of another woman."

He stared at her with narrowed eyes. "You're saying you stopped loving me, but you didn't want my ego to suffer?"

"Yes."

"When did you discover you didn't love me anymore? The night of the argument?"

"No, of course not!"

"A week before? A month?" He hammered at her like a prosecuting attorney.

"I don't... How can I remember? It was a gradual thing," she lied.

"Then you should be an actress instead of a lawyer, because the night before that damn dinner-dance, we made love all night," he said grimly. "And a good part of the time was at your instigation."

Kylie remembered every vivid detail of that night. The knowledge that it was their last together had made her want to touch him, to please him, to give everything and receive even more in return.

She turned away, biting her lip. "Your memory must be better than mine."

He yanked her back to face him. "Look at me and tell me you don't remember the last time we made love."

He was so close that she could feel the warmth emanating from his body and smell the clean male scent of his skin. She wanted to touch his stern mouth and feel it soften as he kissed her fingertips. She yearned to take the small step forward that would put her in his arms.

He caught his breath at the emotions she couldn't hide. "You *do* love me! Then why, Kylie? *Why?*"

It was no use. She'd been lost from the moment he walked in the door. With a tiny sigh of surrender, she curved her arm around his neck and pulled his head down to hers.

Adam's kiss was almost savage in it intensity, but Kylie met it with equal hunger. They were possessed with each other, uttering incoherent sounds while they strained to get closer, although they were already almost fused together.

Adam's tongue plundered her mouth in a demanding male ritual that turned her liquid inside. She dug her naïls into the rigid muscles of his back as the flame he'd lit rose higher.

When he finally dragged his mouth away from hers, they were both shaken. Adam held her so tightly she could feel his heart thundering against her breast. Or maybe it was her own. They were both pounding in time.

"Promise you'll never leave me again." His breathing was ragged.

"I couldn't leave you," she said simply, knowing it was true.

"You don't know the hell I went through all these months!"

She gave him a ghost of a smile. "It wasn't exactly a picnic for me, either."

"You have to tell me what happened," he said urgently.

Kylie's eyes darkened as reality intruded on their joyous reunion. How would Adam react to her news? She couldn't bear it if the love in his eyes faded. He'd live up to what he considered his responsibility, but she wanted so much more.

"Let's get out of here. We have to talk, and then I want to make love with you." His voice dropped to a husky register.

"I can't leave now." Kylie drew out of his arms, trying to make plans. Maybe Mrs. Banachek would stay later. "I'll try to come to your place after work."

"If you think I'm letting you out of my sight, you're certifiably insane," he said roughly.

"Be reasonable, Adam. I have clients to see."

"I don't care if you have an appointment with the President! I'm not budging until we clear up whatever caused this disaster."

Tears filled her eyes. She'd hoped to have one perfect hour with Adam before things changed between them, as they were bound to. But even that was denied her.

He groaned, folding her into his arms. "Don't cry. We'll do it your way. But don't even think of doing another disappearing act!"

"I won't, Adam, I promise," she answered fervently.

"You might as well get used to the idea that I'll never let you go."

"I hope you'll never want to," she said wistfully.

"Would a wedding ring convince you?"

Her eyelashes dropped. Adam was in a mood to promise anything, but taking advantage of his euphoric state wouldn't bring lasting happiness. "That isn't necessary," she murmured.

"It is to me. I realized after I lost you that I'm a very possessive man."

"You said yourself that a marriage license is only a device to keep people together," she said weakly.

"Exactly. I want to bind you so tightly to me that you'll never get free."

Kylie moved away, needing to distance herself from his powerful allure. "We both know how you feel about marriage. Right now you're willing to offer what you think I want, but it isn't what *you* want."

"You're wrong, Kylie. I proposed to you that last night."

She shook her head sadly. "You were doing the same thing then—trying to smooth things over."

His smile lightened the strain on his face. "That's a pretty drastic way to end an argument."

"Can you honestly say you would have suggested it if we *hadn't* argued?"

"Maybe not at that moment," he answered frankly, "but sooner or later. I didn't just pluck the idea out of thin air. It's been lying dormant. I love you, Kylie. I want to spend the rest of my life with you."

She wanted desperately to believe him. She knew Adam had convinced himself, but all his plans revolved around the two of them. It was a rosy dream of passionate love with no responsibilities.

He was watching her with a puzzled frown. "I can't be wrong about how you feel. Why don't you want to marry me?"

"I didn't say that."

"You didn't accept, either."

She moistened her dry lips. "I have something to tell you first. Something that might change your mind."

He turned pale. "You're not ill? Oh, darling, is that why you went away? For some kind of treatment?"

"No, I'm fine," she assured him hastily.

"Thank God!" He gathered her in a smothering hug. "I wouldn't want to live if anything happened to you."

As he tilted her face up to his, the intercom switched on and Marcia's voice said apologetically, "I'm sorry to bother you, but Mrs. Forsythe is in the reception room, and she's raising holy—She's getting impatient."

"Then tell her to get another lawyer," Adam growled.

Kylie was as frustrated as he, but it couldn't be helped. "Tell her I'll be right with her." To Adam she said, "We can't talk here. Come to my house at seven."

Kylie had given up her wistful desire for one perfect interlude in Adam's arms before making her revelation. It would be selfish to let him make love to her, thinking everything would be the same as it had always been.

"You can't just leave me dangling like this," he said indignantly.

"We'll settle everything tonight," she promised.

"That sounds very reminiscent of another date you made with me," he answered suspiciously.

Her blue eyes were clouded as she gazed at his beloved face. "I said I would never leave you again. I hope you'll feel the same way after tonight."

Kylie had specified seven o'clock because she needed time to bathe and feed Michael. Also to prepare herself for Adam's meeting with his son. How could it be anything other than extremely emotional?

Michael had never been more adorable. As he wriggled and cooed happily in her arms, Kylie's hopes rose. Could Adam help loving this perfect child? But as she hurriedly changed from her business suit to a long, flowing caftan, tension gripped her. This was the most important night of her life.

When seven o'clock came she took a deep breath to compose herself. When seven-thirty came and went without Adam, her composure started to crumble. It was useless to tell herself he was merely a little late. With everything at stake between them, she would have expected him to be early. She could make up any number of excuses, but everything pointed to one shattering conclusion. Adam had changed his mind.

Had he panicked when he realized how deeply he'd committed himself? Yet wouldn't he have the decency to call? Maybe he'd decided a letter would be less traumatic all around. And maybe it would be.

She was staring somberly out the window when Adam's Jaguar drove up and stopped with a screech of brakes. He was out of the car almost before the motor died, striding up the walk. Kylie flung open the door and rushed into his arms.

"I'm sorry, darling." He hugged her tightly. "There was an accident on the freeway. I was stuck in a giant traffic jam for a whole hour. I would have left the damn car parked there if I'd had any other way to get here."

"I thought you weren't coming."

"You didn't!" He drew back to look at her incredulously.

"It's after eight," she said in a small voice.

"That's what drove me wild—being cheated out of an hour with you. It never occurred to me you'd think I wasn't coming." He framed her face in his palms, gazing down at her adoringly. "When are you ever going to start trusting me?"

Tonight, she thought. Tonight would show her ultimate trust in him—the trust she'd fought so long and so hard in vain. His mouth claimed hers before she could answer, but her response told him what he needed to know. They were lost in the wonder of each other, alight with love and desire.

Adam was the one who finally drew back, albeit reluctantly. "Tell me what you have to say to me that's so important, because I don't want any more interruptions. After we get that out of the way, I intend to make love to you for a week."

Kylie's blissful happiness faded as she realized the moment of truth was at hand. "First I have something to show you," she said quietly.

Adam followed her into the bedroom, a puzzled frown on his face. In the doorway he started to chuckle. "You brought the crib back. Is this to show me who's boss?"

She stood by the crib without answering, waiting for him to join her. The room was dimly lit by a night-light, so he didn't see the baby till he stood beside her.

His perplexity deepened as he stared at the sleeping infant. "That isn't Thomas."

"No, it's Michael," she said softly. "Adam ... Michael O'Connor."

His eyes widened in amazement as they swung from her to the baby and back. "You mean ..."

She nodded. "Our son."

Adam was so overcome by emotion that he couldn't speak for a moment. The dim light temporarily concealed the fact that the emotion was anger, but when he confronted her, Kylie recoiled from the fury in his voice.

"How could you do such a thing?" His tone was deadly. "Do you know what I'd like to do to you?"

"I ... I hoped you'd be pleased," she whispered desolately.

"Pleased! Are you out of your mind!"

"Come into the other room," she said hastily as Michael began to stir.

Adam stalked after her, almost on her heels. In the living room his hands fastened cruelly on her shoulders. "Why didn't you tell me about this?"

The shattering of her dream broke Kylie's heart but not her spirit. A small kernel of anger began to grow at Adam's callousness. She shook off his hands and drew herself up to her full height.

"You don't have to worry. I don't expect anything from you."

His eyes narrowed dangerously. "What's that supposed to mean?"

"Child support," she answered succinctly. "It's my baby. I had him. I'll take care of him."

"May I remind you that it's my baby, too." His anger flared anew, only to dissipate suddenly as he stared searchingly at her. "How could you have our child without telling me, Kylie?"

"I was afraid you'd react exactly as you are now," she said uncertainly.

He ran his fingers through his hair. "How do you expect me to act when I find out you didn't want me with you during what should have been the happiest time of our lives?"

She stared at him, afraid to believe what she was hearing. "You mean . . . you mean you're not angry about the baby?"

"How could you even think such a thing?" His embrace almost cracked her ribs. "I'm angry that you didn't *tell* me, didn't share this with me!"

When Kylie could breathe she said, "You never expressed any interest in having a family. I thought it was part of your aversion to marriage."

Adam sighed. "I said a lot of stupid things to you. Maybe I even believed them in the beginning. But you taught me what love and commitment are all about. When you left, I went a little bit crazy."

"Is that why you left to live in Paris?"

"Everything here reminded me of you. I hoped a complete change would make life more bearable. But it didn't. I had to come back and keep on searching for you."

She smoothed the tortured lines in his face lovingly. "You found more than you bargained for."

"He's such a beautiful baby. Could I take another look at him?" Adam asked humbly.

Kylie led him into the bedroom again. When she lifted the sleeping infant and placed him in his father's arms, the expression on Adam's face brought tears to her eyes. He was proud and fearful and awestruck all at the same time.

"He's so perfect, like his mother," Adam murmured, holding the baby like a piece of delicate china.

Kylie laughed through her tears. "Not when he squalls in the middle of the night." Michael was making tiny smacking sounds with his mouth. She took him from Adam and put him back in his crib. "He'll be awake soon, and you can give him his bottle."

When they returned to the living room Adam was charged with excitement. "We'll buy a house big enough for my studio. I can work at home and be a house father while you go to the office."

She smiled indulgently at him. "Babies aren't always cherubic. They cry and need their diapers changed. And later on they toddle around and get into everything."

"If I survived what *you* put me through, I'm equal to any challenge." He bunched his fingers in her hair, looking at her with burning intensity. "I was only half alive without you, and that half wasn't good for anything."

"If I'd only known," she said penitently. "I put us both through purgatory for nothing."

Tiny flames flickered in his gray eyes as he folded her in his arms. "Don't you think you should find a way to make it up to me?"

"Any way you like," she murmured, clasping her arms around his neck and offering her lips.

His hands moved slowly down her sides, cupping her breasts briefly before molding her waist, then her hips. Kylie shuddered with pleasure as he pulled her against his taut loins.

He lifted her caftan slowly, bunching it around her waist while he stroked her bare thighs. She pressed against his burgeoning masculinity, conveying a hunger that was equal to his.

Adam drew in his breath sharply at her response. He stripped off her gown in a lightning movement and stared at her nearly nude body with glittering eyes.

"I've lived this moment in my dreams a thousand times," he said hoarsely, feathering her breasts with his fingertips.

"I never thought it would come again." She tilted her head back and closed her eyes as his tongue touched one hardened nipple.

"How could you ever doubt it?"

Adam sank to his knees and continued his devastation, sliding his lips down her body to its most vulnerable point. His firm grip on her hips was the only thing that kept her from falling. Kylie was weak with desire, consumed by the inferno he was creating.

"Please, Adam," she pleaded. "It's been so long."

"For me, too, my love."

He lowered her to the carpet and left her for only a moment. His clothes were flung off in an instant, and he removed the last of hers as swiftly.

Adam poised his body above hers for a heart-stopping moment. His eyes smoldered with passion as he said, "I love you, darling. Now and forever."

She wanted to affirm her own love, but it wasn't necessary. Her joyous acceptance of him spoke louder than words.

Their mating was fierce yet tender. Both gave in equal measure, arching, thrusting, reaching the ultimate peak rapidly, their bodies shuddering with release. The wild storm swept through them in violent waves that crashed over and over again. When the feverish ecstasy subsided to muted satisfaction, they still clung together as though they would never let go.

Kylie was too sated to move for a long time. Adam's gentle caresses were the perfect finishing touch. When she tilted her head to press her lips against his jaw, his arms tightened their embrace.

"What time does the marriage license bureau open tomorrow?" he murmured.

"It doesn't. Tomorrow is Sunday."

He made a small sound of annoyance. "Don't you know a friendly judge who would open up the store for us?"

Kylie smiled. "There isn't any hurry now."

"Speak for yourself. I won't be happy until I know you're really mine."

"How much proof does it take to make you positive?" she teased.

Adam pulled her even closer, gazing down at her adoringly. "Twenty-five or thirty years ought to do it."

* * * * *

Silhouette Special Edition

COMING NEXT MONTH

#499 LOVING JACK—Nora Roberts
Steady Nathan Powell was jolted upon finding impulsive
Jackie MacNamera ensconced in his home. Living with her would
be impossible! But *loving* Jack soon proved all too easy....

#500 COMPROMISING POSITIONS—Carole Halston
Laid-back cabinetmaker Jim Mann definitely wasn't ambitious
Susan Casey's type. So why were his warm brown eyes lulling her
into such a compromising position?

#501 LABOR OF LOVE—Madelyn Dohrn
Alone and pregnant, delicate Kara Reynolds temporarily leaned
on solid John Brickner. But Kara's innocent deception—and
Bric's buried secrets—gave new meaning to "labor of love."

#502 SHADES AND SHADOWS—Victoria Pade
Talented Tyler Welles lived in the shadow of a well-publicized
scandal. Eric Mathias was determined to expose her... until he
discovered the precious secret behind her shady reputation.

#503 A FINE SPRING RAIN—Celeste Hamilton
Haunted by the miraculous and tragic night they'd shared years
ago, Dr. Merry Conrad reappeared in farmer Sam Bartholomew's
life. But could she convince him she belonged there forever?

#504 LIKE STRANGERS—Lynda Trent
Five years ago Lani's husband left on a cargo flying mission—
and never returned. Suddenly Brian was back... but like a
stranger. Could they ever be man and wife once more?

AVAILABLE THIS MONTH:

#493 PROOF POSITIVE
Tracy Sinclair

#494 NAVY WIFE
Debbie Macomber

#495 IN HONOR'S SHADOW
Lisa Jackson

#496 HEALING SYMPATHY
Gina Ferris

#497 DIAMOND MOODS
Maggi Charles

#498 A CHARMED LIFE
Anne Lacey

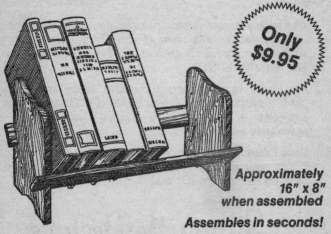

1989
IS THE YEAR
OF THE MAN!

What makes a romance? A special man, of course, and Silhouette Desire celebrates that fact with *twelve* of them! From Mr. January to Mr. December, every month spotlights the Silhouette Desire hero—our **MAN OF THE MONTH**.

Sexy, macho, charming, irritating...irresistible! Nothing can stop these men from sweeping you away. Created by some of your favorite authors, each man is custom-made for pleasure—*reading* pleasure—so don't miss a single one.

Diana Palmer kicks off the new year, and you can look forward to magnificent men from **Joan Hohl**, **Jennifer Greene** and many, many more. So get out there and find your man!

Silhouette Desire's
MAN OF THE MONTH ...